ASK LAURA

GILLIAN JACKSON

BLOODHOUND
— BOOKS —

Re-published in 2024 by Bloodhound Books.

www.bloodhoundbooks.com

Print ISBN: 978-1-916978-75-1

Chapter One

An agony aunt should have all the answers drawn from the experience of her own perfect life, right. She is immensely proud of a loving husband, two-point-four beautiful children, and a charming home which is always neat as a pin, right? Wrong! I am thirty-eight years old, a stone or two overweight, and my husband has left me for a younger, sexier woman. As if this isn't a good enough cliché, she's also his PA at work. I have a sixteen-year-old daughter, Lucy, who currently isn't speaking to me (all to do with a pair of shorts, and I mean, really short shorts) and eleven-year-old twin sons, Sam and Jake. In common with most boys their age, they live and breathe football and suffer from an aversion to soap, water and vegetables. All three children seem programmed to leave a trail of devastation behind them in every room of the house. Said house, anything but charming, requires a massive dose of TLC or, failing that, a nuclear bomb.

Fortunately, however, my employers are blissfully ignorant of my chaotic life as we mainly communicate remotely over the internet. So, once a month, I join the ranks of weary commuters trekking into London, thankful I don't have to go every day to meet with my editor Madeline. She greets me with gushing words and air kisses, her fashionable ensemble complementing a perfectly made-up face and impeccably coiffed hair. If this sounds a little like jealousy, it's because it is, tempered by a strong affection. Over the three years I've worked for Madeline, she's proved to be as beautiful inside as out. My envy is founded simply on my insecurities as my editor is so altogether, whilst I muddle along in a cloud of eternal busyness without the time, or often the inclination, to devote to my appearance.

My aspiration in life is to become a woman who has everything totally under control, with her family so well-grounded, that each day passes in a perfumed haze of idyllic bliss. Ideally, each family member will be fulfilled and confident in their place in the world, knowing they are valued and loved. The reality, however, is so far removed from perfection, and there are days when I'd happily crawl back into bed with a giant bar of chocolate and a bottle of wine. But no! I get up when the alarm rings, not daring to allow myself the luxury of the snooze button, stumble into the shower and wake myself up with a blast of cold water, whatever the season. This ritual reminds me I am alive and functioning, even if only just.

Occasionally I ask myself why I became an agony aunt when there are so many problems in my own life without taking on board other people's. However, I love the work, and even if a proportion of the letters from readers are not genuine, many are, and if my replies help someone, it is totally worthwhile. And did I mention it pays the bills? Well, it goes some way towards them, and with the related articles the magazine occasionally commissions from me, we manage to live quite comfortably with the huge bonus that I don't have to leave the house to work.

When the application form for the job arrived in the post, there were large boxes in which to write my history and qualifications, far more than my single degree needed. After careful consideration, I enlarged my handwriting to match. Admittedly the degree in psychology is appropriate, and I'd been working voluntarily for the last two years for a local counselling charity, which looked pretty impressive in black and white. But what caused me at least one sleepless night was the hypothetical problem to which they asked me to reply. It was sketchy to say the least, presumably lacking in detail to test my skill at reading between the lines:

Dear Agony Aunt,

My husband has told me he wants a divorce after fifteen years of marriage. He says he's bored with me, but I thought we were happy, and this has come totally out of the blue! I feel hurt and angry. What should I do?

Mary

Dear Mary,

This must have been quite a shock for you. Try to persuade your husband to talk about his reasons for wanting a divorce and find out why he is unhappy with your marriage. If he refuses or finds it difficult to speak to you, perhaps he has a friend he could confide in, someone who might act as a mediator. Or you could seek professional counselling as a couple. Fifteen years together is a long time to throw away without discussing and exploring all the options.

If your husband refuses to participate in any dialogue and remains determined to seek a divorce, you must begin thinking of yourself and your happiness. Do you really want to stay in a marriage with someone who doesn't want to be there? On the other hand, if you act calmly and with dignity, you will weather this storm much better than allowing anger and bitterness to take control. I wish you luck with whatever you decide to do.

Laura

It took me three hours and copious amounts of coffee to compose the reply in the specified number of words allotted to me. It must have hit the right tone and depth the magazine was seeking because I was subsequently called for an interview and offered the job. What I really wanted to write in reply to poor Mary was:

Dear Mary,

If your husband has been so hurtful and wants a divorce, then fine, give him one but tell him you want the house, the car and the bank account!
Laura

Now, I wouldn't want you to think I'm flippant about my work, as I do take it seriously. The diversity of people's problems challenges me continually, hopefully keeping my brain from becoming jelly. The articles, too, are exacting, taking me back to my student days, a time I adored when, with my peers, we debated anything and everything, from Freud to Dr Spock, with aspects of physiology in between. The articles, which are tailored to the female, thirty to fifty plus age group, have the usual twee alliterative titles, '*Managing the Menopause*', '*Coping with Crisis*' and my particular favourite, '*Surviving the Surly Student*'. Perhaps with the latter I can draw on my own life experience. In researching the column, I am constantly looking for help with my children, as with '*Life as a Lone Parent*'. I believe life is a constant learning curve, and mistakes are simply lessons that will make us stronger to face the future if we heed them. Ha!

In the bottom drawer of my desk, under a pile of old greetings cards I haven't the heart to destroy, there lies a half-finished manuscript, '*The novel*' (a bestseller, of course) which I began to write during my pregnancy with Lucy. So many people who write for a living have a secret desire to produce a great literary work of art and I admit to being no different. Perhaps half-finished is exaggerating. Ten chapters would be more accurate, plus a notebook filled with random ideas which I always intended to use in a plot for my novel. Admittedly, I've taken it out on occasions and read through it. It isn't good, but it may become something commercial with a few months of editing. Who knows? It's my 'one-day project', but I haven't a clue when 'one-day' will arrive.

Chapter Two

I feel blessed to have a house for the children and me. As Paul was the one to initiate our divorce, he was the one who left the marital home where the children and I still live. To give him credit, he didn't argue the point in our settlement and I've been working towards paying off his share of the house since we split. It's a 1930s semi-detached in a pleasant area of West Finchley. We only live here because an aunt of Paul's, who was unmarried and childless, made him the sole beneficiary of her will, including this house. To buy the same place today would be entirely out of my price range – neighbouring properties are selling for around the million-pound mark. Outrageous, I know, but rising property prices are a sad fact of life in London.

Not being the most fastidious of housekeepers, the place has a distinctly lived-in feel, but occasionally guilt prompts a pathetic attempt to blitz the place. On one of those days, I was brought to a sudden halt in absolute horror. Starting at the top of the house seemed a logical way to get the task done, but I was to get no further than Lucy's room.

It wasn't because I was snooping – I could no longer stand

the mess and was trying to distinguish the dirty clothes from the newly ironed ones, all of which were strewn across the bedroom floor. It was there I discovered them; a packet of birth control pills! My heart skipped a beat and I held my breath, staring at the troubling find. The pills were pushed under the bed but not far enough to hide them effectively. Lucy is sixteen and, according to the law, old enough to sleep with a boy – but not in the opinion of an already slightly neurotic mother. Turning them over in trembling hands, I counted the empty blisters in the pack, twelve missing tablets. So, she was taking them, which presumably meant she had a sexual relationship. My mind went into overdrive, trying to recall if Lucy had mentioned any particular boy of late. She hadn't, which wasn't surprising. We don't have the kind of relationship where we tell each other everything, Lucy has a best friend for such confidences. So, what should I do?

If I approach her with the evidence, I'll be accused of prying, but what's the alternative? My baby, my firstborn child was in a sexual relationship which I knew nothing about, and even worse, I didn't even know her boyfriend! This could definitely be chalked up to another failure in the list I was amassing as a parent, but it couldn't stay on the list without being addressed. Should I ring her father? No, that would be the ultimate betrayal, and Lucy would never speak to me again if I fessed her up without talking to her first. And my ex, Paul, would take it as confirmation I was a lousy parent, a complete failure. But how should I deal with it? Writing a letter to '*Ask Laura*' crossed my mind, and I laughed out loud, my voice sounding strangely brittle, cutting into the silence of a room which usually pulsated with what passed for music in Lucy's world. It needed to be addressed and this afternoon would be the ideal time while the boys were at football practice, and Lucy would be first home from school.

Once I'd decided on my course of action, nothing more

constructive would be done that day. My insides churned with nerves, or possibly it was the half a dozen chocolate biscuits I'd eaten since my discovery. Biscuits always taste better when eaten with stress. The day seemed interminable, but eventually 3.40pm arrived and with it, my daughter. It was no surprise when she slammed the door and ran straight up to her room; I'd been getting the cold shoulder since vetoing the short shorts last Saturday. I own belts wider than they were, and it was freezing outside too. After a few deep breaths, I climbed the stairs and tapped on Lucy's door.

'We need to talk.' I raised my voice as the music was already throbbing throughout the house. When there was no reply, I stepped inside, ignoring the look of irritation on her face. I opened my palm to show her my find and waited for the expected tirade. Instead, there was steely silence as she grabbed the pack from my hand and pushed it deep into her pocket.

'Where did you get these from?' I tried to sound calm, reasonable even.

'The family planning clinic, where else?' Lucy almost spat the words out.

'Didn't you need an adult with you?'

'Mum, I'm sixteen and old enough to see a doctor alone. So why do you always treat me like a child?'

I sat on the bed next to Lucy, who immediately turned away, folding her arms across her body, an act of disapproval. I stood to turn down the music and took my place again next to Lucy.

'Having a sexual relationship with a boy is something you must consider carefully. It's not a matter of being old enough – it's about respecting yourself, saving yourself for someone special.'

'Right, like Dad was your someone special?'

'I'm not claiming to be perfect or to have always made the

right decisions, but I hoped you might learn from me so as not to make the same mistakes I did.'

Lucy turned her head away again, avoiding eye contact.

'Who is this mysterious boyfriend then? Will we get to meet him soon?' I tempered my voice, not wanting to sound accusing.

'You're joking! Bring him back to this madhouse?' she said to the wall.

'Lucy, this is your home; the boys and I are your family. Are you ashamed of us? Because if you are and you think he'll look down on us, then perhaps he's not the right one for you?'

'Who said anything about the right one? I'm not planning a wedding or anything! Look, save the advice for your readers, Mum. It doesn't work on me.'

I stood to leave, saddened our relationship had soured so much.

'We have to discuss this sometime, Lucy, and probably talk to your dad too. Think about it and we'll talk later.' I left her alone, pretending not to hear the disgusted 'tut' as I turned away.

Back downstairs, as I rummaged in the fridge for something to make for tea, my mind drifted back to the day Lucy was born. Okay, she hadn't been planned and we married young, but I like to think we'd have married eventually anyway. She was a tiny baby, petite but perfect, so perfect, with tiny fingers grasping at mine and her little face screwed up against the light, trying to make sense of the new world into which she'd been so suddenly thrust. Cradling her in my arms and guiding those rosebud lips to my breast, I fell in love, and Lucy's presence brought out the best in Paul and me. The three of us were so happy, and my love for this helpless little scrap of humanity threatened to overwhelm me. As she grew, so did my love. Lucy was perfect, with cornflower-blue eyes and honey-blonde hair, like my own – and the way she chuckled when Paul played with her was infectious. I could never imagine that one day the all-encompassing harmony of our little family would be torn apart.

When Lucy was three, we decided I should actively seek a job. Our daughter was at an age when she would thrive in the company of other children at a nursery, and a second income would ease the financial burden on Paul. I was secretly looking forward to returning to the adult world of work and doing something to stretch my mind. However, it was not to be as I became pregnant again, ending our well-laid plans. Who would want to employ a pregnant woman? Yes, it was another unplanned pregnancy, and when we learned we were expecting twins, the pressure began to bear down on our relationship, and tiny cracks appeared in the cement of our marriage. There would be two more mouths to feed, yet no second income to help.

Paul and I were disappointed for different reasons, but when the boys were born, this was forgotten in the joy of those two tiny babies conceived (albeit accidentally) in love. We were sure we would cope and weather the storms of the future. But our joy was short-lived as Paul began to work more hours. By the time the boys were a year old, I was exhausted from the effort of looking after three young children and a home with a husband who seemed more and more unwilling to be with us. His long hours paid off with two pretty rapid promotions, and I dared to hope things would change and perhaps we would see more of him in the future. But I was wrong.

The second promotion brought a PA into the equation, a young, pretty girl who didn't smell of baby sick or talk about teething and the rising price of nappies. I should have seen it coming but was too wrapped up in domesticity and had become a drudge – a boring mummy when Paul wanted a cute, sexy wife to keep him interested. And when the cracks widened, we should have talked. Conversation is what I advocate to my readers when they write to me; talk, communicate, and verbalise. It's so important! But instead, we shouted, sulked and blamed each other. Paul moved out just before the boys' second birthday. I'm amazed he stayed so long, and with hindsight, I don't blame him. If I'd had the choice, I wouldn't have lived with me either.

So, Laura Green, agony aunt, have you learned your lesson? Yes, I think so, but I still struggle to parent my three children alone. Paul sees them regularly; every other weekend, and he picks the boys up one evening a week to take them to one of their endless football practices. His relationship with Lucy these days is mostly through 'FaceTime'. I know she tells him how awful I've been and he sympathises, which is easy for a remote, virtual father to do. But will she tell him about the pills? I think not.

Chapter Three

Sam and Jake are fraternal twins but share many of the same qualities and interests, although not identical in appearance. Football has never interested me, but as it is the single most important thing in my sons' world, I try to keep up with their favourite teams and how they fare in the league tables. Naturally, I make mistakes and almost as soon as I think I have a grasp on which player plays for which team, they seem to move on elsewhere, and the twins look at me as if I come from another planet. Sam is the taller of the two and although they are equally enthusiastic about football, he's the one with the more natural talent. As Paul takes them to their mid-week practice, I get to see them play on the weekends they're with me and stand dutifully in all weathers to cheer on my sons. I'm pretty sure they like me to be there, but my instructions are to remain 'cool' and not display any behaviour which would embarrass them in front of their teammates.

My appearance also has to be approved, and they often remark on my attire before we leave the house, with groans and comments such as, 'You're not wearing that stupid hat, are you?' prompting me to change to something more suitable, even if it's less warm than the one with the fluffy ear flaps. My comments also have to be monitored, ever since I shouted 'offside' rather loudly when to anyone more knowledgeable than me, it was clearly not offside at all. Sam and Jake have given up trying to educate me on the finer points of the beautiful game. Lucy has no interest in her brothers' passion, and on the odd occasion I've invited her to a match, she screwed her face into an expression of distaste as if there was a bad smell in the room.

My regularity at matches has afforded me the opportunity to get to know some of the other parents, and I often stand with a group of mothers, who all seem to have a better grasp of the rules than me. There is also a single dad, whom I try hard to avoid – the fly in the ointment. His name is Richard Ward, and he wasted no time in telling me he was also divorced and suggested we might be able to offer comfort to each other. The way he looked me up and down, his suggestion was clearly a euphemism for sex. He's one of those men who stand far too close, and when I fail to avoid him, I spend my time leaning back to prevent his breath from being in my face. Richard has asked me out occasionally, and my constant refusals don't seem to have deterred his enthusiasm.

Naturally, I've phrased my rebuffs carefully to avoid offending him, but even when these refusals are firm, he doesn't get the hint! It seems as if Richard Ward does not give in readily. His son, Jon, is on the team with Sam and Jake and appears to be a pleasant child, if somewhat quiet and a bit of a loner. Football practice is about the only time Richard sees his son other than occasional night stop-overs, which to the man's credit, he seems to genuinely regret. However, the transparent hints that if he were in a settled relationship, he would be in a stronger position to see more of his boy are wasted on me. Yes,

I feel sorry for him, but there's no way anything will happen between us. I find something about Richard creepy, for want of a better word. Fortunately, one or two other mums have picked up on my dilemma and call me over to rescue me when Richard corners me on the sidelines. I feel safe in the middle of their little group and am much happier with their company than his.

I was somewhat cautious when Jake told me Jon had asked him to go for tea to his dad's house. Perhaps it was a genuine offer of friendship, but I couldn't help thinking Richard may have contrived the situation to pursue me further.

'Are you and Jon close friends at school?' I asked.

'Not really, he usually hangs out with James and Simon but I don't think he's invited them over, just me.'

'Do you want to go?' I asked. Jake shrugged; he wasn't sure himself.

'I suppose I should. There's no real reason to say no, is there?' This was probably as close as my son would get to being kind to a lonely classmate. But, no, that probably does Jake an injustice. He is a kind boy and caring too. He even tries to speak to Lucy despite her moods and sullenness which have caused Sam to give up on his big sister.

'Well if you want to go, you can, but take your phone so you can ring me to come and get you when you're ready to leave.' So it was settled and I was already thinking of an excuse to pick Jake up and hurry straight home.

When the day arrived and Jake went to Jon's straight from school, I prowled around the house, jittery and unsettled, although I don't exactly know why. Sam and Lucy were both home and in their respective bedrooms, transfixed to screens of one kind or another. When the phone rang a couple of hours later, I rushed to pick it up, hoping it was Jake wanting to come home. Instead, however, it was Richard's voice which greeted me.

'Laura, I was just telling Jake I'll bring him home. So there's no need for you to come out.'

I tried to process this quickly and mentally pictured a scenario where Richard was angling for an invitation inside, denial of which would be somewhat rude.

'Thank you, Richard, but I've got to come out to pick up some milk, so it's no trouble. I'll be there in ten minutes.'

Richard tried to insist, but I didn't want him to know where we lived, although I bet he'd been pumping Jake for such information. Winning the pseudo-argument, I set off to pick up my son. Richard asked me in as I anticipated, but the milk excuse came in handy again as I told him I wanted to catch the shop before it closed. Surely this man could see I wasn't interested in him, but he appeared to have very thick skin. My firmness eventually paid off and we managed to leave relatively quickly.

'Did you have a good time?' I inquired.

'Suppose so. We played on Jon's Xbox most of the time. It was a bit boring.'

'Never mind, Jon probably enjoyed your company,' I consoled my son.

'He'd rather be with his mother. He has to stay at his dad's two nights a month but he doesn't like being there and there's not much to do.'

I nodded, concentrating on driving, and the conversation seemed over.

'His dad asks a lot of questions,' Jake volunteered.

'Really, what kind of questions?'

'Well, he wanted to know where we lived and our phone number, and he asked what you did for a living.'

I groaned audibly and felt Jake's eyes turn on me. 'What's wrong? Shouldn't I have told him?'

'No, it's fine, I just think Richard would like us to become friends, but I don't think it's such a good idea.'

'Gross, do you mean he fancies you?'

'No, yes, well... I don't know, but I don't particularly want to see him.'

Jake was silent for the rest of the journey, no doubt concentrating on the fact his mother was a single woman, and it was not entirely out of the question that she could, one day, find a man she could like. Once home, Jake disappeared into his room and I flopped down on the sofa, a mental image of Richard in my mind. It isn't that he is not attractive (although he isn't), but I didn't have time to embark on a relationship, nor the inclination to see Richard any more than was necessary. Finally, the telephone broke my reverie, and on answering, Madeline's honeyed voice greeted me. It surprised me she was ringing on an evening – we usually only spoke during office hours. She asked if we could meet the following day, another surprise as it wasn't our usual time for a get-together.

'We've got some letters in the office for you, and there's something I'd like to discuss too,' my editor said.

'Is everything okay, Madeline?'

'Yes, yes, everything's fine, but I'll have to dash, I'm afraid. See you in the lobby at ten?'

'I'll be there,' I answered, then replaced the phone. It was puzzling; Madeline hardly ever rang me in between our meetings unless it was for a specific query, something she was unsure of in an answer to one of the letters I'd returned to her. To request a meeting was rather worrying, and all sorts of scenarios raced through my mind. Was my job on the line? I was aware the magazine had recently cut down on staff to streamline the company, but it had been mainly office staff. Surely my page and articles would be safe? Finally, I concluded I'd have to wait and see, but in the meantime, I'd try to work on my upcoming feature. '*Battling the Bulge*' was an article on the psychology of eating, why we comfort eat and how to remain in control of our diet. It was an article I should read myself, but while working on it, I gave in to the urge to open the packet of chocolate biscuits which I'd hidden away from the children. Shame on me!

Chapter Four

P rior warning of this latest trip to the city would have given me a chance to dash to the hairdressers in a bid to boost my confidence. Meeting Madeline always makes me long to look as glamorous as she does. Still, getting up early gave me enough time for a long, hot shower. After the children left for school, I dressed in my favourite outfit, a black-and-white check woollen suit (Chanel style, although not the real thing) which fitted me perfectly and made me feel reasonably well prepared for this unscheduled meeting.

Madeline was already waiting in the lobby and greeted me with her usual effusiveness, not giving anything away by her expression.

'Shall we go to my office?' she suggested. 'Carol's brewing coffee.'

Carol was her assistant, a mouse of a girl who jumped and blushed if anyone spoke to her. I liked her and wished Paul's PA had been more like Carol. We rode in the lift to her comfy little glass-walled eyrie on the seventh floor, where the River Thames could be seen from the window, and city life was enacted in real time below us.

When seated, with our coffee before us, Madeline handed over a small pile of letters. The way we work is that she or Carol sorts all the '*Ask Laura*' mail and weeds out the ridiculous and prank letters. Then they shortlist them to about a dozen, which are passed on to me. I then select which ones I'd like to feature, usually between four and six each week, depending on the word count of the question and my reply. Most letters arrive as emails, but a few paper ones arrive by post. I like to see the original as so much can be learned from the reader's handwriting, stationery, and how they express themselves. I tucked the letters into my bag to read later, willing Madeline to get to the point of why we were in her office for an unprecedented, extra meeting.

'There have been some other letters for you, only a couple, which we didn't want to pass on, but our legal team insist we tell you about them for your protection and our own.'

'Protection?' I frowned; whatever was in them? Of course, we get a few rude ones, in every sense of the word, which are generally not passed on, but what was this all about?

'This arrived a couple of weeks ago and then another last Wednesday.' Madeline passed over two letters in plain white envelopes addressed to '*Ask Laura*' at the magazine address. The word '*personal*' had been handwritten at the top of each envelope. Opening the first letter, I was glad to be sitting down. It wasn't a lengthy missive, typed and printed on A4 paper, but it was full of hate. It called me all kinds of disgusting names and accused me of pandering to the whim of '*stupid women who should know their place and stop whining about their men*'. It was sexist, offensive and couched in very angry language. Drawing a deep breath, I opened the second letter and read it. This one was clearly written by the same man, for indeed it must be a man, and if the first had been rude and offensive, then this one was equally as bad and more. The term which came to mind was 'chilling'. Reading it left me feeling nauseous, not for the general accusations similar to the first letter but for the specific references to me. It was more personal, and the writer, as well as accusing me of encouraging women to disobey their men, told me to stop writing my letters page or '*you will regret it!*' It was a threat, a demand that had consequences, although they were unspecified.

'Are you okay, Laura? You've gone very pale.' Madeline was full of concern. I grabbed a biscuit from the plate Carol had left us and ate it in two bites.

'I'll be fine,' I said, reaching for another biscuit and eating it just as quickly before gulping down the scalding coffee. I needed time to process this unexpected development, but Madeline anxiously awaited my comments.

'I don't know what to say.' My brain suddenly fogged, and I couldn't grasp the right words to express myself.

'Don't worry, Laura, drink your coffee. Would you like some more biscuits?' she asked kindly. I was suddenly embarrassed to see I'd almost finished off the whole plate. I shook my head.

'Brian Clark from our legal team said he'd be happy to come and talk to you about this. Would you like me to give him a ring?'

Legal team? Did this mean they were taking the letters seriously? Surely they were from some misogynistic maniac with nothing better to do?

'If you think it's necessary, Madeline,' I agreed, and she went to the phone on her desk to make the call.

'He'll be here in a couple of minutes.' She smiled at me but I had never seen my editor look so serious before.

Brian Clark was a man of slight build. Narrow shoulders and neck supported an over-large head, with a few tufts of hair plastered onto his balding pate. He was about my height, five foot six, and probably weighed considerably less than me.

However, he had a kind face and a voice that would be soothing in any other circumstance.

'Pleased to meet you, Mrs Green.' He smiled.

'Laura, please,' I replied.

'And I'm Brian.' He sat beside Madeline. 'I see you've read the letters.'

I hadn't a clue what to say, so I waited for him to take the lead.

'I'm sure they're distressing for you; we were quite shocked when they arrived. But, unfortunately, because there is a threat, even such a veiled threat, we would advise you to go to the police.'

I could barely speak and was still trying to process the anger and hate directed at me in the letters. I was at a loss to think of anyone who would write such things or why. Would someone really be stirred to such action simply by the answers I gave my readers?

'Do you think that's necessary?'

'I do, and it's not just to cover us. Of course, we hope there'll be no more of this hate mail, but naturally, if there is, then we'll pass them on to you, and you in turn could pass them on to the police.'

I nodded; perhaps he was right.

'If you'd like me to come with you, I can do?' Madeline's face showed such concern, I was touched. 'This afternoon's schedule can easily be rearranged, and we can get it over with today?'

'Thank you, but it's fine. I'm happy to go myself although as you say there may not be any more and the police probably won't be interested.'

'Oh, I'm sure they will.' Brian Clark sounded convinced. 'The letters imply there'll be consequences if you don't stop writing your column; we have to take this seriously, which means bringing in the police.'

Chapter Five

Dear Laura,

I am forty years old and single. Both my parents died in the last two years after I had cared for them for most of my adult life. I now feel my life is over, and I have no job and no qualifications to get one. Friends are almost non-existent as there was never time to develop friendships, and I've never had a relationship with a man either. Being an only child means there are no family members to turn to either and I'm so lonely. The only thing I have is the house in which I've always lived, but at times it feels like a prison. Sometimes I'd just like to curl up and die as any kind of life seems out of reach for me now.

Angela

Dear Angela,

You've certainly had a difficult time and I can understand how circumstances lead you to feel this way. From what you tell me, it's clear you are a caring person, having looked after both of your parents for so many years. But forty is not old, and you still have plenty of time to make a new life for yourself.

My initial advice would be to go and see your GP as I sense you may be clinically depressed. There's no shame in this, we all need a little help during difficult times, and you've seen more than your share of problems.

If you are actively looking for a job, don't be despondent, you have talents and experience as a carer which could open up opportunities for you. Perhaps while you are looking you could try some kind of voluntary work. There are dozens of charities crying out for volunteers, in shops, the WRVS, hospitals... the list is endless, and it may help you to find out what you want to do and possibly lead to new friendships, as would taking a course at your local college. There are many courses suitable for mature students, academic or creative, and you could try to find something which interests you and may prove helpful in seeking paid employment.

You've certainly earned the right to think of yourself, Angela, and I applaud you for such selfless care of your parents, which is not always an easy thing. If you are on the internet you may like to look at the magazine's website which features articles about loneliness and depression. The address is on the inside cover of every issue.

Please don't despair. You are young with so much to offer and so much life still to enjoy.

Laura

Angela's letter struck a chord with me. I've also felt lonely at times as my father died four years ago and my mother lives on a different planet. Dad was stricken with lung cancer which seemed unfair as he'd never smoked a cigarette in his life! Mum was already showing signs of dementia during the last few months of his life, so it was left to me to care for them both. But I'm not complaining. Dad was no trouble and tried hard to carry on as usual so as not to place too heavy a burden on my shoulders. But with a wife slowly leaving him, it was distressing, and I think he was ready to go when his time came.

Mum, by then, was oblivious to the world around her and I was forced into making the awful decision of finding a home for her to live in, for her own safety. So, she now lives quite happily on planet Alzheimer's with others stricken by this same cruel disease. I, too, am an only child and felt very alone and isolated during my parents' illnesses. Paul was also an only child, but his parents are both alive and well, living in Highgate, just a couple of Tube stops away from me. They were terrific with the children during those dark days and supported me in many ways, and I love them for it. Having been disappointed with their son when he left me, Janet and Bob have remained a part of my life, and the children still see them regularly.

Unlike Angela, I'm blessed in having people to turn to, yet I struggled mentally to decide whether to tell Janet and Bob about these hateful letters. Finally, I decided not to, perhaps they were just a couple of random letters, penned by someone with a sick sense of humour, and with luck, there would be no more. However, telling the children was undoubtedly out of the question, so it was to be a waiting game, and I tried hard to put the issue out of my mind.

I did intend to go to the police, knowing if I didn't, Brian Clark would. Yet, it would have to wait until the following day, as my trip to the city had filled up so much time and the children would be arriving home, expecting me to be there.

'Not fish again! We had fish yesterday!' Lucy was first to arrive home.

'Did we?' I honestly couldn't remember what we'd eaten yesterday. I am not a particularly good cook and, despite my aspirations, will never be a domestic goddess. Lucy tutted and turned to go upstairs. I watched her retreating – black hair hanging loosely to her shoulders with a shock of purple half-covering her eyes. Why she'd dyed her hair when she possessed the most beautiful honey-blonde natural colour, I'll never know, but I didn't have a say in the matter. Lucy stayed overnight with one of her friends and arrived home the next day looking like a stranger. Being angry was futile, and I dearly hoped it was a passing phase. We really needed to have a conversation about the pill, but I simply didn't have the energy or inclination after the day's events. Turning my attention back to the fish, I attempted to make it more interesting by coating it in savoury breadcrumbs (from a packet, of course) and making potato fritters – the boys' favourite.

One of our house rules, which I try to keep to a minimum, is that we eat together around the table at least once during the week and again at weekends. It is easy to make a meal and allow the children to eat on the run, watching television, or in their room, hence the rule, and that evening was rule night. When the meal was ready, I called my family from their various locations and we settled around the table to eat.

'Wow, fritters, great!' Sam exclaimed, making me smile at the simple things which pleased my son. Lucy looked at the fish and began pushing it around her plate as if trying to revive it. I hoped she wouldn't attempt the kiss of life next. Observing her closely, I wondered if she'd embarked on another fad diet, something she regularly tries in an effort to lose weight, which she can ill afford to lose. I've attempted complimenting her on her slim figure, which, quite honestly I would swap mine for any day – but Lucy hates the body she has and frequently attempts to alter it drastically. Finally, she took a bite and I breathed a sigh of relief.

'Jon's asked if I'd like to go to his dad's for tea again next week,' Jake told me.

'And do you want to go?'

'Don't mind, I suppose,' was the unrevealing answer.

'Well it's entirely up to you, Jake, but tell Jon when you decide. It would be rude not to let him know until the last minute.' I was secretly hoping he wouldn't go, suspecting Jon had received some kind of prompt from his father and this was another ploy to see me again. Jake nodded his head and pushed a couple of fritters into his mouth while my thoughts returned to those letters. Even though I tried to discipline myself to ignore them as someone's idea of a joke, they still played heavily on my mind. Would there be any more? Hopefully not, but I would take them to the police station tomorrow, sure they would think it was nothing more than the proverbial storm in a teacup.

Chapter Six

The local police station was a satellite office, open only during the week and four hours on Saturday mornings. As I have never had cause to visit it before, I had no idea what it looked like on the inside. Outside it was beautiful, an ornate Victorian building which had once been a large private dwelling, it was now divided into two, with the police station occupying one side and the local library the other. The vast heavy doors were wedged open and I pushed my way through a glass interior door and gazed at my surroundings. It was something of a let-down; having expected the interior to reflect the same era and charm as the outside, I was disappointed. A rather shabby desk, enclosed by a glass partition, stretched the length of the lobby. It was reminiscent of the sixties or seventies, with the wood tired and in need of varnishing or chopping up for firewood. The opposite wall was flanked with grey plastic bucket chairs, the type we had at school years ago. The floor was covered in linoleum and cracking from heavy traffic, with black scuff marks from myriads of rubber-soled shoes. The officer behind the desk looked to be about thirteen, which said more about my age than his, and I approached with a smile, not knowing quite what to say.

'Good morning, I'd like to speak to someone about some letters I've received.' He looked puzzled. Obviously, I needed to be more specific.

'They're abusive letters, sent to my work address and my editor insisted I bring them to you.' My tone was apologetic, knowing they had much more important issues to deal with than my two paltry letters.

'Can I take your name please?' he asked, politely enough, so I dutifully recited my name and address.

'So, you want to see a detective?' He looked at me expectantly.

'I don't know who I want to see; can't I just give you the letters and leave them here?'

He smiled at my naivety.

'It's a matter for CID. If you'd like to take a seat, I'll see if someone's available to see you.'

I obediently sat on one of the bucket seats, glancing at my watch to check the time; it was 9.45am. Ten minutes passed before a young woman in civilian clothes came out to see me. She was also impossibly young and very pretty, with long glossy black hair tied back into a ponytail.

'Mrs Green?' she asked. 'Would you like to come through?'

I stood up to follow her through swing doors to a corridor with several rooms leading off both sides. She took me into the first room on the right and motioned for me to sit down on a wooden chair while she took the other one opposite me; a small table separated us.

'I'm Detective Constable Amy Peters; my colleague says you've been receiving abusive letters?'

'Well, only two, but my editor, who I work for, insisted I bring them in. They were sent to the magazine address, but they didn't show them to me until yesterday.' I pulled the offending letters from my bag and slid them towards her on the table. As she began to open them, she asked,

'So you don't open your own mail?'

'That's right. I work from home as an agony aunt for the magazine. Usually, they only pass on the letters they want me to feature each week, and most of them come by email these days.'

DC Peters nodded as she read the letters.

'Are these the only ones as yet?' she asked.

'Yes, do you think there'll be more?'

'Your guess is as good as mine.'

'I'm sorry, I'm wasting your time, aren't I?'

'No, certainly not! The tone of the second letter is more serious than the first and hints at some kind of threat. You haven't received any at home, you say?'

'No, only these two which were sent to the magazine.'

'That's good. It means the sender probably doesn't know where you live.'

I let go of the breath I didn't know I was holding in relief.

'Is there anything else which has been happening in your life at the moment? For example, have you felt as if someone's been following you or anything else unusual?'

'Goodness, no!'

'Sorry, there's no need to worry. As I said, apparently, the sender doesn't know where you live which is a good thing. You say you work as an agony aunt; do you use your own name or a pen name?'

'My own, but only Laura, not my surname. But there's a photograph of me at the top of the column.' I remembered posing for that picture and trying to set my face to express the right degree of intelligence and empathy whilst still being approachable. I don't think the result was quite what I wanted, but Madeline had the final choice of picture. DC Peters wrote down almost everything I said and then asked for the magazine's name, their address and my editor's name and contact number.

'Is there anyone you've fallen out with lately or someone at work who may have a grudge against you?'

'No, not at all. I don't have many people in my life; I'm divorced with three children, and as for colleagues at work, I barely know them. As I said I work mostly from home.'

'Then you have no idea who could have sent these letters?'

'No, not at all.'

'And your ex-husband, is there animosity there at all?'

'We parted years ago and he's moved on with someone else now. Our relationship isn't wonderful, but we're civil to each other, and he visits the children regularly. I couldn't see him being responsible for this at all.'

'Do you think it could be someone who's written to your page and not received the answer they were looking for?'

'Well, yes, it's entirely possible. I don't give the answers readers always want, but the answers I feel are the correct ones for a given situation.'

'What qualifications do you need to be an agony aunt?'

The sudden change in her questions threw me for a moment.

'Well I'd like to think empathy and common sense are paramount, as well as life experience, but I do have a degree in psychology.'

'Ah, I wondered. So, what do you think these letters are all about?'

I'd read them both several times and formed some ideas but was unsure about sharing them. Surely the police would have a better idea than me? Still, my opinion had been asked for so I went ahead.

'Well, I think the writer is a man and a man who is either a misogynist or not very good in relationships with women. He appears angry about women in general and those references to "women knowing their place" points to chauvinistic tendencies. It could be he's absorbed these views from his father or perhaps there was no father around and he had a very domineering mother. I can see him being a loner and an unhappy, angry man.' As I spoke, DC Peters made notes and nodded her head frequently. That was as much as I wanted to say – it summarised my thoughts since I'd first seen the letters.

'What happens now?' I asked.

'We'll look into it, Mrs Green, and contact the magazine, but in the meantime, try not to worry. Whoever he is, he doesn't appear to know where you live and there are thousands of women called Laura out there. So we'll give it a couple of days, speak to the magazine and then get back to you. But, naturally, if you receive any more letters, please let us have them straight away and the same if anything else out of the ordinary happens too.' Amy Peters gave me a broad smile and stood to show me out of the room and back into the foyer.

Once outside, the cold, bitter February wind whipped at my face and around my legs. I pulled my collar up and dropped my chin to keep warm. It was 10.50 and I decided to treat myself to a latte and a cake; sugar is medicinal, isn't it, and surely I deserved something nice? But my legs felt a bit like jelly, and a strange feeling settled in my stomach like something was stuck there. These letters had affected me more than I'd expected and those hateful words refused to exit my mind, no matter how much I tried to expel them.

Chapter Seven

The coffee and carrot cake barely took my mind off those stupid letters. What I needed was a strong dose of common sense and the best place for me to find it was in Highgate, at the home of Janet and Bob, my ex in-laws. So I rang to see if they were home rather than waste a Tube journey, and hearing Janet's voice almost reduced me to tears. Silly, really, as I kept telling myself the letters were nothing to worry about, just some woman-hating nut letting off steam.

'Can I come round?' I asked rather weakly, and Janet, in her usual pragmatic way, said of course I could, as if it was the most natural thing in the world, which it isn't actually. I generally meet Janet for a catch-up in town when we do our 'ladies who lunch' thing every few weeks, or she and Bob come to our house to see the children. A thirty-minute Tube journey (three stops on the Northern Line), a five-minute walk, and I was entering their charming home, a place of peace and serenity. Not that it was an immaculately presented glossy magazine house, but shabby chic, by which I mean original shabby chic, not simply a décor style. Their furniture was ancient but of good quality and over the years they'd patched and renovated it with an enviable flair. Colourful throws and cushions warmed each room, and the walls were lined with bookcases holding well-thumbed books from Shakespeare and Dickens to Maeve Binchy and Stieg Larsson. It smelled of sunshine and dog, but in a perfectly acceptable, even comforting way. As soon as I sat down my mood became instantly calmer. The dog in question was an elderly chocolate Labrador called Fudge. He made an effort to stand up on his arthritic old legs to greet me, tail swishing from side to side as he waddled in my direction. Having already kissed Janet and Bob, I reached down to fuss Fudge, stroking his silky ears, and was rewarded by him sitting on my feet, so at least one of us was comfortable.

Janet must have had the coffee ready as she left the room for no more than two minutes before reappearing with a laden tray. The three of us sat in the watery sunlight from the French windows and enjoyed the aroma of fresh coffee. I didn't know what to say once actually there with these two lovely people. Perhaps I didn't need to say anything, just simply be in their company, but they would be wondering, even though they wouldn't ask.

'I've had a couple of crank letters at work.' My words caused Janet to raise her eyebrows; Bob simply blew on his coffee.

'What kind of letters?' she asked.

'Well... they objected to my replies, in somewhat extreme terms, and the second one, in particular, was quite malicious and told me to stop writing my column or I'd regret it.'

'Oh, Laura, how terrible!' Janet took my hand and squeezed it. 'Have you been to the police?'

'Yes, this morning. Madeline insisted, and so did a man from the magazine's legal department. They have to cover themselves I suppose.'

'So what are the police going to do?'

'There's very little they can do. I spoke to a detective constable who made copious notes and asked if I knew who the letters could be from, but it's ludicrous, no one I know would send them. So it's probably some husband who objects to an answer I've given his wife – and as they were sent to the magazine, thankfully it appears he doesn't know where I live.'

'They will investigate, though?' Bob chipped in.

'She said they would speak to Madeline and look into it, whatever that means, but quite honestly, they've got nothing to go on. The envelopes were cheap white ones which could be bought almost anywhere and the letter was typed and printed from a computer. By the time it had been passed around to all and sundry at the office, there'll be little chance of fingerprints.' I sank deeper into the sofa. 'I'm sorry to bother you with it, it's probably nothing at all and I don't want you to worry.'

'It's no bother, Laura. You know better than that! I'm just glad you've come to us. You know we'll help in any way we can, don't you?' Janet was all concern.

'Yes, and I'm grateful for it. I don't know what I'd do without you both.'

'Phooey! You should call upon us more often. It's always lovely to see you and the children – you don't call upon us often enough. When was the last time you had a night out and let us babysit?' She all but wagged her finger at me, but in the nicest possible way.

'Where would I go? I'm perfectly happy at home with the children and my job. In fact, I wondered if I could borrow some more books although I haven't brought the last lot back yet?'

'You don't need to ask,' Bob said. 'Help yourself and don't bring them back. Take them to a charity shop or something – we're drowning in books here!'

'Now then, will you stay and have some lunch with us, it's

only soup but I've made a batch of bread and we've some lovely brie in the fridge?' Janet always made her own bread, and her soups were to die for.

'I'd love to,' I answered honestly and followed her into the kitchen to help. I considered telling her about Lucy being on the pill but then thought again. Perhaps I should discuss it with Paul first – he'd be annoyed if his parents knew before him.

'How's Paul? I haven't seen him for a while. He tends to meet the children out somewhere these days and drop them off at the corner afterwards. I'm beginning to think he's avoiding me.' I tried a laugh which sounded rather strangled in my throat. Janet didn't answer immediately, and I wondered if something was wrong.

'He is okay, isn't he? And Zoe?' I almost hated saying her name – it sounded so perfect, beautiful, poised, slim – and young.

'Actually, he probably is avoiding you.'

'But why?' I was shocked.

'Zoe's pregnant.' Janet turned to watch my reaction, concern written all over her face. It was something I'd never even considered would happen. Paul was forty, which isn't old for a man to have a family, but I'd assumed he wouldn't want any more as he already had three children.

'I think it's Zoe more than him who wants a baby; she's only twenty-seven, so it's quite natural.' Janet put her arms around me and I stupidly found myself crying on her shoulder. It wasn't as if I wanted Paul back. I got over him years ago, but news of the baby brought back memories of our children and how happy we'd been. He'd been a good dad, initially at least. Perhaps the morning's events had made me vulnerable too. In the comforting warmth of Janet's arms, I allowed myself a moment of being needy. It was so hard always having to be the adult and the one to offer comfort to others. I took a tissue from my jeans pocket and sat down at the kitchen table, blew my nose noisily, and pulled myself together.

'I'm sorry, Janet. I am pleased for Paul. I just didn't expect it.'

'I know, perhaps it was a bad time to tell you, but he'll have to tell you soon, and the children, goodness knows what they'll think.' She smiled and I returned the gesture imagining Lucy's face and sure the word 'gross' would figure somewhere in her reaction. The boys would probably take it better, but if they felt their relationship with their dad was in jeopardy, there could be some jealousy in store.

'Thanks for telling me, goodness knows when Paul will get round to it, he always did have ostrich tendencies.'

'Zoe's already over seven months.' Janet looked almost guilty.

'Seven months! But why hasn't he told us, what's the secrecy about?' I was shocked, wondering how he could have kept this from the children. Then, mulling it over, a few things dropped into place. Paul's reluctance to see the children of late and their meetings always being on neutral territory now made sense. Perhaps the boys wouldn't have noticed anything but Lucy certainly would have!

'She doesn't look that far gone. Being tall and slim must help Zoe carry the baby well,' Janet observed, reminding me of my pregnancies when I resembled a beached whale, particularly with the twins. I made a comment about this, and we laughed together and got on with preparing lunch. The news, however, stayed with me for some time afterwards. I imagined Zoe looking the picture of radiance and health, with a neat little 'designer' bump, shown off by a slim-fitting jersey dress, accentuating her pert, firm bottom. I was sure she would carry it well, not like me, who waddled like a duck, especially latterly with the boys, and my craving for Toblerone bars and ice cream didn't help in the weight department. Even now, I've never lost all the extra pounds I put on during pregnancy, but I can hardly blame the twins eleven years later, can I? My body sags in all the wrong places which is no one's fault but my own. Somehow, I didn't think Zoe would have any problem with losing her baby weight, and for an instant, I hated her for it.

I made my way home, feeling slightly better for seeing Janet and Bob, but the house felt empty and hollow as soon as I put the key in the lock. Uncharitable thoughts of Zoe still crowded my mind – thoughts I embellished in my head until they became an imagined form of reality. I was sure she would have no stretch marks or varicose veins, unlike me. It was unreasonable to dislike her so much when we'd only met on half a dozen occasions. She'd always been polite and friendly in a cool sort of way and I knew the fault lay entirely with me. Such a long time had elapsed since my marriage break-up, and it wasn't entirely her fault. Paul was as much to blame as Zoe. I steeled myself to be more gracious towards her in the future, and when the baby arrived, to be happy for them both.

It was times like this when I missed Holly, who had been my friend and next-door neighbour for more years than I care to remember. She would have turned my crazy thoughts into laughter, and I missed sharing with her. Holly brightened any room and any situation with her whacky sense of humour and an even stranger dress sense. She was the only adult I've ever known who could wear lime-green woollen tights, with a pink minidress and purple-streaked hair tied up in an orange scarf, and get away with it. I could never decide whether it took ages to perfect some of her outfits or if she threw her clothes on in the dark each morning. Most of her ensembles were recycled bargain finds from charity shops, which she wore with style, calling them 'retro'. Holly's hair too changed colour almost more often than I changed the sheets on my bed, but that was her, and I loved her all the more for her quirkiness.

Holly's friendship had seen me through many rough times

during the last few years. She supported and encouraged me when I needed to work, often taking the children out on special trips to give me time to myself. She listened to my whining when Paul left me for his PA and somehow managed to make me see the funny side and laugh at myself too. Holly helped out when the boys got chickenpox at the same time as I came down with flu, her ministrations being invaluable. I think we might have starved to death without her then.

Holly was also my primary source of fun. At least once a fortnight, we shared an evening at my house when she would bring the wine, often more than one bottle, and I would provide the chocolate. We made a pact never to feel guilty about such indulgences and also, whatever we discussed during those evenings would stay within those walls. Thank goodness the walls couldn't talk! We laughed like schoolgirls and couldn't have been closer if we'd been sisters. Occasionally we'd treat ourselves to lunch in town, always finding something to celebrate, even if it was just the first Thursday in a month or because it hadn't rained for two whole days.

Holly and Brian, her husband, were never blessed with children of their own, and she often said she felt privileged to share mine. (And she was most welcome at times!) She was warm and funny, and the very sight of her had the power to cheer me up. I was devastated when Brian was promoted at work and they moved to Carlisle. It was such a long way to travel, and I knew our meetings would become few and far between. Determined to continue our friendship, we communicated on Skype, usually once a week, often more, and always late at night. But somehow, even though I knew I could Skype Holly, a virtual friend was not the same as a warm flesh and blood one.

Chapter Eight

Dear Laura,

I am sixteen and live at home with my parents. My boyfriend has fallen out with his family, and my mum and dad agreed to him moving in with us. We want to share a bedroom but they won't hear of it and have said he must sleep in the spare room. It is the 21st century, and surely they shouldn't be treating me like a child anymore! Do you think they're unreasonable?

Tricia

Dear Tricia,

Your parents are being incredibly generous in allowing your boyfriend to stay with them, and I don't think it's unreasonable of them to ask him to sleep in the spare room. You don't say whether their objections are based on religious beliefs, but it appears this is their moral belief anyway, and while you and your boyfriend live under their roof, you should respect their wishes. Everyone who reaches sixteen thinks they are grown up – I know I did, but your parents are making a very generous gesture here. You can show your maturity far better by going along with what they want. It will also give you the time and space to learn whether this boy is the right partner for you. If you and your boyfriend are still together in a couple of years, you may wish to find your own home together, and you will have avoided any bitterness with your parents.

Laura

No coconuts for guessing who this letter made me think of. Lucy had said nothing more about being on the pill and coward that I am, I too let the subject drop, but it needed to be addressed. So I decided to ring Paul and ask him to come around so we could talk to Lucy together. Hopefully, Paul would also use the opportunity to tell me about the baby.

I rang him at the office on his direct line so Zoe wouldn't know I was ringing, although I wasn't even sure if she was still working as his PA, probably not with the baby coming so soon.

'Paul Green, hello?' His voice was clipped but friendly.

'It's Laura.' There was a brief embarrassing silence which I felt should be filled. 'We need to get together sometime soon to talk about Lucy.'

'Why, what's wrong?' The tone of genuine concern in his voice pleased me.

'Nothing's wrong in that sense – it's just – she's on the pill and being very evasive about who the boyfriend is.'

'The pill! Why on earth did you let her do that?'

'I didn't let her, she went to a clinic by herself and they prescribed it. I only found out by accident.'

'Well you need to take them off her!' The concern was turning to anger and I was the one conveniently placed to take the backlash.

'No, Paul, we need to talk to her. She's fifty per cent yours as well, you know.'

'It's a bit difficult at the moment...' He was hedging. I should have expected it.

'It's difficult for me too, but you need to make time and soon. Give me a date and time, and I mean this week.' The sooner the better for me.

'All right, I'll come over tomorrow after work, at about five-thirty. Is that any good?'

'Yes, five-thirty, we'll see you then.' I put the phone down before either of us had a chance to say something we might regret.

The following day I worried about Paul coming, yet goodness knows why. It wasn't as if it was me who'd done something wrong. My plan was not to tell Lucy in advance in case she opted out and didn't come straight home after school. But when she did arrive home, I owned up and told her that her dad was coming round and we wanted to talk to her.

'What is it with you?' she almost shouted at me. 'Can't you let me lead my own life?' Then, without waiting for an answer, she flounced off upstairs, where she remained until Paul arrived.

When he did come, I thought maybe we should form some kind of strategy and asked my ex-husband what he thought we should do about the situation.

'How on earth should I know? This is more a woman to woman thing, isn't it?'

'No, it isn't. Lucy's your daughter as much as mine and we need to agree here. Do we insist she comes off the pill, which would almost certainly risk pregnancy, or do we let the matter go but insist on meeting the boyfriend?' I looked Paul straight in the eye when I said the word 'pregnancy', but he didn't flinch even though this would be an ideal opportunity to tell me about Zoe's baby.

'Well, we certainly don't want her getting pregnant, so perhaps being on the pill is the better option.' He looked distant as if he was far away in another land.

'I can go along with that, but we need to meet this

boyfriend. If she's so taken with him and they're sleeping together, we should try to get to know him.'

'Okay, so tell her, will you? I really can't stay. Zoe's not too well at the moment.' Paul stood to leave.

'No way! I asked you here so we could talk to her together. You're not leaving me to do this alone.' I blocked his exit and pushed him back into the chair with the flat of my hand on his chest. He was suitably shocked and sat motionless with his mouth open. I moved to the bottom of the stairs and called Lucy down, which would normally not work as she's generally hooked up to music. However, she must have been waiting for the call and came down immediately. The boys knew their dad was coming but I'd banished them to their rooms until we'd spoken to Lucy, then I'd promised they could see Paul. Our daughter flopped onto the sofa, chin on her chest and arms folded, avoiding eye contact. The silence confirmed that Paul had no intention of opening the dialogue, so I began.

'Lucy, your dad and I have been talking, and we'd like to know a little more about your boyfriend.' Silence filled the room as Lucy and her father both studied their feet. 'Well, does he have a name?' I asked.

'Brad,' Lucy responded.

'Brad who, do we know his family?'

'Johnson and no, you don't know them.'

'So what do you think, Paul?' I lobbed the ball to him, getting increasingly annoyed that he was leaving it all to me. I wanted his support, not for him to be an observer.

'Yes, it would be good to meet him.' But, unfortunately, my ex wasn't very helpful.

'Look, Lucy.' I decided to say my piece. 'Your dad and I aren't happy about you being on the pill or indeed about having a sexual relationship at all. But we know we can't stop you so we'd at least like to meet this boy you're so keen on. Surely it's a reasonable request?'

'You bloody hypocrites!' Lucy was suddenly full of venom. 'Don't you think I've done the maths – you were pregnant with me long before you were married, yet you have the nerve to tell me what to do!'

'I was quite a bit more than sixteen at the time, and Dad and I intended to get married anyway. So we just brought it forward a bit.' I glanced at Paul for support.

'Don't talk to your mother like that, Lucy!' He was losing his cool now, which was all we needed.

'What do you care? You're too wrapped up in that girlfriend of yours! When you left us, you forfeited your right to tell me what to do!'

This wasn't going as I'd expected or hoped. I sat down next to my daughter and tried to slip my arm around her shoulders but she shrugged me off.

'Don't touch me!'

'Lucy, we only want what's best for you,' I pleaded.

'No, you don't. You're too wrapped up in your darling twins – and you!' She glared at her father again. 'If you'd cared about us you wouldn't have left us for such a bimbo!' With that stinging comment, she jumped up and ran upstairs leaving us both stunned.

'Well that went well.' Paul's voice dripped with sarcasm.

'And it was no thanks to you!' I retorted, angry at myself as well as him. 'What do you think she'll say when you tell her about the baby?' I couldn't resist adding.

'How do you know…?' His puzzled expression gave way to a dawning. 'My dear parents, couldn't they have waited to let me tell you?'

'Which would be when? As Zoe goes into labour?' I didn't want to row with Paul like this but we seemed to spark off each other these days. 'Well, your sons want to see you even if your daughter doesn't, so I'll let them know they can come down now.'

'I don't have the time, Laura...' Paul stopped when he saw the look in my eyes.

'Okay, if you don't have the time to see them, you can tell them so yourself!' I marched upstairs to tell Sam and Jake they could come down and see their dad. Paul stayed for another fifteen minutes, not nearly enough for the boys, and left with promises of seeing them again soon and taking them to play ten-pin bowling, then out for a pizza. I only hoped he kept his promise. I hated seeing the disappointment on their faces when he cancelled visits.

Tea was a gloomy affair with only the boys' chatter to lift the atmosphere. Another attempt at speaking to Lucy was shrugged off and I found myself alone after tea while she sulked in her room and my sons kicked a football about in the garden.

The situation with Lucy was troubling, not just the pill thing but what she'd said in her anger. Did she honestly think I was more concerned with her brothers than her? And I'd never heard her call Zoe a bimbo before; where did that come from? Perhaps we'd not handled the separation well if there is a proper way to do such a thing. The boys weren't even two when Paul left and probably can't remember him ever living with us, but Lucy was six. Maybe I'd expected her to cope better because she was older, which was apparently wrong. At six years old, my precious little girl had completed her first year in school, a difficult time for any child, had two new and demanding brothers who sucked up all my time and energy, and her beloved daddy deserted her. How could we have got it so wrong? Was I so wrapped up with the twins and my own sadness that I'd not paid enough attention to Lucy? Was it too late to apologise and make it up to her? Most certainly, I'd have to try, but it wasn't going to be easy. Had Lucy turned to this Brad for the love and comfort she felt was lacking at home? How dare I call myself an agony aunt.

Chapter Nine

M any of the letters I receive come from women with family problems, the majority of which are complex and involve immediate family, parents, partners, children, the entire spectrum. Stupidly I'd never thought of my own family as being in any way dysfunctional, but after the previous evening with Paul and Lucy, guilt began to gnaw away at my mind. My daughter was my firstborn child and, as such, held a special place in my heart. With her birth came great happiness and a sense of wonder that I've never lost. Sadly, somehow I'd not managed to convey this to Lucy – she didn't know how special she was to me. We take such things for granted at times, thinking that our loved ones know how we feel. Lethargy sets in, and we neglect to tell them how special they are to us and how much we love them. It's not that I love the boys any less. I adore them every bit as much, but a daughter is special, and my heart ached for Lucy's unhappiness.

Whilst reflecting on this, the telephone rang. It was DC Peters asking if she and a colleague could come and talk to me about the letters. Naturally, I agreed. I should have been writing an article about '*Holiday Harmony*' – a feature which would run ahead of the school summer holidays, and one which I now felt utterly unqualified to write. It was almost 10.30am and Amy said they would be with me in fifteen minutes, so I boiled the kettle and set a tray in anticipation of offering my visitors coffee. When the doorbell rang, I pasted on a smile which I didn't own and invited them in. Amy introduced the other officer as Detective Sergeant Steve Radcliffe and we assembled in the living room with coffee and questions on both sides. The DS was about six feet tall with broad shoulders and an athletic build. He was handsome in a rugged way, and I would guess somewhere in his early thirties. Amy spoke first.

'There's been another letter, Mrs Green,' she said matter-of-factly as if it had been expected.

'But I've not had one; surely the magazine would have passed it on to me?'

'They gave it straight to us. We'd asked them to pass on any more letters unopened so that we might have a chance of some forensic evidence,' Amy explained. It made sense.

'And did you? Get any forensic evidence, I mean?'

'It's too early to say. We've sent it for examination but it will take several days as it's not a priority case.' That at least was reassuring.

'So what did it say?' I wanted to know yet didn't want to know.

'It's couched in very similar terms to the last ones but a little more forceful and specific.' DS Radcliffe took over the conversation as Amy Peters took out her notebook and a pencil.

'Can I read it? It was addressed to me.'

'Well, we can tell you the gist of it if you're sure you want to know?' The sergeant seemed reluctant.

'Yes, I do.'

He took the notebook from his colleague and began to read

out some of the letter; he spoke slowly, paraphrasing the points and missing out some of the more distasteful words. Even his edited version was more chilling than the others had been and my stomach was churning by the time he'd finished. A few moments of silence ensued when I thought I was going to be physically sick. Then, taking a deep breath, I concentrated on focussing on the letter objectively, a tactic that had helped me cope with traumas in the past. Unfortunately, it didn't seem to help, the room seemed suddenly cold and I wrapped my hands around the mug of coffee, trying to draw warmth and comfort from it. The DS looked at me sympathetically then attempted to move on to more general questions.

'I always thought these agony aunt columns were fictitious, with the letters made up by journalists. I can't believe that you're actually '*Ask Laura*'.' He spoke as if he'd heard of the column.

'Are you familiar with my page?' The question brought a blush to his face, which rose from his neck up to his hairline.

'My mother sometimes gets the magazine so I've seen it on occasions.' He was flustered and even his DC looked at him now and smiled to herself. Could we have discovered his guilty pleasure?

'Can you explain how it works?' He again moved things on quickly and I went along with it even though I'd already told the constable.

'The letters arrive at the magazine address where the paper ones are sorted with a selection sent on to me. I decide which ones to answer, between four and six a week, and send them back with my answers by email. Some readers send their problems via email, and the process is the same. Madeline, my editor, has the final say in which ones are published.'

'Do you ever enter into correspondence with your readers directly?' he asked.

'No, that's not possible. Occasionally I refer readers to

articles I've written previously and which are archived on the magazine's website if I think it will help their situation.'

'So you never get involved personally in any reader's problems?'

'That's right. I try to signpost readers to organisations that could help, for example, Relate for marriage guidance, bereavement groups, Gingerbread for single parents, etc. But the magazine policy is never to get involved personally.'

'Then you wouldn't give out your address, phone number or email address?' he asked.

'No, never.' It seemed an obvious question but presumably they had to ask the obvious.

'There were a couple of inferences in this latest letter that lead us to believe the writer might know a little more about you than we previously thought, perhaps even where you live.' DS Radcliffe seemed reluctant to tell me this and nothing he'd read to me from the letter made me think the same.

'So you didn't read the whole letter to me?' My anxiety was increasing, surely knowing precisely what was in the letter couldn't be any worse than the scenarios my imagination would weave. 'Can I see the letter in its entirety, please?'

He reluctantly turned back in the notebook to the page from which he'd read.

'This is only a copy. As I said, the original is being examined.'

I scanned the page and almost immediately was aware of the blood draining from my face. The words were full of venom and talked of the vile things he'd like to do to me, physical violence and even sexual references. There was mention of my honey-blonde hair and my 'pretty face'. The writer almost casually dropped into the letter that it would be a shame for such a face to become scarred. It was shocking – especially when he wrote that he knew where I lived in my comfortable home with my beautiful family, and if I didn't stop writing my column, he'd be 'paying me a visit' one dark night. I dropped the pad onto my lap. DS Radcliffe picked it up and asked if I was all right while his colleague went to the kitchen to fetch me a glass of water. I drank the water too quickly and coughed and spluttered all over. Then, flapping my hands to indicate I was okay, I regained my composure, outwardly anyway.

'I'm sorry,' I mumbled. 'It's certainly not pleasant!'

'That's why we didn't want you to read it all, but you can see why you need to take this seriously. Have you had any more thoughts on who this could be? Have you argued with anyone lately, your ex-husband perhaps?' the DS asked.

'We're not on the best of terms but I'm certain it's not him. I honestly can't think of anyone who would want to scare me like this. But the references to my home and family are very general. They could apply to any number of women throughout the country, and he'll know what I look like from the headshot on the page each week.'

'Yes, we realise all of that, which is why we can't offer you any kind of protection,' DC Peters spoke up.

'Protection, I wouldn't expect it! I'll admit to being a bit unnerved by this, well more than a bit really, but I'm pretty certain that this isn't anyone I know, or even who knows me.'

'That's our thinking now too, but we would ask you to be extra vigilant until this is sorted out.' Amy Peters smiled reassuringly at me.

'It's a pity it's not like the old Agatha Christie stories,' I mused, 'when the culprit was caught by the faulty letter on his typewriter. Printers are so impersonal and tell you nothing about the writer.'

'Actually, many modern printers include some form of tracking information which can associate a document with the printer's serial number. Apparently, it's something to do with a yellow dot, or similar mark, which forensic investigation can decipher.' The DS suddenly looked embarrassed as both DC Peters and I stared at him.

'Of course, it's not widely used, only in cases of serious fraud and the like.' He blushed again, trying hard not to come over as some kind of techno-geek.

'So the forensic team won't be using such high-tech knowledge on my nuisance letters?' I smiled at him, rather enjoying his discomfort. He shook his head and stood to leave.

'If you think of anything at all that might help, please ring. And could we have the address of your ex-husband too? I know you think he's not responsible, but we still need to check him out, just to eliminate him if nothing else.' He handed me a card with his contact details and I gave him Paul's address, thanked them both and then showed them to the door.

My concentration was gone entirely. It would be impossible now to do any work. So I boiled myself an egg and ate in silence whilst considering getting a cat. A purring ball of fur on my lap could be just the thing to calm my increasingly edgy nerves, or maybe I should consider a Rottweiler.

Chapter Ten

Madeline's call was unexpected, although I had thought about calling her myself to find out why she hadn't told me of this latest letter.

'Darling, this is so horrible for you. The police asked that any further letters be sent directly to them – I'm so sorry!' she gushed.

'That's okay, I understand.' And I did.

'We've had a meeting with the legal department and the executive editor and have decided to suspend the '*Ask Laura*' page for the time being.' Madeline spoke softly now, knowing this wouldn't go down well with me.

'But why? The police agree that it's probably someone who doesn't know me. Why give in to this monster? It's blackmail and if we give him what he asks, he'll have won!' I was angry and afraid simultaneously; angry at the man writing such letters and fearful for my future! If they decided to cut out my page, I'd be looking for another job, and I loved this one.

'We simply can't take the risk. If anything did happen to you, I'd never forgive myself. Put yourself in my place, Laura. Wouldn't you do the same?'

'I suppose so, but this is only temporary, isn't it?' I asked, needing reassurance.

'Only until the police find whoever is doing this. In the meantime, we'll continue paying your salary and perhaps you could concentrate on writing some more features? Our readers will miss your problem page, but they enjoy the regular features you write so beautifully.' Madeline was always so calm and annoyingly right. All I could do was to thank her and accept the decision to suspend my page. They had been generous in continuing to pay my salary, but we both knew it wouldn't be indefinite. We ended the phone call, by which time I felt more than a little deflated. Perhaps it was time to pull out my unfinished (barely started to be more accurate) novel, but I had no heart for it. Maybe tomorrow?

That evening, Jake was going to Jon's house again, and I'd given him the same instructions about ringing when he was ready to come home. Lucy was in her room, and Sam absorbed in a computer game, so I'd spent my time trying to write, although the words wouldn't come. Then, just as I was beginning to wonder if I should ring Jake, the door opened and he walked in, followed by Jon and Richard. My heart sank.

'Hello, I was just about to come and get you.' I tried to sound upbeat but felt the situation was suddenly not in my control, even though it was in my own home. Jake gave me a weak smile and went upstairs, followed by Jon, while Richard edged towards me.

'Jake was ready to come home and wanted to show Jon something, so I thought I'd bring them over to save you the trouble.' His face had a peculiar expression on it, a mixture of anticipation and something else which wasn't easy to interpret.

'Thank you, but it wouldn't have been any trouble to come for him. I hope he's behaved himself?' What a stupid question. Jake, probably the most sensitive of my children, always behaved himself at other people's homes; I knew he could be trusted.

'Oh yes, he's been great. They get on so well together it's a pleasure to see.' Richard sat down next to me on the sofa, uninvited. I stood up and offered coffee, not that I wanted to prolong this visit but simply to move away from such uncomfortable proximity to this man. He patted the seat beside him, saying, 'No, don't worry about coffee, come and sit down and get comfortable.'

The only way I could have been comfortable with Richard would be by sitting in the next room.

'Richard, you'll have to forgive me, but I have a lot of work to do tonight, so I'll just go and see if Jon's ready...'

Richard stood and moved over to me, and before I was able to protest, his arms were pinning me to the door-frame and he was trying to kiss me. I pulled away and almost ran to the other side of the room. His face darkened.

'Come on, Laura, don't be a tease. I know you're lonely and we could have a bit of fun, a diversion, you know? So, you scratch my back and I'll scratch yours, literally if you like?' He laughed, snorting at his joke.

'Yes, I do know what you mean and I'm sorry but you've got the wrong idea entirely! I'm not looking for another relationship or even a bit of "fun" as you put it!' My whole body was trembling as Richard's face grew darker. He came towards me again, his face contorted into a grin or a leer. I couldn't decide which.

'Think you're too good for me, do you? You with your pathetic little life, pretending you can solve other people's problems when you can't even get yourself a man!'

If the children hadn't been in the house, I was convinced he would have struck me or something worse. I froze, afraid to move as Richard pushed past me and went to the bottom of the stairs.

'Come on, Jon, we're going home, *now!*' he shouted. Fortunately, Jon came down immediately and I watched as his father grabbed his arm and almost dragged the poor boy out through the door. I remained still, breathing deeply to calm myself. Jake came downstairs and jolted me back into the world of the mundane as he asked what he could have for supper. If he noticed the state I was in, he said nothing, and I forced myself to find my son something to eat.

Sleep didn't come easily that night. My mind raced with the events of the day and I had to admit to being shaken by the unpleasant encounter with Richard. He'd clearly been engineering a friendship between our sons, in which probably neither of them had an interest. Perhaps now that would stop and Jake wouldn't receive any more invitations from Jon. The memory of Richard touching me made me shudder. The man must be so thick-skinned as I'd told him on previous occasions that I had no interest in seeing him at all. Surely now he would realise that I wasn't being coy or teasing. I simply didn't like him.

As I mulled over the incident, a strange thought crossed my mind; could it possibly be Richard who was the source of these hate letters? Surely not! I tried to form some kind of timeline to piece together events in relation to the letters. I'd certainly been aware of Richard for the past year, but he'd only approached me a few months ago when he first asked me to go out with him. Since then he'd hovered on the periphery of school events, and I'd been very much aware of him watching me on occasions. He'd even suggested another date, which again I refused. The invitations from Jon to Jake had been more recent but was it possible that Richard wrote those letters, and if so, why? Could it be an attempt to make me feel vulnerable so he could play the knight in shining armour and offer comfort? And should I tell the police about him? It was a tough call; if I did speak to the police, they would almost certainly interview him, which, if he were innocent, would be a dreadful accusation no matter how tactfully the police approached it. Yet they had asked me to inform them if anything out of the ordinary happened or if I had any suspicions about who this letter writer could be. I tossed and turned in bed, unable to decide what to do, and sleep refused to rescue me from my troubled mind.

Eventually, I went down to the kitchen to warm some milk in the hope of getting sleepy, purposefully turning my thoughts from Richard to the other bad news of the day, the suspension of my page. It grieved me to think that '*Ask Laura*' wouldn't be appearing in the magazine and for an indefinite period too. I loved answering those letters and liked to think that my advice helped those readers who perhaps had no one else to turn to. Switching on my laptop, I began scrolling through some of those old letters that I could never bring myself to delete. One of them jumped out at me; it was sent nearly two years ago from a mother estranged from her daughter.

Dear Laura,

My daughter, Alice, left home last year to live with her boyfriend. I didn't want her to go, but she's seventeen and we'd not been getting on too well at the time. I hoped we could build a new relationship and perhaps become friends, but she refuses to see me. She never comes home and when I've called at their flat, I don't get an answer, even though I'm pretty sure she's in. She still sees her sister, who is fifteen and living at home, but even she won't tell me why Alice refuses to see me or answer her phone. What can I do?

Sally

Dear Sally,

This is such a difficult time for you and I can feel your pain throughout your letter. Teenage years are never easy, and as parents, we sometimes fail to pick up on things our children see as important. Perhaps there was a particular incident or even something you said which Alice misunderstood? You could try writing a letter, asking her what it is that you have done to cause this estrangement, and telling her how much you long to see her again. If there is no response, maybe you could tell your younger daughter how upsetting this is for you and ask for her help telling Alice how you feel.

You don't say what your relationship with Alice's boyfriend was like – could you approach him to talk about the situation?

If these suggestions don't work, there's very little you can do except to remain constant. Continue to send birthday and Christmas cards, with chatty messages asking how she is and telling her how much you would like to see her again. Hopefully, in time, Alice will realise what she is missing and how much you love her.

Laura

If I'd expected to read something that would help me sleep, this was certainly not it. I remember this letter, even though it was so long ago, and I remember thinking that this would never happen to Lucy and me. How foolish I was! Two years ago, Lucy and I were still friends, but now I was all too aware of a shift in our relationship. Gradually, she stopped telling me things we would normally have discussed and laughed at together and confided in her best friend instead. It was a time of pushing the boundaries when Lucy was testing me to see how far she could go, and I, with my shiny degree in psychology, thought I knew it all! Feeling confident that I could handle adolescence, it never occurred to me that we were growing further apart. I put it down to a phase and ignored those subtle changes when I should have been proactive, when

I should have reassured Lucy that she was so precious to me and talked to her more, not less. But was it too late? Would Lucy end up hating me for not understanding her? I must make it clear to my daughter that I love her more than life itself, that I'd backed off to give her space to grow when I should have been nurturing and guiding her through the trauma of those teenage years. I must apologise to my daughter and try again to gain that unique closeness that mothers and daughters can share. I only hope it's not too late.

Chapter Eleven

When morning finally arrived, the problems of the previous day dawned as inevitably as the sun. The mental debate of ringing the police about Richard, or not, was still troubling me as I showered and dressed in a trance. Pulling myself together, I tried to be cheerful at breakfast, particularly for Lucy. My daughter has never been a morning person and all attempts at conversation were ignored or responded to with sullen, incoherent grunts. Once the children left for school, I tidied around until procrastination had to be put aside. I moved to pick up the telephone, only for it to ring before I had the chance. It was Paul, and from his cold greeting, I gathered the police had been to see him.

'Did you have to tell them I might have written those letters?' he demanded.

'I didn't tell them that at all!' My tone was equally brusque. 'They have procedures for this kind of investigation and an ex-husband is always in the frame. So you needed to be eliminated from the investigation, it makes sense really...'

'It wasn't a good experience, finding the police on my

doorstep. I've even got to go down to the police station to be fingerprinted! Couldn't you at least have warned me?'

'Like you told me about the baby?' I regretted saying it as soon as the words left my lips.

'It is rather different.'

'Yes, it is, and I'm sorry, it was uncalled for and I apologise.' Paul went on to ask about the letters, which I played down as if they didn't bother me and we finished the call. Next, I dialled the police station and almost immediately was put through to DS Radcliffe. I found myself struggling to find the right words to say – not wanting to blacken Richard's name unnecessarily – which was precisely what I was about to do. After telling the sergeant the purpose of my call and attempting to explain the events of late, he stopped me and offered to come round. Gladly I accepted the offer – surely it would be easier to talk over a cup of coffee and I would be able to explain that this was simply a long shot and I didn't actually think Richard was the crazy letter writer.

Again, the DS was at my home within a very short time; it was pretty comforting knowing how near the police station was. As he walked into my lounge, it struck me as strange how pleased I was to see him. His physical proximity had a reassuring effect on me, emphasising how vulnerable, and yes, afraid I felt until the presence of this man banished some of that negativity.

For the first time I noticed his eyes, which were an unusual shade of blue, fringed with long dark lashes. His nose was perhaps a little too large for his face, but the eyes drew attention from this, together with a pleasant mouth arranged in a reassuring smile. DS Radcliffe accepted my offer of coffee, and we were soon facing each other across the coffee table in the lounge.

As I began to recount the previous night's incident with Richard, my hands were trembling. It had unnerved me more than I realised. The sergeant listened attentively, nodding to encourage me until my tale was finished.

'Can you tell me the history of this man, Mrs Green? Any other times he's approached you, that kind of thing.'

I nodded and began to think back.

'Do you think you could call me Laura, or is it not protocol in this situation?' I would feel infinitely more comfortable with someone who used my Christian name. He nodded and smiled, so I began to tell him of every contact with Richard I could remember. These didn't amount to many and it crossed my mind that I was making a fuss about nothing until again my hands trembled at the memory of Richard's angry face. The time Richard Ward first appeared on the scene was certainly well before the letters started, but why would he be writing them if he was attempting to begin some kind of relationship with me? I voiced this uncertainty and the DS offered one or two possible reasons.

'On the first occasion when you refused a date with him he could have been offended. He may have thought up the idea of the letters to make you feel vulnerable. On the other hand, his reasoning could have been that you might be more willing to let a man into your life if you were upset and needy. Or maybe he was being purely malicious, angry at being turned down.'

'Then why would he pursue the issue, and why come on to me last night? It's probably not him and I shouldn't even be suggesting it!' I wished I'd simply forgotten the incident. 'Will you have to interview him?' Stupid question, of course he would. How else could he rule him out as a suspect?

'Yes, but we'll be very discreet. If you're frightened of any repercussions, and this man sounds an angry sort, we'll warn him off. If he's stupid enough to approach you again, we can get a court order to keep him away from you.' The sergeant took down Richard's address and promised to let me know how he got on with him.

'Thank you, DS Radcliffe,' I said.

'It's Steve.' He smiled. 'Here's my mobile number. If this man does contact you, ring me on here any time, day or night.'

'Your wife won't be too pleased if I do,' I said with a laugh.

'There is no wife, so don't worry.' He finished his coffee, thanked me and left. Standing in the kitchen, holding our empty coffee cups, I felt a right idiot. Had I really just fished to find out if he was married? Stupid, stupid me! He was years younger than me. What on earth was going through my mind? Still, there was comfort in being on first-name terms with him, and he'd given me his mobile phone number. When my cheeks cooled down, my thoughts turned from silly schoolgirl fantasies to Richard Ward. With no idea of when Steve would see him (I should have asked him, instead of admiring his eyes) it was impossible to know when to expect any fallout. But I trusted Steve to handle the interview sensitively and possibly warn Richard against contacting me. The next few days were going to be anxious ones for sure.

With time on my hands and no enthusiasm for writing a feature, I decided to bake a cake or some biscuits, perhaps even both. Amazingly the necessary ingredients were to be found in my kitchen and a pleasant hour or so was spent reacquainting myself with domesticity. The finished results looked edible enough, and hopefully, the children would appreciate my efforts.

There was still an afternoon to fill. Not wanting to stay in, I decided to visit my mother. The home she lives in is, in my opinion, the best one in the area. When she became unmanageable and the decision inevitably needed to be made, I visited all the facilities within travelling distance from my home. Some were, quite frankly, appalling and places I wouldn't consider, despite their claims of '*a home from home*' and '*friendly, dedicated staff*'. My visits were all purposely unannounced to enable me to see the homes as they were, without prior warning giving the staff notice to be on their best behaviour. The first home was ruled out because they refused me entry, and I could hear shouting in the background. A very young girl opened the door and was almost rude as she informed me that I must make an appointment, and the door was closed in my face before there was even a chance to request a prospectus. I didn't make the suggested appointment, having already seen enough.

A couple more places welcomed me in to view their facilities and talk about practicalities. The first of these was in an ancient building with a smell of damp and of urine, diluted by bleach. Almost every room needed a complete overhaul, and there was no need to ask why they had so many vacancies. Most of the residents were in the same large, cold room, many of them oblivious to their surroundings but moaning and groaning as if in pain. There appeared to be very few staff on duty, and when I asked about staff/resident ratios I was told there was a sickness bug going around and several staff members were off sick. I couldn't wait to get out myself and therefore didn't even consider it for Mother.

The next one was a significant improvement with an enthusiastic matron who welcomed me warmly, even though my arrival was unannounced. She cheerfully showed me around personally, answering any questions which cropped up. Residents were either in small community rooms with staff encouraging them to participate in activities or in their bedrooms, napping or watching television. There was a good feel about the place and the matron told me how almost half of their residents had dementia. She had a positive ethos and explained that they tried to find the person who had once inhabited the diseased body, to remember they were someone's mother or father, stricken down by this terrible affliction. The staff were encouraged to be patient and kind, even though verbally or physically abused by residents. Matron was selective when hiring staff members, which showed. Yes, there was noise, a little moaning and groaning, but staff were speaking soothingly, holding those old gnarled hands and gently stroking them to calm and settle residents down. As I had made an impromptu visit, the acts of kindness I witnessed couldn't have been manufactured. Cedar Lodge was to my mind the right place for my mother, but, as expected, vacancies did not arise often and her name would have to be added to a list, which I did there and then.

A couple of other places seemed adequate, but Cedar Lodge put them in the shade by comparison. However, after Dad died, the situation was suddenly urgent, and I accepted a place for Mum in a rather large care home with a secure wing for people with Alzheimer's. It had scored reasonably well on my list of possibilities. But, to cut a long story short, Mum did not settle and I received constant telephone calls from the home asking me to call in to 'discuss' her condition.

There was no reason to believe Mum was any more difficult than the other residents with the same disease, but she seemed to cause insurmountable problems for the staff. Each time I was summoned, pressure was exerted to allow them to sedate my mother, an idea which horrified me. Was this usual in cases of Alzheimer's, or was it to make life easier for the staff? Putting off making a decision, I began to ask around in a bid to learn if this was standard practice. It was a constant worry and a dilemma which was miraculously solved when a very welcome call came from Cedar Lodge, offering an immediate place for Mum. Aware how a move could prove unsettling, I decided to go ahead, feeling the benefits far outweighed any disruption, which thankfully proved correct. Mum is now in a lovely room of her own with an en suite and a television lounge close by. Regular activities stimulate her, and she has settled in so well that I regularly thank God for this place. Matron is always available to discuss any aspect of care, and shortly after moving Mum in, I asked about their policy on sedatives.

'Yes, we do recommend them on occasions. When a resident becomes over-anxious about something and all else fails, we will consult her GP and the family and decide what course of action to take. Most residents who are on sedatives only take them at night to aid sleep, and we find that when they are properly rested, anxieties are no longer such a problem. This is one of the reasons we put so much effort into offering stimulating activities each day.' As she explained, a piano could be heard playing in the background, accompanied by cracking voices singing along to 'We'll Meet Again'. I smiled, reassured. My mother moved into Cedar Lodge seven years ago, and it has undoubtedly been the best place for her.

Visits to Cedar Lodge are bittersweet experiences. Mum rarely knows who I am, although I like to think there are occasional moments of clarity when the woman she used to be can once again be glimpsed. During the afternoon my head was spinning with thoughts of Richard Ward and the possibilities of repercussions, as well as the situation with Lucy. But I forced myself to smile at Mother, who looked at me and asked, 'Who are you then?' She eyed me up and down. 'You'll need a mop and bucket to clean that floor – it's filthy!' Mum emphasised the words with several swatting movements of her hands as if getting rid of an annoying wasp. It was all too much. I dropped onto the chair beside her, put my head in my hands and burst into tears. I couldn't stop and was thankful we were alone in the room. After a moment, I felt my mother's hand on my head, her thin, bony fingers caressing me, stroking my hair as she did when I was a child. She was mouthing soothing sounds, *shh... shh...* as she'd done years ago. How I longed to have Mum back, to put my head on her shoulder and pour out all my troubles – to be the child again with a loving mother who would solve all my problems with a few wise words and a hug.

I cried for my parents, both gone, for my marriage which could have been beautiful but had soured, and for my daughter, whom I love more than life itself. Finally, I cried for myself, for my loneliness, insecurities and my failings. I felt weak and ineffective, with my livelihood in the balance, and some unknown person who hated me so much he would send such hateful letters. What had I done to deserve all this? Suddenly, Mother's arms reached out to hold me and I dropped onto my knees with my head in her lap. She continued to hold me as I wept. I don't know how much time elapsed, but the tears were cathartic. When I eventually looked up, I saw my mother. Not the shell she had become, but the loving mother she had once been, with compassion in her watery old eyes. The look was fleeting – and then she was gone once more.

'I don't want to buy any double glazing, you know! My husband does all those things himself, so you'd better get on your way before he comes home!' my new mother said, and I laughed.

Chapter Twelve

Sam was the first through the door after school, sniffing the air like a terrier.

'What's that smell?' he asked.

'Chocolate cake and lemon spiced biscuits.' My pride was shattered as he wrinkled his nose. Jake seemed more impressed and sneaked one from the plate while my back was turned. I pretended not to notice the crumbs on his face and asked him about his day.

'Did you see much of Jon today?'

'Not really. He was in class but other than that we didn't see each other. Did something happen between you and Jon's dad?' Jake's perception surprised me.

'Well, he did suggest we spend some time together and I said no. He wasn't too pleased.'

'Good, I'm glad. I don't like him – he's creepy.'

'Creepy? How do you mean?'

'He just is. He always watches us, as if he doesn't trust us to hang out without doing something wrong. I'm glad you don't want to see him, Mum. You're too good for him.'

I embarrassed my son by giving him a hug, my kind,

sensitive boy. It's funny how you can miss a whole other side to your children. Jake surprised me and a sudden rush of love welled up inside me for him, but at the same time, nervousness filled my stomach. Will Steve have been to see Richard yet? Probably not. Richard would have been at work during the day, so it could be a while until he was interviewed.

Lucy arrived home and ran straight upstairs without speaking to her brothers or me. We were getting used to it. She was still brooding about our last confrontation but how much longer this would go on for was impossible to say. As yet, she'd not given me an answer regarding meeting her boyfriend – in fact we'd barely exchanged more than a dozen words since then.

Dinner was a relatively quiet affair with only the boys chattering about school and football. Lucy sulked, and I found it difficult to concentrate on what the twins were talking about, although they didn't need me to participate in the conversation. After homework and an hour's television, the boys went to bed, and Lucy remained in her bedroom. It was just after nine o'clock and I was considering going upstairs to see if we could talk. The situation was getting me down but would never be resolved if we both ignored it. The telephone rang, allowing me to delay the difficult conversation with my daughter. I picked up the receiver.

'Hello?'

'You bitch! How dare you accuse me of sending threatening letters! You think you're quite something, don't you? Well you're not! You're a pathetic, frigid cow and I wouldn't have you if you threw yourself at me!'

Stunned, I listened to Richard's tirade of abuse, frozen to the spot. His voice was full of venom as he went on to call me some of the most horrid names imaginable, and I was terrified. Unable to find a voice to answer him, putting the telephone down and cutting him off seemed the best course of action to take. Collapsing onto the sofa, my whole body trembled and I had to take deep breaths until my heartbeat steadied and I no longer felt the pulsation of blood in my ears. The phone rang again and I stared at it, unsure what to do. Should I try to reason with him? His anger would probably make reasoning a fruitless exercise. After half a dozen rings, I picked it up and immediately put it down, then took it off the stand and left it off.

Perhaps this would make the situation worse, and Richard might come round. Having never been so afraid in my life, I hadn't a clue what to do. It was too late to ring Janet and Bob; they would insist on coming round, which wouldn't be fair to them. But I felt so vulnerable and alone; what if Richard was the letter writer and I'd inadvertently pushed him over the edge by sending the police round to see him? After listening to his words on the phone, it seemed a credible assumption to make. I was very conscious of the children upstairs. The only positive emotion flowing through me was one of maternal protectiveness. Strangely, although feeling unable to protect myself, when my focus was fixed on the children I could dredge up some kind of feral strength – a natural instinct to defend my offspring. I stared at the phone, uncertain. Then I did what seemed to be the most sensible thing of all and rang Steve Radcliffe.

Steve assured me I'd done the right thing by ringing him and as he was still working, it was no trouble to call round, although he was about half an hour away. My apologies sounded lame and confused, which exactly matched my feelings, yet knowing he was on his way calmed me down somewhat. I checked that all the doors were locked and put the kettle on to boil before going upstairs. The boys were reading, so I told them to put the light out and go to sleep. My gentle knock on Lucy's door was ignored, so I opened it quietly and went inside. She was lying across her bed with earphones on, oblivious to my presence. Walking over to the bed to get her attention, I asked if she would like a hot drink.

'No thanks,' was the curt reply, but at least she'd added 'thanks'. I returned downstairs to wait and prowled aimlessly around until Steve arrived, by which time I'd eaten four Kit Kats and was thoroughly disgusted with myself, not just for the chocolate but for everything. Perhaps I should forget the novel and write a handbook on how to mess up a life! My credentials for writing such a work include: unplanned pregnancies, messing up a marriage, alienating a daughter, and not handling an unwanted admirer. The list grew in my mind until interrupted by the doorbell.

Had it only been this morning when this man had last been here? It seemed so much longer. Steve looked at me with concern.

'Let me make you a drink,' he said.

'I'll do it. What would you like?'

'Hot, sweet tea. You need it more than me.' He followed me into the kitchen and watched me make the tea, asking no questions until we were back in the lounge.

'What time did he call?'

'Shortly after nine.'

'Do you think you can tell me what he said?'

'I'll try.' It was embarrassing repeating some of the disgusting things Richard had said and avoiding eye contact, I repeated most of the one-sided conversation.

'I was taken completely off guard and barely responded until it became too much and I put the phone down. It rang again within a minute or two. That's when I took it off the hook.'

'Have you had any calls since then?'

'Well, no, but it's been off the hook for most of the time.'

Steve picked up the phone and dialled 1471, listened to the number, and noted it.

'Right, Laura, this is what's going to happen. After you rang, I sent a couple of uniformed officers to Ward's address. They should have seen him by now and they'll make sure he doesn't get in touch again. Tomorrow I'll send someone to fit a security camera outside your front door. This can only be a temporary measure for as long as the threat lasts. We can't fit them permanently, but it might be an option you'd like to consider yourself. I would also suggest you get a telephone which has a caller ID display, so you'll know who's ringing and have the option of answering or not.'

I nodded feebly, feeling like a useless woman who couldn't sort out her own pathetic little life.

'When we visited Ward earlier, we took his fingerprints, so they'll be on file to compare as soon as forensics sends the results over. It could be what angered him, but in my experience, the ones who make the loudest noise are the ones who are least likely to take action.' Steve was trying to reassure me, which I appreciated. His presence was in itself a comfort. Strangely, living alone with only my children had never frightened me before, but I was truly scared then. However, he seemed in no hurry to dash off and asked if he could look at the doors and downstairs windows to check for any security issues. It didn't take long to do the tour of my home and Steve seemed satisfied that it was reasonably secure.

It was half past ten by then, and I knew he would have to leave, although irrationally, I longed for him to stay.

'Be sure to lock the door after me,' were his parting words. As well as locking it, I wanted to barricade it with furniture. But I refrained from such excessive measures, making my way upstairs to bed instead, weary yet with little hope of sleep. Reliving the day's events in the silence of my bedroom, I drifted in and out of sleep, restless and listening to every sound. Even the familiar creaks and groans of my home brought fear rather than the comfort they usually afforded. It began to rain, and as the windows rattled with the high wind, my mind started to play tricks on me. Shadows from the trees outside the window took on fearful, ugly shapes, which in my half-dream, became people trying to enter the house. A bolt of lightning illuminated the room and I sat upright, suddenly wide awake. The storm was worsening, and I began to wonder if all the doors were secure. Once the thought took root in my head, it was impossible to sleep without checking.

Downstairs, the phone was still disconnected and I picked it up to check for any missed calls, of which thankfully there were none. Richard must have been warned off and hopefully wouldn't trouble me again. Everything was secure, so I made my way back upstairs to look in on the children before returning to bed. All three were sound asleep, oblivious to the storm outside and the even fiercer one raging inside my head.

Chapter Thirteen

A workman was on my doorstep by nine-thirty the following day to fit the security camera. It was a relief that the children had already left for school, but there would be some explaining to do when they came home this afternoon. Exactly how much to tell them was a dilemma. My instinct was to protect them from the world's realities, but they were growing up so quickly. Perhaps they were old enough to know what was going on, and although I hadn't directly lied to them about current circumstances, I'd been evasive.

Mid-morning, the phone rang, and I almost dropped the dishes in my hands. Surely it wouldn't be Richard again? The only way to find out was to answer and when I did, a flood of relief washed over me as Janet's voice greeted me warmly.

'We were wondering how things were, Laura. Are the police any nearer to finding out who sent those dreadful letters?' Her voice was comforting, and I took the phone and sat down to tell her the latest happenings.

'So do you think it could be this Richard who's sending the letters?'

'I honestly don't know, but he's certainly a problem.

Hopefully, the police will have scared him off and he'll not be in touch again, and they've taken his fingerprints too.'

'Have they managed to get any fingerprints from the last letter?' Janet asked.

'Sadly, not yet. It's too early. This might be a major incident to me, but it's not very high on their list as far as priorities go. I'm sure they'll let me know as soon as they can.' I was deliberately vague about the police, for some reason, not wanting to mention Steve by name. He was concerned and helpful, which is probably the sort of man he is. But, of course, I was stupid reading any more into it.

'Why don't you come over for lunch? We'd love to see you again and I've got some jam for you. As usual, I've made far more than we'll be able to eat.'

The thought of Janet and Bob's comforting presence and their lovely home beckoned, the workman had finished fitting the camera, so there was no reason to say no. I was achieving nothing productive in my own home and their company would surely give me a lift. So, replacing the phone, I ran upstairs to tidy my hair and apply a little make-up, then set off to the Tube station and on to my in-laws.

As usual, they greeted me warmly, and even Fudge made an effort to stand up and waddle over, wagging his tail enthusiastically. Pasta and salad were waiting on the table, making me feel suddenly very hungry. I enjoyed the food and probably had more than my share of the bottle of wine they'd opened but only for medicinal purposes, of course. Sitting in the warm lounge with coffee afterwards, we discussed the storm from the night before. Huge branches had come down in their street and smaller ones littered their garden. Naturally, I didn't tell them the effect the storm had on me and the irrational fear it had induced, but I began to open up a bit more to these lovely people about some of the things which troubled me.

'The magazine has suspended my page until this is all over,' I admitted as if I'd done something wrong.

'Oh, how awful, but surely they'll find this menace soon and things can go back to normal?'

'That's what I'm hoping too, but what if they don't find him? Even if the letters stop they will still be there in the background and the magazine might decide to finish '*Ask Laura*' permanently. There aren't many magazines which still feature problem pages, and they have been trying to streamline lately. So they might use this as an excuse to cut out the page for good.'

'Well it would be their loss. You do a great job, Laura,' said Bob, giving me his vote of confidence.

'Thank you, but it's a possibility I'll have to consider.'

'But you still have your articles, they're always so good, and perhaps you could write for other magazines too?' Janet always looked on the bright side.

'Yes, I've been trying to think about some features, but quite honestly, it's so hard to concentrate with all this going on.' I paused, wondering if I should tell them about the situation with Lucy. They were her grandparents and had a right to know.

'Things are a little difficult at home too at the moment.' The tale about Lucy, her mysterious boyfriend and finding the pills came out, and it was such a relief to be able to talk about it.

'So when are you going to meet this boy?' Bob asked.

'We haven't agreed on a date yet. Lucy is putting great effort into avoiding me and has hardly spoken a full sentence to me since I found the pills.'

'What did Paul say?' Janet's face was all concern.

'He did come round, and we spoke to Lucy together but it wasn't a very fruitful dialogue. With everything else going on I suppose I've let the matter slip. We'll try again and see if we can arrange a time to meet him.' I spoke determinedly, but the phrase '*the road to hell is paved with good intentions*' was ringing in my mind.

'Do the children know about the letters?' It was an obvious question and something about which I was still undecided.

'No, not yet, but when they see the CCTV outside the house, there are bound to be questions, so tonight might be a good time to talk to them.' It wouldn't be an easy conversation, and to be quite candid, I was weary with worry. It seems our little lives had been invaded with unwelcome events and I was no longer in control.

With that thought in mind, I left Janet and Bob, having enjoyed their company and the chance to talk openly to someone other than the police. But, yes, it was time to tell the children, if only for their own security. Until we knew who was sending the letters, they should be more vigilant too.

Sam was the first to spot the camera and ask the question why. When his brother and sister arrived home, I gathered them around the kitchen table to explain what had happened. Trying to make it sound like everything was under control wasn't easy when the reality was, it wasn't. Nevertheless, I attempted to keep my voice calm and even and explain the letters as simply and as well as possible.

'It's not Jon's dad who's sending them, is it?' Jake looked worried.

'I did mention him to the police and they've been to see him. Has Jon said anything to make you think he might?'

'No, but I don't like his dad,' Jake said. At least there was no fallout from this quarter. Hopefully, Richard would be too embarrassed to tell anyone, especially his son.

'How does the camera work? Can we see everything which is happening outside?' Trust Sam to be the curious one.

'Probably not. We won't have to do anything as the camera belongs to the police, not us. The man who fitted it talked about video compression and motion detectors. It's only activated by something moving into the camera's range. He said it could be connected to a computer to view any images, but that's for the police to do, not us.'

'Cool, can I try?' Sam was excited. At least he didn't seem concerned about any threat. Jake and Lucy were harder to read. Jake was quiet, he always was the one to keep his thoughts to himself, and Lucy remained silent and sullen.

'No, Sam, we can't touch it. It's not ours, and when this is over the police will take it down, and it probably won't record anything more interesting than the neighbourhood cats chasing mice through the night.' Only Sam laughed.

'This letter writer is probably only someone wanting to cause trouble, but it doesn't mean we shouldn't be extra careful. Tell me if anything unusual happens so we can tell the police, and I don't need to tell you about talking to strangers, do I?'

Lucy rolled her eyes, already bored with the whole subject. Jake nodded and Sam asked, 'What do you mean about anything unusual?'

'Well, if you think anyone's watching you or the house. Other than that, I don't know, just be careful, please.'

'Did you really have to go to the police over a few cranky letters?' Lucy didn't actually tut her disapproval, but I heard it anyway.

'The magazine insisted on contacting the police, and I agree with them. Just all take a little extra care, will you?'

The children left the kitchen, Sam, to look at the CCTV camera and Jake and Lucy upstairs to their respective rooms. It was a relief when the situation didn't appear to frighten them. To Sam in particular, it seemed to be exciting, whereas I simply longed for it all to pass so we could get on with our normal, if somewhat dull, lives.

Chapter Fourteen

A week passed without incident, which in itself was somewhat worrying. I hadn't heard from the police other than a courtesy call from DC Amy Peters to say they expected the fingerprints from forensics any day. I didn't know exactly what to expect from the police as this was hardly the case of the century, so I asked if there'd been any more letters, to which she answered no. Whether this was good news or not was debatable. If the letter writer had stopped, feeling he'd achieved the goal of the '*Ask Laura*' page being suspended, then we would probably never find out who he was. But if the magazine reinstated my page, would the letters begin again, or would they decide not to take the risk and cut out my page permanently?

Admittedly I was somewhat disappointed when Amy rang and not Steve, which is rather silly of me, I know. Steve's presence was reassuring and had a calming effect on me, but he would have many other cases which were far more important than mine. Very little had changed with Lucy either, although I did press her again to invite Brad for a meal so we could meet him. She looked horrified, but when she saw the determination in my face, she reluctantly agreed. Conveniently, Brad was away on holiday for a couple of weeks, so a meeting would have to wait until he returned; Lucy enjoyed telling me that one.

My new phone, with caller ID, rang mid-morning and I recognised the number as the school.

'Mrs Green? This is Marjorie Wilson; I'm the pastoral care tutor for the lower sixth.'

'Oh yes, hello.' I vaguely remember meeting her at one of the parents' evenings. 'Is everything all right?'

'I was going to ask you that. Lucy hasn't been in school this week. Is she ill?' Her words hit me like a slap in the face.

'But she has, surely? She's left the house as usual each morning. Are you certain she hasn't been there? Could she have been late and missed registration?'

'No, Mrs Green, we're sure. Perhaps you could come into school to discuss this with Mr Bennett? Are you able to come today?'

'Yes, of course. Shall I come now?'

'Mr Bennett has a gap at one o'clock if it's any good?'

'Yes, I'll be there.' I was stunned. Lucy had left as usual every day that week, so where had she been going? My first thought was to dial her mobile number, but unsurprisingly, my daughter's voice told me she could not take the call and please leave a message. I did, perhaps a rather angry message, letting her know the school had called to ask where she was. If she got the message and knew she was rumbled, it was unlikely she'd call me back, which sadly was the case. After an early lunch, I tried again telling her I was on the way to school to see the headmaster, softening my tone a little and saying how much not knowing where she was worried me. It was pouring with rain, so I decided to take the car rather than brave the twenty-minute walk, not wanting to be soaked through when I arrived.

West End Academy, where all three children attend, is my

old school too, but it was called West End Comprehensive then. Since my day, there are many other changes, including a swimming pool and a new science wing. For parents' evenings or productions of one kind or another, my visits to the school invariably prompted uncomfortable feelings. Having been a shy, self-conscious child, school had been an anathema to me, and I cannot concur with those who insist they are the best years of life. For myself, I couldn't wait to leave, and going to university was a much more positive experience. There'd been a culture of bullying at West End in my day, which thankfully is not the case today. But there was a different attitude to bullying then, and I would never have told my parents about it. They would only have lectured me about standing up for myself. It was part of the growing up process which I was expected to deal with on my own.

Those unpleasant memories came flooding back on entering the school, and heading to the headmaster's office evoked the same nauseous feeling from my school days. The corridors were much narrower than I remembered, and the classrooms seemed smaller, almost claustrophobic. Knocking gently on the headmaster's door, I waited for a reply.

Mr Bennett was a small, stocky man with a balding pate and deep-set, dark eyes, which gave the impression he could see directly into your mind. He possessed thick eyebrows which reminded me of caterpillars and made me want to laugh aloud, but I resisted; after all, this was a solemn occasion. His office heating was set far too high and I was most uncomfortable in my winter coat and thick scarf. He was in shirtsleeves but still looked far too warm with ugly damp patches under his armpits; hopefully, this interview would not take long. Mr Bennett spoke first, revealing badly stained, crooked teeth. He must be a heavy smoker or imbibe coffee as if it was going out of fashion.

'I gather you're not aware of Lucy's absences, Mrs Green?'

'That's right; Mrs Wilson's phone call was quite a shock and I've been trying to reach Lucy on her mobile phone since then, but she's not answering.'

Nodding, he looked down at a file, then lifted his head, placed his elbows on the desk and steepled his fingers, making me wonder what was coming next.

'Lucy's been rather distracted lately. A couple of her tutors have raised concerns about her lack of interest and failure to hand in homework, and she doesn't appear to be engaging with her studies as she usually does. Has anything been going on at home which might have disturbed her?'

Instantly I thought of the letters, but Lucy had only just become aware of them, surely they wouldn't be a reason for her to stay away from school.

'There's nothing I can think of which would cause this, but she has mentioned a new boyfriend in the last few weeks. Perhaps you could see if he has been absent too?'

I felt protective towards my daughter, even though I was furious with her. Mr Bennett didn't need to know all the details of our family problems and definitely not the argument over the pill!

'What's this boy's name?'

'Brad Johnson,' I replied. He stroked his chin thoughtfully.

'The name's not familiar. Are you sure he comes to this school?' he asked.

I blushed. 'Actually no, I assumed he did, but we haven't met him yet, he's away on holiday, so he may go to another school.'

I felt as if it was me who'd been playing truant and was embarrassed at how this must look to him. I had no idea where my daughter was now, was unaware that she'd been skipping school, and she had a boyfriend whom I hadn't met. What sort of mother did this make me? We could discuss little more without Lucy being present, so I left the school with a promise to return the next day, with my daughter, to hopefully sort this all out. Mr Bennett stressed the importance of school, particularly as Lucy had already embarked on studying for her A levels, but it wasn't me who needed to hear his lecture.

Once back at home, I tried Lucy's phone again but without success. It seemed I would have to wait until she came in for an explanation. The children would be arriving home in about an hour, and I was antsy, prowling around the house again and munching on chocolate biscuits, which only served to make me feel worse. What I wanted to do was to ring Steve, which was ridiculous. He couldn't help in a professional capacity, and just because he was a good listener didn't give me the right to offload my problems on him. Yet his face was in my mind, his warm smile and the safe feeling his presence elicited. Yes, I was definitely thinking about him in an inappropriate way, but dreams couldn't hurt, could they?

Chapter Fifteen

There've been only two occasions since Paul left when I've dated other men. The first one was only a few months after the split. David was the manager of the local branch of our bank, who I'd known to pass the time of day with for a few years. When dismantling my marriage, it was David who advised me on all matters financial. Naturally, he knew my circumstances, which gave him the advantage over me, and he always seemed to be around when I visited the bank. His friendliness helped to smooth over a difficult time and everyone appreciates service with a smile – I was no different. Our conversations became more frequent, and the topics we discussed broadened. It was no surprise when he asked me out, and I was delighted. David was very handsome, always immaculately turned out and no single woman under fifty would have failed to be flattered by his attention.

However, I could barely remember dating as Paul and I were married so young, and I was nervous. Janet and Bob readily babysat for me, and I went out on a first date with a good-looking man. It was terrifying! The evening went quite well, but when he drove me home, he was clearly expecting me to invite him in, which I felt obliged to do. My in-laws tactfully left, and the children were all asleep in bed. It sounds stupid now, and I feel a right idiot, but I thought David wanted to come in simply to have coffee and prolong a pleasant evening. When he suddenly turned into an octopus and became very physical, I was taken aback and out of my depth. Perhaps I'd expected a goodnight kiss or two, but he apparently had more in mind, much more! Don't get me wrong, I'm not a prude, but making love is something special and the clue is in the phrase, making *love*. It's an expression of love – of closeness and tenderness, something not just for recreational purposes, to my mind anyway. I didn't feel I knew David well enough, or had those feelings so early in our relationship. He was angry; apparently, buying dinner for a woman these days obliges her to return a sexual favour, something I naively hadn't expected. He left before the kettle boiled, and I changed my bank.

It was a long time before I accepted a date again and under very different circumstances. Robert was an old friend from schooldays and someone I felt I knew. He and his girlfriend were both at our wedding and they married shortly afterwards. About a year after Paul and I separated, an email arrived from Robert out of the blue, telling me that he and Jane had split up too. We exchanged emails for a while, consoling each other and trying to cheer the other up until he suggested we meet one day. Robert lived about an hour's drive from my home and offered to come over one Saturday. As Paul was having the children over the weekend, I agreed, confident the awful experience with David wouldn't be repeated.

I was right; Robert was the perfect gentleman and made no unwelcome advances at all. Our relationship blossomed and I even began to think I could be falling in love! Finally, after six months together, I was ready to commit and made my feelings clear to Robert. He, however, began to get edgy and slightly withdrawn. We saw somewhat less of each other, which was

Robert's doing, not mine, and he suddenly became very busy at work. I couldn't understand what had changed; we'd been getting on so well. When I challenged him about where our relationship was going, he told me he was living with Jane again! Their separation had only lasted a few weeks, but because, he told me, he couldn't make up his mind which of us he wanted to be with, Robert had remained silent. Naturally, I was furious and very tempted to tell Jane, but I didn't, and that was the last I saw of Robert.

Dear Laura,

My husband has been seeing another woman but says he still loves me. He wants me to let him continue seeing her until he's 'got her out of his system'. Is this a reasonable request, and should I go along with it? It hurts me to think about him with another woman. He says she knows he's married but doesn't want to give him up. I feel so depressed and cry all the time. What should I do?

Marylyn

Dear Marylyn,

Your husband is being unfair in asking you for permission to see another woman. You need to sit down and decide what you want. If you still want your husband, tell him, but insist he stops seeing her. He cannot have his cake and eat it too! Explain how the situation makes you feel, and if he loves you, he will stop seeing her. If you both want to continue with your marriage, perhaps you could seek counselling to help you recover and move forward.

Quite honestly, if he doesn't agree, then he's not worth holding on to. Regain your self-respect and build a new life for yourself. You deserve to be happy, and it could be that your happiness doesn't lie with your husband but elsewhere.

    Laura

Marylyn's letter was one of the first I ever received as '*Ask Laura*', and I often wonder what happened to her. Did she get rid of her selfish husband, or were they reconciled? I shall never know. The situation with Robert reminded me of Marylyn, and Robert was why I gave up on men. But that was before I met Steve Radcliffe. I know the idea of a relationship with Steve is ridiculous, he's younger than me and although not married, he could be in a relationship – a good-looking man like him surely wouldn't be single for long. Perhaps my flight of fancy was simply borne out of loneliness during a difficult time. Whatever it was, I needed to bring it under control and act my age. Fantasies about handsome policemen were so inappropriate. The children were my priority now, particularly Lucy.

The confrontation with my daughter was every bit as tricky as I'd expected. She arrived home at the usual time, dropped her school bag in the hall and ran upstairs to her room. It was evident this situation couldn't go on. Lucy ignored me most of the time, which I found hurtful. It was hard playing the 'bad' parent all the time, doling out the discipline when I just wanted to hug her and tell her how much I loved her. But she wouldn't let me in. When the boys were both home and occupied with other things instead of hanging around the kitchen wanting food, I went up to see Lucy.

Knocking on the door of her room, I didn't wait for an answer and went straight in. She was sprawled on the bed and looked at me with a scowl before turning to face the wall, tapping furiously on her mobile phone. Moving to sit on the bed, I pulled her shoulder to turn her round.

'Lucy, we have to talk. The school rang me this morning to ask why you haven't been there this week.' She didn't even have the good grace to blush or apologise. Silence was her weapon of choice.

'Look at me, please. We need to sort this out. Is something bothering you at school?' Perhaps like me, she was being bullied? A shrug was her only reaction.

'I need more, Lucy. Sentences, reasons, arguments, come on, Lucy, you're a bright girl. Don't you see you're wasting all the potential you have?'

'School's boring!' she said, which at least was a phrase.

'So what have you found to do which is less boring than school?'

'Just hanging out with friends.' Excellent, almost a sentence!

'Which friends would they be?'

'Brad and a few others.'

'But Brad's away on holiday, so where did you hang out today?'

'The shops, the park...'

'The park? It's February, Lucy; it would be freezing in the park!'

My daughter shrugged again. How on earth was I going to resolve this?

'Mr Bennett wants to see you and me first thing in the morning and I've promised him we'll be there.'

'I'm not going. I'm done with school!' She sounded angry now, which was good. Any reaction is better than none, surely?

'But what about your exams? You're in line for such good grades and will almost have the pick of universities.'

'I don't want to go to uni, so I'm not going back to school.' She turned away to face the wall again.

'Okay, I'm going downstairs to ring your dad. He needs to

know of your plans, so you can talk to him.' There was no response from Lucy so I went to do as I'd said.

'Look, Laura.' Paul sounded annoyed over the phone. 'I can't keep coming round every time you argue with Lucy.' He was as unhelpful as ever.

'This is rather more than an argument; she hasn't been going to school! All she'll tell me is that she's hanging out with Brad and some of his friends. I can't handle this on my own anymore, Paul. I need your help!'

'Okay, I'll ring Zoe and let her know I'll be late home.'

'Thank you.' I put the phone down, disappointed that Paul wasn't more concerned. He always seemed too busy to give the children the time they needed with him. Everything I asked of him was begrudged, but I wasn't asking for me. It was for our children.

Chapter Sixteen

Although still furious with Paul, a sense of relief washed over me when he arrived. He looked weary, and I couldn't help wondering how he would cope with a new baby in just a few weeks. Yet even at the risk of being called a nag, I did not intend to let him shirk his responsibilities with our children either.

'Where is she?' he asked.

'Up in her room. I've tried to talk to her and got nowhere, perhaps if you go up on your own?'

'Come on, Laura, I thought you wanted us to do this together!'

'The last time we spoke to our daughter together, it didn't work. I've tried, so it's your turn now.'

Paul ran his fingers through his hair and sighed. He was beginning to look his age and any youthful vitality he once had seemed to have drained from him. I felt rather sorry for him.

'Look, Paul, I know you don't like confrontation any more than me, but Lucy's slipping away from us, well from me anyway. I've tried, but perhaps I'm too close. Perhaps she'll open up to you. Please, help me with this.'

'Okay, I'll try.' Paul briefly stroked my cheek and looked at me with an unreadable, enigmatic expression. He turned and began to climb the stairs, wearily as if climbing a mountain.

Fifteen minutes can at times seem like an eternity but hopefully it was a good sign. Did it mean Lucy was opening up to her father? Whilst waiting downstairs, I made a coffee, assuming Paul would need one, a strong one when he came down. I also managed to eat a whole bar of milk chocolate, which made me feel good until it was finished and the guilt took over. Eventually, Paul came downstairs and into the kitchen.

'Well?' I pushed a cup across the table to him as he sat down opposite me. 'How did it go?'

'She's adamant that she's not going to school anymore.' He sighed.

'But did you tell her it wasn't an option?'

'I tried but you know how stubborn Lucy can be and we can't physically drag her there, can we?'

'Well, I'll certainly try! But, doesn't she legally have to go to school?' I was unsure.

'Not at sixteen.'

'That's ridiculous,' I replied.

Paul shrugged, he looked exhausted and I felt guilty for adding to his burden. 'Did she tell you anything more about this Brad and where she's been going when she's not been to school?'

'Brad's away, but apparently, she has a key to his flat which is where she's been.'

It struck me like a bolt of lightning. Brad isn't someone from her school or any other school. If he has his own flat, he must be older than Lucy, but how much older?

'Paul, we have to go up and speak to her again. We need to know where this flat is and how old this boyfriend is too.' My ex didn't protest. Instead, he drained his coffee mug and stood wearily to follow me back upstairs.

'Lucy.' I knocked and opened the door. Our daughter had been crying. Was this a sign that she was coming round? I sat on the end of her bed while Paul took the chair by the desk. How I longed for the days when her problems could be fixed with a hug and a magic kiss.

'I'm not going back to school, and you can't make me!' She sobbed. I tried to reach out to her but she pulled back.

'Lucy, there must be a reason why you don't want to go to school – this has come on so suddenly. We can't help if you don't tell us what it is.' I looked to Paul for support.

'Your mother's right. We only want what's best for you and leaving school now isn't in your best interests. We'd also like to know how old Brad is and where exactly is his flat?'

'What's age got to do with it?'

'When you're only sixteen, quite a lot.' Paul sounded firm, but Lucy only shook her head. We were making no progress. Goodness knows what I was going to tell the headmaster the next day.

'Will you at least come with me tomorrow to discuss this with Mr Bennett?' I had told him we would be there. Lucy shrugged.

'I know you think you're grown up and know what you want, but we see this as a mistake. You've shown such promise in your studies and could have endless opportunities in the future. If you throw it all away now, you'll regret it, Lucy.' I tried to speak gently, my little girl was hurting and I was powerless to take the hurt away.

'All right, I'll come, but Mr Bennett isn't going to make me change my mind either.'

It was a concession, and I smiled my thanks. Lucy had neatly avoided telling us where Brad lived but we were both reluctant to push her further. Agreeing to accompany me tomorrow was a step in the right direction. Solving this would take patience, and we needed to take it one step at a time. We left Lucy's room and returned to the kitchen to talk.

'Thank you, Paul. It's so much easier to cope with you beside me.'

'I know, and I'm sorry I haven't been around much lately. Things at work have been manic since Christmas, and there's talk of redundancies. Zoe's not coping well with the pregnancy either, so I feel pulled in all directions.'

'I'm sorry, this won't help either but we have to show a united front to Lucy. I haven't a clue what's made her like this. Perhaps it's just this boyfriend or something more deep-seated. Sometimes I wish I could rewind time and parent the children all over again, avoiding the mistakes we've made. But sadly, we only get one chance with each child.' I was well aware that past mistakes can't be undone, but hopefully, we could learn not to repeat them.

'Is there a school counsellor who Lucy could talk to?' Paul asked. Now why hadn't I thought of that?

'What a great idea! I'll ask about it in the morning. Talking to someone outside of the situation could be just the thing she needs.'

Paul nodded thoughtfully and I suddenly felt sorry for him.

'Off you go home now. Thanks for coming – it made a difference.'

'Do you want me to come with you in the morning?' he asked. In all honesty, the answer was 'yes', but I declined, telling him instead that I'd ring and let him know how it had gone.

Paul went to find the boys and have a few minutes with them before leaving. Making more coffee, I took two mugs up to Lucy's room. She looked directly at me, understanding the olive branch I was handing her.

'Thanks for the coffee, but just because I've agreed to go to school tomorrow doesn't mean I've changed my mind.' It was the longest sentence my daughter had spoken to me for weeks and I couldn't help but smile. I would give anything to put this all behind us and have the kind of relationship we'd had when Lucy was a little girl.

Chapter Seventeen

I watched a DVD with the boys during the evening. Lucy declined the invitation to join us, turning her nose up at their choice of viewing. I, however, settled in to brave the transforming robots or whatever the film was about. A little past eight o'clock, the doorbell rang and I felt relief at being saved from the last half hour of the film. As I opened the door, it was a surprise to find Steve Radcliffe on my front step. We smiled at each other, and then, as I stepped back to let him in, my mind began to race with questions. Had they found the letter writer? Had another letter been sent? Were the forensics back, and with what result? It turned out to be a combination of two of the above.

'I'm afraid there's been another letter.' Steve spoke gravely and my heart sank. 'As before, the magazine didn't open it, so we've sent it off for comparison with the previous one. The forensics has come back for the last one and we managed to get some pretty clear prints.' He paused, maintaining eye contact as he told me, 'They don't match either your ex-husband or Richard Ward.'

I sighed, unable to decide if this was good news or bad. Quite honestly, it was what I'd expected. To my mind, Paul was never a suspect. As for Richard, I'd been unsure and now felt terrible for casting suspicion on him at all.

'So we're no further forward then?' I asked, disappointed.

'Not necessarily. We ran the prints through our database and didn't find a match, but, as we do now have prints, if anyone else comes into the frame as a suspect, we'll be able to confirm almost immediately if he is the letter writer.'

'Do you think I should apologise to Richard Ward? I feel terrible about naming him as a suspect now.'

'No, that would most certainly be a bad idea. Ward doesn't seem to be the sort of man who would forgive and forget, so I'd recommend you keep well away from him in the future. He might even take advantage of an apology to try to see you again, and I'm assuming you don't want to?'

'You assume right.' I smiled. 'Can I get you a coffee, Steve?'

'That would be great. I've just knocked off shift so coffee would be very welcome.'

I smiled inwardly at this, pleased that although he'd officially finished work, he was happy to be in my company. I was certainly delighted to be in his. With all these inappropriate thoughts filling my head, I'd completely forgotten to ask about this latest letter. After rectifying this, Steve answered.

'I could let you see my notes on it if you like, but it's very similar to the last one with nothing new to make us think this man does actually know you. I'm beginning to think if he did know you or where you lived, he would have used the knowledge by now.'

'In what way?'

'Perhaps by directing the letters here or boasting about

what he knew. People who do this kind of thing enjoy the
power it gives them. He would want to step up the pressure, let
you know what he knows in an attempt to scare you even more.
Having no new information in this latest letter convinces me
that he doesn't know your address or you personally.'

I nodded. It made sense and was a relief.

'Having the security camera outside has been a comfort,
and the boys think it's amazing.' I was grateful to Steve for
arranging it.

'Good, it will certainly be a deterrent to any unwelcome
callers.' He smiled. Steve had such an infectious smile – I
grinned back at him.

'How old are your children?' he asked. It was a relief to
talk about something unconnected to those awful letters.

'The twins are eleven and Lucy's sixteen now.' The
mention of Lucy took my smile away.

'Is something wrong, Laura?'

'Sixteen is a bad age.' I attempted a smile. 'Lucy hasn't
been to school this week and I'm ashamed to say I knew
nothing about it until the school rang me this morning.' Was it
really only this morning?

'Hmm, a difficult one. Has she told you where she's been
going?'

'Apparently to her boyfriend's flat, which is another worry.
I've only just found out there is a boyfriend and assumed he
was someone from school until she mentioned his flat. Lucy
won't tell me his age, but he must be a good few years older
than her.'

The phone rang, and I picked it up, annoyed at the
interruption to our conversation.

'Laura? It's Angela here, from Cedar Lodge. Sorry to
disturb you so late, but your mother's not well at all. The
doctor's on his way, but I think you should come too.'

'What is it?'

'Well, we thought she'd picked up some kind of virus which was affecting her breathing, but whatever it is, it's looking serious... and you should prepare for the worst.'

Stunned, I thanked the matron and replaced the phone in a daze. Could this day get any worse? Steve looked at me, concerned.

'Is something wrong?' It was the second time in only ten minutes he'd had cause to ask me the same question. The kindness in his voice suddenly weakened me and I burst into tears. Steve took the two steps between us and enfolded me in his arms. He held me as I sniffed and sobbed onto his shirt. It was a relief to have his arms around me, and I wished I could stay there forever. Pulling myself together, I explained how my mother was ill and the matron feared the worst.

'I'll have to ring Janet to see if she can come round and sit with the children – they're nearer than Paul. I must tell the children too.'

Sam and Jake had never really known their grandmother. The real woman, that is, not this ghost of the person she now was. Lucy perhaps had a few more memories but hadn't visited much during the last few years. There was no point. Mother could be angry and aggressive at times and I wanted to protect the children from those unpredictable moods.

'I'll take you if you like?' Steve's voice broke into my thoughts.

'I couldn't possibly ask you to do that.'

'You're not asking, I'm offering.' His smile would be my undoing.

'It's very kind... and yes, I would appreciate the company.'

Janet was all business.

'Of course we'll come! Don't worry about a thing. We'll stay all night if necessary.' What a blessing they were to me. I don't know how I'd manage without them. Telling the children was the next thing. The film had just finished and the boys came bounding into the kitchen, hungry as usual. If they noticed I'd been crying, they didn't let on, but they were curious about who the stranger was.

'Boys, this is Detective Sergeant Radcliffe. He's been helping to find out who's been sending those letters I told you about.'

'Cool! So you fitted the camera outside. Can you show me how to run it through the computer?'

'Sam, don't be so rude. I've told you the camera is not ours to experiment with.'

'Your mum's right, Sam. I'd be happy to show you, but it's not allowed.' Steve smiled at him.

'Boys, listen. I've had a call from the nursing home where Granny is. It seems she's not at all well and the matron wants me to go and see her.'

'What, now?' Jake was puzzled.

'I'm afraid so. Granny's very poorly, and there's a chance she might not get better.' Was there ever an easy way to explain such a thing to children? They exchanged looks then Sam spoke up for them both.

'We'll be all right, Mum. Don't worry about us.'

'I've already rung for Grandma and Granddad to come round. They'll be here soon.'

'We don't need babysitting – we're eleven now!'

'Yes, but as I don't know how long I'll be, I'll feel much happier knowing someone's with you. Now, it's time for bed. So off you go and get ready, and Grandma will be here soon.

'I'll just tell Lucy,' I said to Steve and followed the boys upstairs. Lucy surprised me when I told her by beginning to cry. She allowed me to hold her for a minute before shrugging me off and drying her tears. Perhaps it wasn't simply this bad news which affected my daughter but a culmination of recent events; it was all getting to me too!

Janet and Bob arrived soon. After briefly introducing them to Steve and explaining how he'd kindly offered to drive me to Cedar Lodge, we left, heading off to just one more catastrophe in the life and times of an agony aunt.

Chapter Eighteen

The journey passed in silence, although not an uneasy one. I was lost in memories of the past, of happier times when my mother was the intelligent, vibrant woman I'd adored. Steve didn't intrude on the silence, for which I was grateful. It gave me the space to prepare for whatever awaited me. It was a wet night and the windscreen wipers worked hard to clear the rain, their rhythmic movement almost hypnotic. The rain made for very little traffic, and when we arrived, I presumed the few cars in the car park to be staff vehicles. It wasn't the time for visitors.

Cedar Lodge was only dimly lit. Having never been so late in the evening, I found it somehow different, peaceful perhaps without the brightly lit rooms and the background noise of the television and cups rattling on the trolley. Matron's office was adjacent to the main entrance. She must have seen us approach as the door buzzed open and we entered into the home's warmth which was usually welcoming, but this evening felt almost inhospitable. Angela was beside me within seconds and her arms reached out to embrace me. Fighting back the tears, I introduced Steve, giving him the status of 'friend' to avoid confusing explanations.

'Is there any change?' It seemed right to ask. It was well over an hour since she'd telephoned.

'No, the doctor's with her now. Let's go and find him.'

Steve, holding my arm for support, quietly asked if I'd like him to remain in the entrance lobby.

'I'd rather you came with me if that's okay?' I felt in need of his presence and strength. He smiled and followed on to Mother's room.

The doctor was coming out as we approached. It was the duty doctor, one I'd never met. Matron introduced me, and the doctor spoke gently.

'I'm sorry, Mrs Green, but your mother is slipping away. She's peaceful at the moment and not in any pain, but I don't think she'll last the night.'

I nodded and felt Steve's reassuring squeeze on my arm.

'Can I sit with her?' I don't know why I asked permission. She was my mother.

'Of course, Laura, and I'll get another chair for your friend,' Matron offered.

The room was warm but when I touched Mother's arm, she felt cold. Her breathing was raspy and laboured and her colour a deathly pale; it was apparent, even to my untrained eye, she did not have long to go. Steve again asked if I wanted to be alone with Mum and Matron took over.

'Perhaps if you come with me I'll get some coffee for us all, and you can bring Laura a cup?'

She must have been in this situation hundreds of times. Steve dutifully followed her out, leaving me alone with Mother. She looked so thin and frail under the sheets. I held her hand and, shuffling closer to the bed, began to talk to her.

'I love you, Mum. It's been difficult these last few years but I know you're still in there somewhere. I'm going to miss you, but you'll be with Dad soon and...' I didn't know what else to say. Dying is still a taboo subject to many people and not something we generally give much thought to. I desperately wanted to think Mum would be reunited with Dad, and in some way, it was what I believed. The concept of heaven is one I gladly embrace, simply because I find the alternatives difficult to accept. Yes, the human body weakens and dies but what about the spirit? I cannot imagine my spirit, the very essence of me, simply dying with my body. As for God as the Creator, I have always accepted that too. It seems far more credible that the earth and humanity were planned and designed by an intelligent, heavenly being, rather than other theories, like the 'Big Bang'. Now there was nothing more I could do for my mother, it was comforting to picture her, once again in her prime, entering heaven and being with Dad again.

Steve brought coffee and sat beside me in silence as we drank. It took little more than an hour before Mother finally took her last breath. I kissed her brow then allowed Steve to lead me from the room. Matron took over once again, instructing me to go home and rest. She would call the doctor back, and the usual arrangements could be made in the morning. All the details she needed, like the name of an undertaker, were to hand in Mum's file on forms which I'd filled out years ago.

The biting, icy wind hit us full-on as we hurried through the driving rain to Steve's car and he helped me in with such care and gentleness that I cried. Before I knew it, his arms were around me for the second time that night, and he stroked my hair as I sobbed for a full two minutes or more. It wasn't only for Mum I cried, but for Dad too, for Lucy who was hurting but wouldn't let me in, for those vile letters and the probable loss of my job. It all came out in loud, ugly sobs.

Eventually, the tears stopped and I reached for a tissue to

dry my face. Steve looked at me and asked, 'Do you want to go home now?'

'Yes, I've taken up enough of your time. I'm so sorry.'

'Don't be, please. You introduced me as your friend, which is what I'd like to be. And friends help each other out, don't they?'

I nodded as he started the engine, then we moved away. It was 1.45am. Had I been alone, this experience would have been so much harder to bear. Steve had been a true friend. I couldn't thank him enough.

Janet and Bob too were amazing. Steve came into the house with me and we told them what had happened. They'd been dozing on the sofas and insisted they stay for the rest of the night. Steve took his leave, giving me another hug as he left. I experienced a sudden urge to sink deeper into his embrace, to draw strength and comfort from this caring man, but what on earth would he think? After the door closed behind Steve, I felt strangely alone, even though my in-laws were with me. Janet packed me off to bed, where surprisingly, I fell almost immediately into a deep sleep.

Dear Laura,

I'm in love with my best friend. We grew up together as our mothers were friends and we even go on family holidays together. John's always been like a big brother to me, and I know he thinks of me as his sister, but lately, it's not been enough. I think about him all the time and dream of being with him, as a couple and not just as friends. I'm eighteen, he is nineteen. I've had other boyfriends but they never measure up to John. I'm scared to tell him how I feel in case he backs off and I lose him altogether. He hasn't got a steady girlfriend at the moment, although he has dated other girls in the past. What should I do?

Sharon

Dear Sharon,

Unrequited love is so complicated, and I feel for you in this position. But then is it unrequited? The obvious way to find out is by telling him of your feelings. If you have felt this way for some time, maybe now is the time to be brave enough to say so. He may even feel the same way, but you will never know if you don't act. If he doesn't share your feelings and your friendship is strong, as I suspect it is, there is no need to lose John as a friend. Some things are worth acting upon, and you may never get another chance.

Laura

I remember urging Sharon to act on her feelings and often wonder how it worked out for her and John. Is this how I feel about Steve, or is it too early to call it something as all-encompassing as love? And isn't it difficult to distinguish between love of a romantic nature and the kind of love you feel for a good friend? Those blue eyes and his comforting presence lingered in my thoughts until I told myself how ridiculous it was. I was almost fantasising about a man who was considerably younger than me! Perhaps my vulnerability was making me susceptible to these flights of fancy. Steve is a good, kind man. His kindness to me could simply be due to my present predicament. Okay, to put it bluntly, I think he feels sorry for me, but that's not what I want. In my saner moments, I remind myself how he is so much younger than me – and I am a divorced woman with three children. Not such a good catch for Steve, or anyone else for that matter.

Chapter Nineteen

The next morning after waking at the usual time, the events of the previous night were forgotten for a few brief moments. But the memory soon came flooding back, jolting me into reality and reminding me my mother was dead. I groaned, wanting to prolong the oblivion of sleep, yet painfully aware there was way too much to do for such a luxury. Telling the children was first on the list, but as I passed their rooms, they were all still sleeping, so I headed downstairs to see Janet and Bob. Typically, Janet had the kettle on to boil and the table set for breakfast. I hugged them both in turn, grateful for their loyalty and support.

'We'll have a bit of breakfast with you and then pop home to shower and change. We can be back in a couple of hours.' Janet had it all mapped out and my protestations were waved aside.

'Bob can run you about, there are places you'll have to go, and I can be here for the children.' It was a relief to allow Janet to take charge; she was much more capable than me.

After a welcome cup of tea, I decided to wake the children and break the news. Again, the boys took it in their stride. It wasn't that they were insensitive, but their grandmother had never really played a big part in their lives. However, it seemed they could feel my pain and when Jake reached up to hug me, Sam joined in too.

'When will the funeral be, Mum?' Sam asked.

'Goodness, it's too early to know yet. I need to see the undertaker today and go back to Cedar Lodge. There are dozens of things to do before the funeral.'

Lucy was next. I knocked on the door and entered only to find her already awake, earplugs in, and her eyes closed. She became aware of my presence only when I sat next to her on the bed. On hearing of her grandmother's death, her eyes filled with tears. Would it be insensitive to say this pleased me? It was a sign that my thoughtful little girl was still somewhere inside this seemingly unhappy teenager. She too asked about the funeral and I replied as I had to her brothers.

All three children came down for breakfast, and as we sat around the table, Janet fussed over us. The mood was somewhat sombre, but I took comfort in us being together for something as mundane as eating breakfast. Then, as arranged, Janet and Bob went home while I began to make phone calls, the first one to the undertaker, the same one who had arranged my father's funeral. His tone was sympathetic but practical and we fixed a time to meet in the afternoon to discuss arrangements. My mind was blank pertaining to the details and organisation of a funeral, yet I knew the undertaker would guide me through the process.

I had a couple of distant cousins and a few of Mum's friends to inform of her death, but her address book was still at Cedar Lodge, so the calls would have to wait until later.

The boys left for school but only after Sam appeared by my side with a cup of coffee. This little act of thoughtfulness almost set me off crying again, but I bit my lip and smiled my thanks. Even Lucy stayed downstairs longer than usual and didn't rush away when I sat beside her, offering me a chocolate biscuit before withdrawing to her bedroom. The pretence of going to school was over. I would have to ring the headmaster to cancel our appointment; today was not the day for such an interview.

Janet and Bob arrived back as promised, looking tired but in fresh clothes and wearing fixed smiles on their faces. Bob drove me back to Cedar Lodge. Matron wasn't on duty. Mother's death had prolonged her evening shift and now her deputy was in the office. She handed me a large envelope with a few valuable pieces of mother's jewellery and a small amount of cash which had been in the safe.

'You don't have to clear the room out for a few days, but we would appreciate it being emptied in the next week. Our policy is to redecorate for the next resident, and we do have a waiting list.'

'Of course, I'll probably come on Monday if it's okay with you?'

'That certainly works for us, thank you.'

Bob and I made our way to Mother's room. Unable to face opening the wardrobe and seeing all of her clothes, I took just a few photographs, her address book and her watch from the bedside table. It was a pretty gold watch which Lucy might like as a keepsake, so I dropped it into my bag with the photographs. I was anxious to be away from the place which still had my mother's essence imprinted on its walls, so we left after only a few minutes. I would be better prepared to clear the room on Monday.

Arriving home, I found a large bunch of flowers waiting for me in the hall. I say 'bunch', but they were more than worthy of being called a bouquet. Janet smiled as she told me 'that nice young policeman' had brought them round. How thoughtful of him. My mother-in-law looked at me with a smile on her face.

'What?'

'He's very good-looking.'

'I suppose he is.' I tried for nonchalance but she wasn't biting.

'He seems to be very fond of you.'

'We hardly know each other, Janet! He just happened to be here when the matron rang and offered to drive me to Cedar Lodge. The flowers are lovely, but he's that kind of thoughtful man. He would do the same for anyone.'

Janet pressed her lips together, the smile becoming broader. I shook my head and went to put the flowers in a vase. I would ring Steve and thank him, but perhaps later when I was alone.

Michael Morton, the undertaker, arrived promptly at 2.30pm. I'm sure he was wearing the same suit he wore four years ago, when Dad died, it was worn and shiny. He was a tall, thin man who put me in mind of a Dickensian character, but he was practical and efficient. The following Friday, there was an opening for a funeral at the crematorium, and I jumped at the chance. It may seem rather cold, but my mother was lost to me even before Dad died, and my grieving was mostly done years ago. Alzheimer's is like death by instalments, a cruel disease which strikes at the very heart of a family. So the funeral would be in a week. Mr Morton talked me through the service and patiently answered my questions. By the time he left, I had a timeline to work with and knew the practicalities of death would carry me through.

For the next half hour, I made telephone calls, accepting condolences and listening to memories of past, good times. The recurring theme was that perhaps it was for the best. Mum had no kind of life as she was. The practical side of my mind agreed, but the other half wanted to remonstrate and shout, 'But she was my mother and I wanted her to live!'

Later that evening, I rang Steve to thank him for the flowers. He shrugged his kindness off as if it was nothing and repeated his offer to help in any way he could. I wanted to ask him why – to find out if he felt the same attraction to me as I did to him. It was, however, neither the time nor the place to go into such things. I promised I'd let him know if he could do anything, and we said our goodbyes.

Chapter Twenty

The week between Mum's death and the funeral passed in a haze of activity. There were the usual practicalities, which thankfully were not too onerous. After Dad died, I struggled to get through the maze of bureaucracy, sending copies of the death certificate to the bank, building society and anyone else who needed notification. My parents had employed a financial advisor to invest their savings, and at the time of Dad's death, I relied heavily on his experience. Later, we simplified everything; Dad's shares were sold on his death, with the proceeds going into one bank account in Mother's name, with me having power of attorney. Finally, there was the house to clear out and sell, a sad task which Janet and Bob made so much easier with their help and support. Some of the money from the sale of my parents' house was used to pay for my mother's care. There was still enough left to pay the funeral expenses, with the rest as a small legacy for me. All that previous effort made life so much easier now, leaving only the funeral service to arrange and Mum's room at the care home to empty.

After the first, rather solemn weekend, Janet accompanied me to the care home, and we arrived at Cedar Lodge armed with black bin liners. It's a sad fact of life that the possessions we accumulate over the years are eventually disposed of in an almost clinical fashion. I knew pretty much everything Mum had in her room, as I had been the one to move those treasured possessions in with her all those years ago. Now it was time to decide what to keep and where to dispose of the rest. Janet offered to bag the clothes, which I'd already decided to take to the local charity shop. It left me the task of going through Mum's drawers, pulling out old photograph albums, a few birthday cards from Dad which she had kept from over the years, and some pieces of costume jewellery of no intrinsic value. The photographs I put into a bag to take home and look at later, along with the cards. I would read them all once more before disposing of them, knowing they would remind me of my parents and their love for each other in happier times. Perhaps Lucy would like to read them with me. I could only ask. Within an hour we'd finished our task. It seemed sad that it had taken such a short time, an epitaph to Mum's life and the tragic way it had ended.

Back home, Janet made tea to warm us through while I lifted the bags into the utility room, sorting them into what was to go to charity shops and what needed looking through again. Lucy appeared in the kitchen, asking if she could help, which gave me the hope that Mum's death could be the catalyst to restoring our relationship. I replied that her help would be appreciated with taking the bags to the charity shop after lunch. She nodded before disappearing upstairs again. I was still conscious that we needed to go to school to discuss her absences with Mr Bennett. We couldn't put it off indefinitely.

While Janet made lunch in the kitchen and Bob was picking up a few groceries, I again worked the telephone, ringing Mr Bennett first to rearrange our visit for the following day. Of course, Lucy wouldn't be pleased, but it had to be done. If she was old enough to leave school, she was old enough to face her headmaster and tell him why. Madeline was also on my list to ring to update her on circumstances and ask if they had considered reintroducing my page.

'You poor thing!' Madeline gushed when she heard about my mother. 'If I can do anything at all, just let me know.' I thanked her, knowing the offer was sincere, then asked about '*Ask Laura.*'

'It's too soon even to consider it, Laura. I'm sorry, but there have been four letters now, so the consensus is to keep your page mothballed. But at least it gives you the time you need at the moment and we'll keep paying your salary, certainly until the end of the month.'

It was generous of them, but was Madeline's final phrase a clue that my salary would soon cease? It was indeed a possibility and not a very welcome one. It was also apparent that the magazine and the police were still in communication, as Madeline seemed to know the content of the letters even though they were passed on unopened. She did go on to tell me how they'd had letters and emails from readers asking why my column was no longer featured, and it was comforting to know I was missed. I thanked my editor for her concern and replaced the telephone.

After lunch, Lucy helped me load the car with four black sacks of my mother's clothes, and then we set off for the local charity shop. She was quiet on the way, fiddling with the radio until she found an acceptable station, and music filled the silence in the car. It seemed so sad that Mum's entire wardrobe consisted of only four bags. Most of the clothes I bought for her were comfortable, practical items, no buttons and zips, which she found frustrating, and easy to wash. Her life appeared to have gone full circle, from being a child herself to becoming a wife and mother, and latterly almost a child again, who needed help with the most basic tasks we usually take for granted.

I told Lucy we had an appointment with Mr Bennett the next day on the way home. She did not comment but silently disappeared upstairs again when we arrived home. Janet had made a casserole for us, and she and Bob left to go home, instructing me to ring if we needed anything, even if it was only a chat. I thanked them both then decided to have a relaxing bath before the boys arrived home from school. I thought the water would soothe my mind and my body, but it didn't work. Childhood memories of when my mother was young and vivacious flashed across my closed eyelids. I had always felt safe in her protection. When did those roles reverse? Alzheimer's stole her mind and strength, leaving a frail, weakened body in place of the mother I adored and had believed would always be there for me.

Later in the evening, I Skyped Holly and when her smiling face appeared on my laptop, it was an effort to keep the tears at bay. We hadn't spoken for a couple of weeks, but she's one of those friends with whom you pick up the friendship where you left off, which we did. I told her about Mum and she offered her sympathy, frustrated as we were so many miles apart.

'Are you okay?' she asked. 'I mean, other than your mum, you seem so low.' Holly was nothing if not perceptive.

'No, I'm not.' If I couldn't be honest with my best friend, who else could I turn to? 'Lucy's sleeping with her boyfriend and some pathetic idiot is sending hateful letters to the magazine and '*Ask Laura*' has been suspended.' That was it in a nutshell, but I knew Holly would want to learn more. She thrived on detail.

'So, it's been a pretty average week then?' she asked with a grin. Despite myself, I laughed. This is one of the things I love about Holly; she can always see humour in any situation.

'Start at the beginning and tell me all about it.' She shuffled into her chair and pulled her laptop closer, making our contact seem more intimate, and I began my tale of woe. Holly didn't interrupt and listened with a concerned expression. When I was finished, she asked one or two questions which I answered, aware of the chronology of events getting muddled in my mind, so goodness knows what she thought of my ramblings.

'We're going to see the head at Lucy's school tomorrow,' I continued. 'How it will go is anybody's guess but at least she's agreed to it. She's probably taken Mum's death more to heart than the boys have. Lucy remembers her grandmother from before the Alzheimer's; the boys don't have those memories. I'm so grateful they've got Janet and Bob; they're such a help, and children need grandparents.' As I mentioned my in-laws and thought about Holly, my mood lightened. My life wasn't all bad, and I made a mental note to be more thankful for the positives.

'Look, why don't you all come up here for a few days? It's half-term soon, isn't it? We've bags of room and I'd love to see you again. It sounds like you could do with a break as well and as you're not working, nothing is stopping you.' Holly sounded keen for us to go, but I wasn't sure.

'Thanks, Holly, it's a lovely idea, but quite honestly, I should be here just now. The police will need to reach me easily, and with Lucy and this school business, it's just not the right time. You could always come here, though?' The thought of seeing my friend other than on a screen was more than a welcome idea. She grinned.

'I might just take you up on that, but for the moment, Brian's so busy at work and we're in the middle of refitting the kitchen. But I'll think about it and see if I can escape the rubble for a few days.'

We said our goodbyes and I headed upstairs with a few more positive thoughts on my mind for a change. Seeing Holly would be great, but first, there was a funeral to plan and a sullen daughter to get through to. Yes, life was certainly anything but dull at the moment.

Chapter Twenty-One

M r Bennett began by offering his condolences, then Lucy and I took the seats opposite him with his oversized desk separating us. My daughter found something riveting to look at in her lap and I waited for the opening comments to begin from the other side of the desk.

'Now Lucy, why is it you haven't been in school lately?' he said kindly. It was an open-ended question, putting the ball firmly in my daughter's court. Typically, she shrugged, not even looking at her headmaster.

'That's not good enough, Lucy.' The caterpillar eyebrows appeared to join together in a frown. 'If you don't intend to continue at school, you need to tell me why and also what alternative plans you've made.' Nice one, Mr Headmaster. I looked expectantly at Lucy, who lifted her head briefly to meet his eyes.

'School's boring and I just don't want to come anymore.' Her head dropped again.

'So, what is the alternative? Have you been looking for a job?'

'No.'

'Well, if you're not actively searching for a job, how are you going to support yourself?'

Another shrug, but Mr Bennett wasn't having it. In a firm but kind voice, he said, 'Lucy, you're old enough and intelligent enough to know that if you want to get anywhere in this world, you have to work hard for it. You were doing so well in school until a few weeks ago and all your teachers are impressed with your ability. Your GCSE results last year were excellent, so what's changed? Why has school suddenly become boring?'

'It just is!' This was not a particularly mature answer and all three of us knew it wasn't good enough.

'I'm sorry, Lucy, but I can't accept that. Your mother tells me you have a boyfriend. Has he persuaded you to leave school?' All credit to the man – he was doing well. Lucy flashed me a quick look as if I had betrayed her, which in a way was true.

'No, it's my decision. I just don't want to come back.' She looked Mr Bennett in the eye for a moment before studying her hands again.

'Well then, before you can leave school, we have a responsibility to offer you career guidance. Have you given any thought as to what you would like to do in life?' He must have known she had no answer, but he waited patiently for a response. Lucy remained tight-lipped. I toyed with the idea of interjecting to fill the uncomfortable silence but decided against it. Mr Bennett was right. If she was old enough to leave school, she was old enough to make plans for her future and tell us both about them. After a full minute or more, he again took charge.

'Look, Lucy, I know this is a difficult time for you and your mother. What I'd suggest is that next week, when things are a little more settled at home, you come back with your mum, and dad too if he can make it, and we'll talk some more. I'll also ask our career guidance teacher to make time to see you. We'd be failing you if we didn't help you to plan for your future. This will give you time to think and decide what you want. Think about your A levels too. You've done most of the first year's work now, and it would be such a shame not to build on it when I'm sure you'll do well.' His words made sense; even Lucy would be able to see, surely. I thanked him for his time and said I would ring to arrange an appointment next week, and then we left.

Once we were in the car, Lucy turned to me.

'Did you have to tell him about Brad?'

'No, but it seems to me that wanting to leave school has come at the same time as your relationship with Brad. It's logical to think the two are related. I thought Mr Bennett was very kind and raised some valid points. If you want to take responsibility for your own future, you need to have some sort of plan. Make time this week to think about it, and when we go back to school, perhaps you'll have some idea of what you want to do. And don't forget – when Brad comes back from holiday, Dad and I would like to meet him. You can bring him home for coffee or a meal, whichever you would prefer. Just let us know in good time so Dad can make arrangements.'

Lucy remained silent for the rest of the short journey home and I prayed that some sense had got through to her. I couldn't bear to see my daughter throwing away her future for whatever fanciful thoughts were in her head.

Dear Laura,

My first baby was born three weeks ago and I'm not coping well at all. I seem to cry at the slightest cause, and emotionally I'm up and down for the silliest of reasons. I'm not sleeping for fear she wakes up and I don't hear her, so I'm exhausted all the time. It's not because I don't love my baby – in fact – I love her so much it scares me! But, if I'm not coping well now, how will I parent her in the years to come?

Louise

Dear Louise,

I get many letters like yours from new mothers who feel they're not coping. Your body has undergone an amazing change and the mood swings you mention are due to hormones and perfectly natural. It could be you have a case of the 'baby blues', which again is a well-documented hormonal condition. Your body will settle down in time, and although you feel you're not able to cope, the love you feel for your little girl shines through in your letter and I'm sure you'll make a great mother! During these early weeks and months, accept any help offered by friends or family members, or ask for help from professionals (GP, health visitor etc) if you need it. You don't have to do this all on your own, and perhaps if you have someone to take care of your daughter on occasions, you could take the opportunity to catch up on your sleep? Or take turns with your partner so at least some nights you will be able to sleep, knowing if she wakes, her father will look after her. This gives the added advantage of bonding time with her daddy too.

Try to make an effort to attend the baby clinics in your area as well. These not only keep a check on baby's progress but will give you the chance of meeting other new mums and you'll realise you are not alone in how you feel.

As for your parenting abilities in the future, we all learn as we go along. Yes, a child is a big responsibility, but the love you express for your daughter tells me you will be a great mother! A loving home is the first essential of childcare and your desire to be a good mother will carry you through.

Enjoy every minute of your daughter's life, and don't put pressure on yourself to be 'perfect', none of us are.

Laura

When you bring a child into the world, the joy and wonder of this tiny miracle takes you by surprise. Fierce protective instincts rise from somewhere deep inside and you instantly know you would do anything to protect this child, your flesh and blood. But, of course, you don't look too far into the future as you touch those tiny, perfectly formed little fingers and toes and smell the sweet newborn smell of your baby. It's enough to enjoy living in the moment, thinking no further than the first milestones, a smile, a tooth, a word. How could I have looked further ahead and anticipated these awful problems with Lucy? How could we have known what was in store? But no matter what, it changes nothing. That protective instinct is still there, under the surface maybe, but ready to tap into at difficult times. What you don't expect to find is that you will be protecting your child from themselves, they will be the ones to present the very problems from which you want to save them. And they will not see the bigger picture. They will not understand that you only have their best interests at heart; after all, did we trust our parents when we were teenagers?

Chapter Twenty-Two

Mum's funeral was a quiet, solemn affair. The cold, late February morning made me thankful it was a cremation rather than a burial. Even so, the biting wind tugged at my clothes, chilling me through to the bone. The crematorium was a small, sparsely furnished room with artificial flowers adorning the windowsills. Very few mourners attended but I was pleased to see Angela, the matron from Cedar Lodge, with one of the carers I recognised from my visits. They were standing outside the crematorium with the vicar as our car pulled up. Two elderly ladies who had been friends of Mum from years ago were also there, and a lady I recognised as a distant cousin, being pushed in a wheelchair by her husband. Paul, too, was waiting in the cold, solemn and appropriately dressed, standing beside his parents. The children were with me in the car and as we stepped out into the bitter wind, I almost stumbled and fell. Paul moved forward and grasped my arm, steadying my balance and saving any embarrassment. I was grateful he had taken time off work to be there and smiled my thanks to him.

With the boys on one side and Lucy on the other, we followed the coffin inside and sat at the front of the tiny chapel, as the undertaker directed. The vicar had visited me at home during the week to ask about Mother's life and to help me decide what form the service should take. He suggested a couple of hymns, for which I was grateful, and explained how such services usually went. As expected, the singing was abysmal. Perhaps only Angela was familiar with the hymns and her sweet soprano voice rose above the feeble efforts of the rest of the mourners. The vicar gave a potted history of Mum's life, garnered from the snippets I'd told him. It was sufficient, a tribute to the woman she had been, delivered with compassion and even a little humour. Readings from the Bible brought comfort, and my lasting memory of the service was the thought the vicar planted in our minds, of Mum and Dad, reunited in heaven.

When the formalities were over and we filed outside, I found myself thinking what it must be like to watch all your contemporaries die. Perhaps Mum's illness saved her from many such heartaches but it inevitably brought pain to her family. I wanted to remember her as the bright, smiling woman of my childhood, my problem-solver who helped with homework and made everything better when I cried. But the image which would probably remain with me was of the old woman in Cedar Lodge, the woman who switched moods in a heartbeat, who didn't want you to get too close because she didn't trust you, who scowled suspiciously at everyone because we had all become strangers.

After the service, I invited Angela and her colleague to come back home for coffee, which she declined, giving me a warm hug as they took their leave. Mum's cousin also declined the invitation, saying they had to cross London and didn't wish to be caught up in the rush-hour traffic. Paul made his excuses and went back to work, leaving only the children, Janet, Bob and me. Some wake.

At home, as Janet again took charge of my kitchen, Sam and Jake began asking questions.

'What happens to the body when the curtains are closed?' Sam enquired.

'Well, a cremation is burning. Grandma isn't in her body anymore, so a cremation is a way of disposing of the body.' I struggled to choose the words – what a time to ask such grim questions.

'Why are some people buried then?' Jake chipped in.

'It's a matter of preference, really. Sometimes relatives want to have a grave to visit, a place to remember their loved one. Grandma's ashes will be sprinkled in the Garden of Remembrance, beside the crematorium, so we can visit there if we want to.'

'But if they're no longer in their bodies, why do people visit either place?' Jake posed a valid question and one which wasn't easy to answer.

'Well, different people believe different things. I like to think of Grandma in heaven now with Granddad, as the vicar said. Perhaps it's how you would like to think of her now too?' Janet saved me from further grilling by bringing in a tray of hot drinks to warm us up and some scones she'd made earlier that morning. Even Lucy stayed downstairs with us as we did justice to Janet's baking and talked in happier terms about my parents. Guilt washed over me as it became apparent none of my children knew much about them. I could blame circumstances, but the reality was, I should have talked more positively about my parents, and I made a silent promise to do precisely that in the future. Perhaps we could attempt to build a family tree. Bob would be able to supply information from his side of the family, and I could tell the children everything I could remember about mine. Good intentions, but maybe I'd left it too late.

We ordered pizza after Janet and Bob left and ate together in front of the television. A feeling of calm descended on the room, which, considering the day's main event, was more than welcome. I simply enjoyed my children's company and allowed them to stay up long after their usual bedtime. When they finally went upstairs, I opened a bottle of wine and an extra-large bar of chocolate whilst watching a sentimental film from the 1940s. By 11.30pm I was in floods of tears. It suddenly hit me – I no longer had a living parent. Janet and Bob were terrific substitutes, but first and foremost they were Paul's parents, not mine. I cried for my dad and my mum, for the children who only had a part-time father and me, and for myself, a lonely, miserable woman with no job and someone out there who hated me enough to send those awful letters. Wrapped up in my cloak of misery, I didn't notice Lucy standing in the doorway.

'Mum, are you okay?' Her voice was feeble and crackled with emotion. I waved her over and sniffed back the tears.

'Yes, love, I'm fine! I'm just feeling sorry for myself, that's all.'

Lucy sat beside me and allowed me to put my arms around her. I stroked her hair, an act which comforted me as much as her.

'I'll miss your grandma, but she really left us years ago. She'll be happy now, I'm sure.'

My daughter said nothing but stayed in my arms for a few more precious minutes. 'We should probably both get some sleep now, Lucy. It's been a tiring day.' I smiled at her as we stood to go up to bed and experienced an unexpected lightness in my heart. Could it be from those little things which have drawn Lucy and me closer together over the last week? I even dared to hope she would see sense about the school issue and we could begin rebuilding our relationship.

The reflection of a red, blotchy face confronted me in the bathroom, a woman I hardly recognised. I blew my nose, washed in cold water and brushed my teeth. Then, flopping exhausted onto my bed, I fell into a deep and dreamless sleep.

Chapter Twenty-Three

Saturday morning dawned with a covering of snow. As I looked at the garden from the kitchen window, the scene was exquisite. It is only a small garden but the bare trees and naked shrubs were covered in crisp, powdery snow, lighting up the whole garden and brightening my mood considerably. Snow was still falling in large, clean flakes and I suddenly wondered if the boys were too old to make snowmen. They were down first, hungry as always, and as it was the weekend, I offered to make pancakes for breakfast. After we'd eaten far too many, I decided to wake Lucy and see if she wanted to come with me to the boys' football practice. Knocking on her bedroom door brought no response, so I went inside, expecting to find my daughter still sleeping. She wasn't. In fact, her bed was neatly made with a piece of paper held down on the pillow by her ragged old blue teddy bear. My heart leapt into my throat as I ran the few steps towards the bed, fearful of what I might find.

Mum. You'll all be much better off without me.
Lucy.

That was it. No clue as to what the note meant or where she was going! A thousand different scenarios flashed across my mind, and not one of them was good. I half collapsed on the bed, clutching the note. My hands trembled as I read the sentence over and over again. Was this a suicide note? It was too horrendous to even think about! Surely Lucy wasn't so low she'd consider ending her own life? Please, God, no. I could feel the blood throbbing in my ears as I struggled to breathe properly. Was my daughter running away? Where would she be if either of the above was correct? Instinctively I knew I needed to act and ran downstairs to the kitchen.

'Have either of you seen Lucy this morning?' I barked at the boys. Both heads shook as they looked to me for an explanation.

'She's gone...' It was all I could say. It was all I knew! Reaching for the telephone, I dialled Paul's number. Zoe answered.

'Put Paul on!' I ordered, frustrated that he hadn't been the one to answer the phone. Zoe could be heard grumbling to him about my rudeness, but this was no time for polite chit-chat.

'Paul, Lucy's gone!' It was only then I sat down on the floor and sobbed. Jake took the phone from my hand, and I could hear his side of the conversation with his father.

'Mum's crying... I don't know, she asked us if we'd seen Lucy this morning but we haven't... She's holding a note... Right.' He replaced the phone then sat down beside me.

'Dad's on his way. Where's Lucy gone, Mum?' Jake's voice quivered. Sam sat down and I gathered both my boys into my arms, taking comfort from the warmth of their bodies, which, like mine, were trembling.

'I don't know.' My voice cracked. 'Has she said anything to either of you lately?'

'Lucy says nothing to us unless it's to shout at us,' Sam

replied, sniffing and wiping his eyes with his sleeve. Both boys were upset and I knew I must try to be strong for them. Standing up, I tried to think rationally and do something, anything! Calling Lucy's mobile proved fruitless, it was switched to answerphone.

'Lucy, please ring me back, where are you? Please, sweetheart, ring me and we can talk about this…'

I rang Janet and Bob next, in the hope Lucy might have gone to their house. She hadn't, and the call only served to alarm her grandparents, who insisted on coming round as soon as they could. Next, I called her best friend, Molly, and spoke to her mother. They hadn't seen Lucy for weeks, she told me. Lucy and Molly seemed to have had some kind of falling out and Molly's mother wasn't sure they were even speaking to each other. She promised to talk to her daughter, who was still in bed and would ring me back if Molly knew anything at all which might help. I tried other friends too, but no one seemed to know where Lucy might be. It occurred to me to phone the police, but would they be interested? Didn't they have to wait for so many hours, or even days, before declaring someone a missing person?

'Mum, do you think we should call the police?' Jake's face was ashen, his eyes brimming with tears. I hugged him close.

'We will, but let's wait until Dad gets here first.'

'You could ring DS Radcliffe, couldn't you?' The same thought had crossed my mind, but it wasn't Steve's problem. However, I nodded at my son.

'Good idea, Jake. I'll do it now.' Who cares what he would think of me and my dysfunctional family. Finding Lucy was all that mattered. I reached for the phone.

Steve was at work but, without a moment's hesitation, said he'd be round as soon as possible. Relief washed over me; surely he would know what to do?

Steve arrived before Paul, Janet and Bob, and I almost fell

into his arms with relief. He studied the note from Lucy carefully.

'What time did you see her last night?' he asked.

'Just before midnight. We both went up to bed at the same time.'

'And you didn't hear anything from her after that?'

'No, nothing.' I asked the boys to go and watch from the window for their father so I could talk openly to Steve. When they'd gone, I voiced my worst suspicions.

'Do you think it's a suicide note?' The words almost choked me, so painful were they to say or even think, and I felt suddenly nauseous.

'I wouldn't assume the worst yet, Laura. Have you checked her wardrobe to see if she's taken anything?' Of course, how stupid of me not to have thought to do so! I practically galloped up the stairs and into Lucy's room, followed closely by Steve. As I threw open the wardrobe door, relief washed over me as it registered her leather jacket and a few of her favourite pairs of jeans were gone. Looking around the room, I saw her dressing gown was missing from the hook on the back of the door. Tears of relief began to fall. Steve smiled and took hold of my arms, looking directly into my eyes.

'Well, I think this pretty much rules out suicide, don't you?' He smiled and I nodded, feeling so foolish. But my daughter had still run away. What did this say about my aptitude as a mother? I hated myself then. How could I have failed so badly? But running away was infinitely better than suicide, wasn't it? The sound of the boys hurrying to the front door brought me back to reality, and Steve and I went downstairs.

Paul was in the hall, shrugging off his overcoat. The look he gave me as he saw Steve following me downstairs was one of fury.

'Did we need to call the police in, Laura?' He spat the words out in anger, assuming whatever Lucy had done or wherever she'd gone was entirely my fault. Sadly, at that moment in time, I agreed with him.

'I'm here more as a friend than a police officer,' Steve replied, which didn't seem to make Paul's mood any better. He ignored Steve and spoke to me.

'So, what have you done to find her?'

'Obviously, I've tried her mobile several times, but she's not answering. I've rung all her friends, without any luck. She left this.' I handed over the note, which I'd been grasping in my hand since I first found it. I wanted to tell him that at least it didn't appear to be a suicide note, but the boys were listening, and I didn't want to scare them any more than they already were.

'Sam, Jake, would you go outside to see if there's any sign of your grandparents yet?' Obediently they went out through the front door, needing to do something and for once not arguing with me.

'She's probably just gone to meet her new boyfriend, Laura. This note doesn't tell us anything much.'

'Of course it does!' My anger spilt over. 'She says we'll be better off without her! Our daughter could be contemplating suicide for all we know!'

'She'd never do such a thing!'

'How do you know, you hardly ever see her these days!' We were shouting at each other and getting absolutely nowhere. 'Look, we've just checked her room, and she's taken clothes with her, so it at least looks like she isn't thinking about suicide.' I took a deep breath.

'Well, the most likely place to look is probably at this boyfriend's place. Where does he live?' Paul asked. My embarrassment must have shown in my face.

'You don't know, do you?' Paul looked at me with contempt.

'And neither do you! She said he was on holiday, remember,

so we haven't been able to arrange a time to meet him yet.' It sounded a pathetic excuse, even to me.

'If you have a name, I could get someone at the station to run it through the computer to see if we can find an address,' Steve offered.

'It's Brad Johnson. Lucy said he has a flat and it can't be too far away. She's been going there instead of school recently.' As I spoke, I was aware of Paul rolling his eyes. Choosing to ignore him, I watched as Steve took out his phone and began to thumb the numbers. He moved away to speak as the boys came in, followed by an anxious-looking Janet and Bob.

'You didn't need to come round,' Paul greeted them.

'Of course we did! Laura needs as much support as she can get at a time like this,' Janet chastised and then turned to me.

'Is there any news yet?'

'No. I've rung round Lucy's friends with no luck, but she's taken some clothes which at least suggests she has some kind of plan. Steve's ringing a colleague now to try to find her boyfriend's address.'

'But isn't he on holiday?' Bob asked.

'That's what Lucy said, but I'm inclined to think it was a convenient lie to put us off meeting him.'

Janet nodded towards Steve. 'So, are the police officially involved?'

'No, you can't report someone as missing until some time has elapsed. Lucy's sixteen too, so legally, she has the right to leave home.' Even speaking the words seemed so wrong; at sixteen she was still a child. Steve came back towards us.

'Right, I have an address and it's not far away. I can be there in twenty minutes or so.'

'Hang on a minute.' Paul raised his hand as if trying to silence Steve. 'If anyone is going, it'll be me. She's my daughter.'

'And mine too!' I wouldn't be left out of this either.

'If a police officer turned up on his doorstep, this Brad would be more likely to co-operate,' Steve explained. I nodded – it made sense – even Paul would have to agree.

'Do you think he's holding her against her will?' Janet asked.

'No, I don't, but you never know what to expect,' Steve answered.

Eventually, it was decided, Paul, Steve and I would all go, but Paul insisted on taking his car. I hadn't a clue what to expect and only hoped Lucy was there and would agree to come home with us. As to what we'd say when we found her, again I hadn't the slightest idea and suspected Paul too would be out of his depth.

Chapter Twenty-Four

Brad Johnson's address, although not far away, was in an area I'd never been to before. We drove into an estate comprised of several tower blocks and one of the first things which struck me was that there were no trees or grass verges to be seen anywhere; a veritable concrete jungle. Youngsters rode around the flats on bikes or skateboards, shouting to each other in language, which at their age, they shouldn't even know. Was my daughter really here with her boyfriend, and if so, what was the attraction? We pulled up in front of a block covered with graffiti, like most others around it. The smell of urine greeted us as we climbed a ramp, heading for the lift. Unsurprisingly the lift was broken and I was thankful Brad's flat was on the fourth floor rather than the tenth. Paul strode out ahead, determined to be the first to get there, although I was sure he would have no more idea than me of how to play this scenario out.

The door to flat 410 had been damaged at some point and poorly repaired, with cardboard covering an area where presumably one of the glass panels had been. I'm not overly house-proud, but the dirt on the front door alone appalled me, giving me the ridiculous urge to reach for some Cif and a pair of rubber gloves. Paul knocked briskly and then rubbed his hand down the side of his jeans. There was no answer. A second knock didn't register either. Steve moved to the window and cupped his hand against the glass to peer inside the flat.

'There's someone in. I saw movement.'

Paul knocked even harder, but it was clear visitors were not welcome. Steve opened the letter box and shouted through, 'Johnson, it's the police! Open up will you?' A sound from inside grew louder until finally, the door opened a fraction. Steve immediately put his foot on the step so the door couldn't be shut in his face.

'Brad Johnson?' he asked.

'What do you want him for?' the surly young man asked.

'Are you Brad?'

'Yes, why?'

Paul was itching to take control of the situation and edged nearer the door as if he intended pushing his way inside. The sight of this person horrified me. He must have been well into his twenties, unshaven in a lazy, rather than a trendy way and wearing only dirty jeans with his chest bare. As much as I wanted to find Lucy, I began to hope she wasn't inside this awful flat with him.

Steve remained calm and asked, 'Is Lucy here?'

'What if she is?'

'We'd like to speak to her; these are her parents. Let us come in, Brad. We don't want things to get out of hand, do we?' Reluctantly Brad stepped aside to allow us access. I was suddenly grateful for Steve's presence and the calm, authoritative way he handled things. Had Paul and me been alone, Brad probably wouldn't even have answered the door. Once inside I wanted to retch! Torn brown curtains covered the window, blocking any natural light and making the room appear dark and gloomy. The floor was covered with a filthy, brown, patterned carpet which looked as if it had been down since the flat was built. A huge television filled one corner, almost obscured by empty beer cans and discarded crisp packets littered on the unit on which it stood. My eye was drawn to the old, worn sofa at the far wall, where my daughter sat, legs curled up beneath her as if attempting to be invisible. She held a grubby green cushion in front of her, for comfort or protection, it wasn't clear. Instinctively I ran towards her but was stopped by the expression on her face.

Our presence was so obviously unwelcome and I honestly didn't know how to deal with the situation. My beautiful sixteen-year-old daughter had chosen to be in this squat, for it's what it seemed to be, with this man who was far too old for her. Several thoughts crowded my mind, which I could barely process. Why would she prefer a place like this instead of the clean, comfortable home in which she'd grown up? What was *he* thinking about by having a relationship with such a young girl, who was still only a child? I froze just a few feet away from my daughter. Paul, on the other hand, pushed past me, ordering her to come home immediately. Even I could see this was overkill and would almost certainly have a negative effect. As Paul reached out to pull Lucy from the sofa, she wrestled out of his grasp.

'Go away, will you! Can't you just leave me alone?' Her face was contorted with annoyance and embarrassment. She desperately wanted to control her own life but was far too young to understand the mistake she was making.

Steve had been talking quietly to Brad, but when Paul began to get physical, he turned his attention to him.

'Perhaps we could talk this through, Paul. Get Lucy's perspective on the situation and see if we can come to some agreement.'

'Don't you tell me how to treat my daughter! She's coming home, now – that's all there is to it!'

'I'm not going anywhere; I want to stay here!' Angry tears streamed down Lucy's face.

I took a couple of steps forward and perched on the edge of the sofa beside her, not daring to touch her but simply to ask, 'Is this really what you want, Lucy?'

'Yes!' she sobbed. 'Why can't you just go away and leave me alone?'

Paul began to remonstrate again but Steve put his hand on his arm.

'We need to talk it through, not force the issue,' he said gently, and he was right.

For a moment, I thought Paul was going to hit him, but he restrained himself, then turned abruptly and left the flat with the parting words, 'Fine, then *you* sort it out!'

In some ways, I understood his anger and felt the same, but even greater was the pain of knowing Lucy would choose this grubby flat and a man as coarse as Brad Johnson instead of our home and me. The atmosphere changed when Paul left. There was slightly less tension. My eyes were growing accustomed to the gloomy lighting, and I could now get a good look at my daughter's chosen boyfriend. He could have been anywhere in his twenties, with lank, greasy hair and an unremarkable face. He was short, about the same height as Lucy, with a slim build. Down the left side of his chest was a tattoo. The design was intricate and I had no desire to move any closer to inspect it, but it appeared to be some kind of snake, coiled from just below Brad's armpit, down to his hip. I could also make out several piercings in both nostrils and around the top of his ears. Steve gently ushered Brad into the kitchen, leaving me alone with my daughter.

'Lucy, I was beside myself when I found your note! Whatever makes you think we'd be better off without you?' I didn't wait for a reply. 'I love you, the boys love you, and so does Dad. This isn't the place for you. Surely you can see.' I didn't simply mean the flat itself, but it was how Lucy interpreted my words.

'We're going to sort it out.' She spoke defensively, her chin rising as if in defiance. 'Brad's getting the paint on Monday when his money comes through, and then we'll decorate and make something of it.'

I simply nodded. How could I get Lucy to see what a colossal mistake she was making?

'Won't you come home with me now so we can talk about it? Perhaps, if you continue to see Brad without living here, you'll not be under so much pressure. Let's take it slowly and talk about it some more. If you like, Brad can visit you at home, then your dad and I will have a chance to get to know him.' My whole body was trembling, knowing if I said the wrong thing, I risked losing my daughter completely, something too horrendous to contemplate! But Lucy didn't want to lose face; the dilemma was reflected in her eyes. Maybe, loathsome as it was, I might have to leave her here and work things out from a distance. We couldn't afford to alienate her altogether, and if it meant taking things slowly, then so be it.

I asked once more, 'Will you come home, Lucy?' She was so obviously torn but slowly shook her head. I swallowed hard to suppress the sobs which were threatening to engulf me.

'Then will you bring Brad round tomorrow for lunch, so we can get to know him better?'

Lucy seemed surprised at the suggestion and answered in a whisper, 'I'll ask him.'

Steve and Brad came back through from the kitchen. It didn't take much imagination to picture what it was like, and the rest of the flat, too.

'Lucy,' Steve said, 'Brad says you're here by choice, but I need to hear it from you. Are you here because you want to be, or do you feel threatened or intimidated in any way?'

'Of course I'm here because I want to be! Brad didn't force

me to come – he's not like that. He cares for me and I'm happy with him.'

Steve seemed convinced she was speaking the truth. He turned to me.

'We can't make her come home, Laura. Can you accept that?' I nodded, exhausted and upset, then stood to leave.

'Give me a ring, Lucy, about tomorrow, yes?' She nodded and I followed Steve out of the flat. We descended the stairs in silence to find Paul was waiting beside the car.

'So all your fancy words didn't get her to come home then?' His tone was sarcastic, but it was unclear if his comments were directed to Steve or me.

'Legally, there's nothing we can do to make her come home, and after speaking to them both, I'm satisfied Lucy's there of her own free will. Being heavy-handed isn't the way forward here.' We drove back in silence, having failed, but at least we knew Lucy was okay; if we hadn't found her, I'd have gone mad with worry. My daughter was alive and relatively safe – I could cope with that for the time being.

Chapter Twenty-Five

Paul refused to come in when we arrived home, not even to see his parents or the boys. He was sulking, an unpleasant trait which had occasionally surfaced when we were married, but he insisted I ring him to keep him informed of any developments. I didn't need to be reminded. He was Lucy's father and had a right to know. Of course I would keep him in the loop. Paul appeared to be blaming me for the situation, which, as I was blaming myself too, did little for my self-esteem. As he drove away, Janet came hurrying out to meet us, her face a picture of anxiety.

'She's okay, Janet.' I forced a smile. 'Let's get in out of the cold and I'll tell you everything.' The snow was falling again, creating such a beautiful, crisp scene in contrast to what was, for me, such an ugly day. Janet disappeared into the kitchen, the place where she felt most comfortable, returning shortly with a tray of tea. My mother-in-law believes there is not much in life which cannot be sorted out with a good cup of tea. Steve seemed to be quite comfortable in my home too, a fact which hadn't gone unnoticed, not only by me but by Janet too. Bob had taken the boys to football practice, yet there was a fair chance they would be back early with the weather being so bad. I wanted to ask Steve so many questions, so when we were settled with our tea, I took my chance.

'Can Lucy stay with Brad if she wants to, or is there a court order or something similar which we could use to bring her back home?' He shook his head slowly, concern in his eyes.

'Because she's sixteen, legally she can choose to live wherever she wants. The exceptions aren't applicable here. We could only bring her home if she were in some way vulnerable or if Brad was on the sex offenders register.'

Janet gasped. Her mouth dropped wide open as Steve's words sank in.

'It's okay, Janet. When I rang in to find Brad's address, I also asked for any other information we might have on him. His name isn't on our system for anything other than a speeding offence, which was a couple of years ago, so he's clean.'

Janet sighed audibly, pleased her granddaughter wasn't living with some kind of monster or drug dealer. I echoed her sigh. Steve's involvement in my family's problems brought a degree of sanity. His down-to-earth common sense and knowledge of the law helped me look more objectively at this latest catastrophe.

'Who would decide if Lucy is vulnerable or not?' I asked, grasping at straws and hoping we could somehow make her come home.

'I know what you're thinking, Laura, but sadly Lucy doesn't fit into any category which would give you leverage. If she had special needs or a life-limiting disability, there would be grounds for declaring her vulnerable. But she's a bright girl and so there's nothing we can do. Besides, forcing her into coming home will almost certainly have a negative effect. Maintaining contact with her is paramount in such a situation and the best way forward for now. If you try to force her into anything, you'll lose the ongoing dialogue you've established now, and probably your daughter too.'

They were harsh words to hear, but I did not doubt Steve was right. Janet still looked horrified and asked about Brad and his flat. Not wishing to upset her, I played it down to some extent, but she probably realised how bad it was from what I didn't say.

Our conversation was interrupted as Bob came through the door with the twins. He looked at me, an unspoken question in his expression, and I was able to reassure him and the boys we knew where Lucy was and she was quite safe.

'Football's off.' Sam was unhappy. 'A bit of snow shouldn't make any difference, but they called it off anyway, wimps! What time's dinner, Mum?'

'It's hardly a couple of hours since breakfast, Sam; you should still be full of pancakes.' Sighing, he shrugged, and both boys ran upstairs to their rooms.

'We'll be off now, Laura, but you know where we are if you need us.' Janet reached for her coat.

'Thank you so much. I don't know where I'd be without you two – you're amazing.' I meant every word. They were such a support, and I was genuinely grateful. When they left, with warm hugs and words of love, Steve stood to go too.

'Won't you stay for lunch? It's the least I can do after all the help you've given.' I didn't want him to go.

'Officially, I'm still on duty and although I'd love to stay, perhaps another time?' His smile made me believe he meant what he said.

'Of course, I'd forgotten you were working. If it hadn't been for you, Brad probably wouldn't even have opened the door. Thank you, Steve, you're very kind.' There was so much more I wanted to say, to ask him why he was so kind to me, to find out if he felt the same way about me as I did about him, which was laughable really, but he left and the words were unspoken.

The day seemed interminable. I kept my phone in the pocket of my jeans, hoping Lucy would ring and tell me she and Brad would come for lunch the next day. The call never came and I didn't dare phone her. Steve's wise words about not forcing the issue and keeping a dialogue open rang in my ears. There must be a middle ground. Perhaps I could ring her in the morning under the pretext of needing to know how many I was cooking for?

The rest of the day seemed to drag. I was fearful and jumpy, reacting to even the slightest noise in the house. The problems with Lucy, coupled with the vicious letters, were almost too much to bear, but what could I do? The safety of my family was paramount and I would keep going purely for them. I longed for this all to be over, for normality to return, but it was not in my power to alter things. It was a waiting game, but the fear of what would happen next at times threatened to overwhelm me.

Sam and Jake played football in the garden, despite the snow. For me, settling to anything productive was out of the question. Saturday was generally the day to catch up with household chores, but my mind was restless. Playing music didn't help, nor did the endless cups of tea and biscuits. So it was a relief when the boys went to bed, and I decided to have an early night too. Unsurprisingly sleep once again was elusive. An hour after going to bed, I was back in the kitchen, firing up my laptop to distract my thoughts by going over some old files.

Dear Laura,

I am fifteen years old and in my GCSE year at school, and I'm in love with my form tutor. He's only in his twenties and very good-looking.

GILLIAN JACKSON

All the girls fancy him, but my feelings are so much more than a crush. I think about him all the time and dream about him every night. He's always very kind to me, with endless patience if I don't understand something. (He's also my maths teacher.) I'm pretty sure he has feelings for me too. Should I make the first move and tell him how I feel? I'm so confused and have no one to talk to who will understand.

Coleen

Dear Coleen,

I do sympathise with how you feel, but you need to do a reality check here, and the answer to your last question is 'no', certainly not! At fifteen, your body is changing and your emotions are mixed up and difficult to understand, and so they shouldn't be trusted!

Firstly, anything between you and this teacher would be totally inappropriate and also illegal. Yes, he may be kind to you and patient in helping with your work, but this description fits many teachers. He went into a teaching career because he likes helping children and has patience with them. Secondly, he may be in a relationship or even married, with responsibilities to his family. Thirdly, at fifteen, you are still a child, and he is a man, so there can never be any kind of relationship between you other than one of teacher/student. Trying to force the issue will only end in disaster for all concerned, and if you tell this teacher about your feelings, you will put him in a very difficult position.

You may think he has feelings for you, but you don't tell me anything which suggests this. If he does, it would be inappropriate for him to act on them and, as I said before, illegal. It's almost impossible to trust our feelings alone, especially at your age, when you're under pressure with school work.

Concentrate on your exams and try to put this teacher out of your mind. I'm not saying it will be easy, but one day you will realise this was the right thing to do. I know my reply is probably not what you

want to hear, but if you act on your feelings, I can guarantee you will
regret it one day.
    Laura

I often wonder what Coleen did. When letters arrive for the '*Ask Laura*' page, I try to put myself in the shoes of the person writing to me. I, too, can remember having a crush on a teacher at school. Many girls do, and probably so do boys. However, looking at Coleen's letter now, prompts me to think of my feelings for Steve Radcliffe. Is it just as inappropriate as this schoolgirl crush? Perhaps not, but Steve's relationship with me is a professional one. He is kind and understanding, as was Coleen's teacher, so am I as deluded as she? Haven't I enough complications in my life without falling for a guy who is so much out of my orbit? My wild hopes and dreams, in which Steve features as the main event, are impossibly unrealistic. It is almost on a level with a teenage crush, an impossible dream which could never happen. Perhaps I also need a good strong reality check to banish such ridiculous thoughts from my head.

Chapter Twenty-Six

By Sunday morning Lucy still hadn't rung, and I really did need to know if we would have a guest for lunch. I intended to cook a traditional roast dinner, one of the few meals I don't mess up. After all, anyone can chuck a few vegetables into a pan to boil and a joint in the oven, can't they? At 10.30am, I decided to send her a text, partly because I was afraid to ring in case she didn't answer and also because I didn't want to hear the unfriendly tone in my daughter's voice. I kept the wording brief, 'are you coming' sort of thing, then waited for a reply, steadfastly refusing to allow my thoughts to stray on to what Lucy and Brad might be doing at that particular time on a Sunday morning. Procrastinating, I went into the kitchen to put the kettle on for a cup of tea which I didn't want.

The phone rang, making me jump, and I hurriedly picked it up. It wasn't Lucy but the boys' football coach to let me know they'd arranged an extra practice match that afternoon to make up for the cancellation yesterday. The boys would be delighted; the snow had almost completely melted, making the pitch soft but inevitably muddy. It would have been better for them to play on snow. I called upstairs to let them know the good news.

My phone pinged with a text. I didn't care what it said; it was simply incredible Lucy had responded. The dialogue was still open, as Steve said.

> Sorry, not today, busy getting flat ready for painting tomorrow.

Well, at least she'd replied, we were on speaking terms again. I texted back, saying briefly, perhaps another time, and left it there. So, there was no dinner to prepare. The boys preferred pasta to a roast dinner, and I'd read somewhere how it's good for energy levels when playing sport, so pasta it would be.

The beauty of the snow yesterday had turned into grey slush. As I drove to the practice field after lunch, my mood was heavy and as gloomy as the spindly bare branches of the trees lining the road. I hoped Richard wouldn't be there, but he was.

Sam and Jake happily ran off to get changed while I strolled over to join two of the other mothers at the edge of the pitch. Richard moved to within about twenty feet of where we were standing, probably knowing it would unsettle me. I tried not to look in his direction, but it's rather like when you're a child and your mother tells you not to pick the scab on your knee, you just have to pick it anyway. Each time I looked in his direction, Richard was staring directly at me, probably in a deliberate attempt to unnerve me. So it continued as the game got underway, making me feel decidedly edgy. Half of me wanted to run away, while the other half wanted to march over to him and give him a piece of my mind. In the end, I did neither. The threat of a court order might prevent Richard from approaching me, but nothing could be done about him looking in my direction. Why should he have the satisfaction of knowing I cared one way or the other? So I simply ignored him, not looking at him for the remainder of the game and joining in the banter with the other mums, laughing somewhat too enthusiastically at their comments even though they were not funny.

It was only a friendly game, more for the practice than anything else, but our team won. It was a much-needed win, as the season had been poor, and confidence was low. The boys piled into the car, covered from head to toe in mud but buzzing at such a good result. When we arrived home, I was tempted to make them take their clothes off at the door but settled for their boots, which I threw into the utility sink. They could wash them themselves later. Hurriedly I made tea as they showered; they were always so hungry after football. We filled our plates and took them to the lounge to watch a bit of mindless television and relax.

Fortunately, Sam and Jake showed the minimum of interest as to where their sister was and accepted my vague explanation of her staying over at a friend's house for a few days. It was a sad reflection on the current dynamics of our family that they displayed little or no sign of missing Lucy. They went up to bed at around nine, and I intended to follow shortly afterwards, yet whether or not I would sleep remained to be seen. However, the telephone rang – three times – but stopped before I reached it. I thought nothing of it until it happened again – and then again. The caller ID display showed the number to be withheld. With the events of the weekend consuming my thoughts, the hate letters and their author were relegated to the back of my mind, although not entirely forgotten. Now I wondered if this caller was the letter writer. Or could it be Richard who would have been reminded of his humiliation by my presence at the game earlier? Exhaustion overruled my fear so I hardly cared.

'Aw, sod it! Let them do their bloody worst!' I almost shouted and unplugged the phone.

It occurred to me what a relief it would have been if Richard's prints had been on those vicious letters. If it had been him, things would have fallen into place, and the fear surrounding the situation would be lessened. Knowing Richard to be the letter writer would have been in some way understandable, and as the justice process rolled out, there would have been closure. But Richard was proved innocent of this crime, at least. So, the uncertainty remained to wrestle in my mind and pose the questions of who and why. Not knowing is probably a worse state of affairs. Fear of the unknown is always more frightening than the knowledge of who your opponent is. Had it been Richard, I could have dealt with it, but how could I deal with someone who hated me so much, who threatened my family and me but was only a shadow? How could I know where to turn and what to do, when who or what I was up against was unknown? At that moment, life seemed pretty unfair. I wearily climbed the stairs, hoping for sleep to blot out my increasing fears and bring much-needed revitalisation to continue the fight.

Sleep did come, but only after sobbing into my pillow, indulging in a lengthy self-pity party. Images of Brad Johnson's filthy flat swam before my eyes, even though they were closed, prompting me to wonder again how my daughter could abide living in such a pit. Would they clean it up and freshen it with new paint? It was doubtful. If Brad had lived for any length of time in those conditions, he was probably not inclined to expend much effort in decorating. I would have to be patient and hope Lucy would come to her senses and return home, but patience has never been my strong point.

Chapter Twenty-Seven

Monday morning arrived and the boys left for school as usual. Lucy's birthday was in two days, and I hadn't a clue what to do about it. Generally, the choice would be hers, a meal out, or her choice of takeaway with the boys and me, and maybe a friend. My dilemma now was what to do. Would she think it was nagging if I sent another text? But perhaps this could be the occasion to meet Brad socially, yet dare I suggest it? Deciding what to do was a fine line between showing love and concern or driving her away. Finally, I decided on another text asking if I could take her to town and treat her to something nice for her birthday. If she agreed – and Lucy loved shopping, the opportunity might present itself to eat out with the boys and Brad and get to know him better. Sliding my phone into my jeans pocket and hoping for a quick reply, I knew even as I hit the send button, I was setting myself up for another disappointment. The phone remained annoyingly silent until early afternoon when it pinged with a text.

> Would prefer money if you don't mind, to help
> with the flat. Not able to go out for a meal, too
> busy.

I should have expected as much. Lucy was answering my texts but refusing the olive branches they carried. Could this be a calculated response, and was it Lucy or Brad who was calling the shots?

As I continued to ponder my daughter's living arrangements, it dawned on me – perhaps I'd been negligent in not considering financial matters. Lucy had a bank account into which her father paid ten pounds each week. I gave her a similar amount in cash, and she usually deposited any monetary birthday or Christmas gifts into the bank until she decided how to spend it. However, I'd been remiss in not asking what financial arrangements Lucy had with Brad. He didn't appear to have much unless the state of the flat was purely a life choice, and we couldn't expect him to keep Lucy.

But on the other hand, was giving her money condoning their living arrangements? As I pondered what to do, the problem seemed to grow bigger. I should talk to Paul but was pretty sure he'd be against giving her any money and might even stop her regular pocket money if it was brought to his attention. So, not wishing to ring Paul at work, I left it until later, concentrating on other matters which needed attention.

One of the day's tasks on my list was to ring Mr Bennett and put him in the picture about Lucy. He'd been helpful and concerned, and I only wished I could tell him Lucy had decided to resume her studies, but sadly this wasn't the case, for the present anyway. The school secretary put me through to the headmaster, and I began to explain and apologise for wasting his time. Mr Bennett, however, was very polite and genuinely seemed concerned for Lucy. He asked if there was anything he could do to help, which sadly there wasn't, and also said if the situation changed, they would make every effort to enable Lucy to catch up with her studies. Thanking him, I promised to get in touch if my daughter had a change of heart.

For the rest of the day, I tried to concentrate on a feature for the magazine, but by early afternoon I'd deleted more than half of the original word count and was going to have to start afresh. My mind simply wasn't on it; my head was too full of family problems. I would try another day. There was still time to Skype Holly before the boys came home. Perhaps she had a few words of wisdom to offer me or could at least cheer me up a little. My friend answered almost immediately, her smiling face flecked with pale-blue paint and her hair coiled back and tied with what looked like a dishcloth. She waved a paintbrush at me enthusiastically.

'Hi, I've been thinking about you. I was going to call you tonight. How did the funeral go?' Her voice softened with concern.

As I described the virtual non-event, she sympathised with me before asking if there had been any more letters.

'Actually, the letters seem to be the least of my problems lately.' The saga of Lucy and Brad living in a hovel all poured out. I mentioned Steve's involvement, and Holly stopped me before I could skip swiftly past this part of the story.

'Hold on here, Laura. Is this Steve the same policeman who's looking into those letters?'

'Yes,' I admitted.

'And the same Steve who arranged for the security cameras? And the same Steve who drove you to the care home the night your mother died?' I had to admit to it all, knowing precisely what Holly would make of it.

'Quick description please; age, marital status, you know the ropes!' she demanded.

'Honestly, Holly, he's simply a very kind man who would help anyone in the same situation.'

'Now I know you're lying. Come on, spill the beans.'

I knew she wouldn't be satisfied until every last piece of information was in her possession, so I gave in and told her, but not the bit about my daydreams, although she seemed to hear those words in amongst the ones I spoke.

'Well, has he asked you out yet?'

'No, of course not! It's a professional relationship, nothing more.'

'Liar! You might as well admit it. If you don't fill in all the blanks, I'll simply have to make the answers up for myself.'

And she would, too, so I began to tell her what she wanted to hear. Strangely enough, actually verbalising the words instead of simply allowing them to float around in my brain made it all seem real. I admitted to liking Steve, and it felt good to share it with someone.

'Do you think I'm just imagining that he's interested in me?' I asked Holly.

'It doesn't sound like imagination to me. There's one way to find out, though, isn't there?'

I dreaded what my friend might suggest.

'Invite him for a meal. You could use the pretence of it being simply to thank him for his support and then come right out and ask him if he fancies you!'

'Holly, it sounds.... so schoolgirlish! I can't do that.'

'Well, okay then, but you might not get another chance. What if they get the guy who's writing those letters? Or even if they don't, they won't keep on seeing you if the letters dry up.'

She had a point.

'Okay, I'll think about it,' I conceded. 'But what about Lucy and the money issue?'

'Hell yes, what an awful predicament. You'll have to talk to her and even to Paul about it. I can see how it goes against the grain to give her money to live with someone so totally gross, but then she's got to eat! I wish I had an answer for you, Laura – it's quite some dilemma you're in.'

Holly was right – Lucy had to eat. We eventually said goodbye, and after thanking her for loaning me a shoulder to cry on, I went to make a cup of tea.

Although not yet 3pm, it was growing dark outside. Rain was beating against the window, and the house felt strangely silent, almost eerie. A sudden crack of thunder made me jump, then a flash of lightning split the sky, and the rain poured even heavier, falling in sheets which drummed so hard on the window I thought the glass might crack. The phone rang three times again and stopped before I could pick it up. I groaned inwardly. It rang again after a minute, and I didn't even get out of the chair to answer. My whole world seemed to have shrunk around me, and at that moment in time, it consisted only of me, surrounded on all sides by the storm outside and, even worse, the storm within my life.

Paul rang later in the evening to ask what we should do about Lucy's birthday. It was comforting to know he was still actively thinking about the situation, and we held a reasonably adult conversation about our options until I told him I'd sent a text and what our daughter's reply had been.

'We can't just hand over money! He could be buying drugs or anything!' Paul was horrified.

'Yes, and naturally, I feel the same, but this is our daughter – she needs to eat and pay her way.'

'Well, I'm going to stop the weekly payments into the bank. Unless Lucy comes home and behaves herself, I won't be a party to her living with that yob!' My ex's reaction was about what I expected.

'If you do that, Paul, then I'll have to give her even more money and to be quite candid, with my job being in question at the moment, I really can't afford it.'

'You don't have to give her money; she'll have to get a job and take responsibility for herself!'

'But what if she turns to petty crime to feed herself? As you're always pointing out, we don't know anything about Brad. He could get her into all sorts of trouble.' I didn't want to think about such things, much less plant the idea in Paul's mind.

'So, you'd give her the green light to live with someone totally unsuitable and condone it by giving her money? What kind of example will it give to the boys? You must be out of your mind, Laura!'

'I'm trying to find some middle ground here. As Steve said, we need to keep the lines of communication open, can't you understand?'

'Oh right, so now Steve knows what's best for my daughter, does he? It's probably him sniffing around which made Lucy leave home in the first place!' His anger was palpable.

'Don't be so ridiculous. Steve's not "sniffing around", as you put it. He's been helpful, that's all.' I should have known better than to mention Steve, but it just kind of popped out, and he does talk more sense than Paul was doing at the moment.

'Look.' I didn't want to prolong the conversation; we were getting nowhere. 'I'm going to give Lucy money for her birthday. You can do what you want, as you keep reminding me, she's your daughter too.' The call ended and left me feeling worse than ever. The boys had gone to bed, and once again, a dark feeling of loneliness engulfed me. The rain still lashed down. I shivered, then opened the curtains and sat staring out into the inky black night. When would we be able to get back to normal, whatever normal was? My whole life seemed to be on hold, and I felt utterly powerless to do anything about it.

Chapter Twenty-Eight

Tuesday didn't prove to be any better than Monday. I risked sending another text to Lucy asking for the okay to call around on Wednesday and hinting how much I'd love to see how the decorating was getting on. The reply was brief.

> Too messy for visitors. I'll come for tea tomorrow to see you and the boys.

I should have expected another rebuff, but at least she was coming home for tea. It had only been a few days, but could she be missing us? However, a nagging little voice inside my head was telling me it was only the money she wanted. My reply said it would be lovely to see her and Brad would be very welcome too. I also included the fact that her grandparents were going on a three-week holiday and had left a parcel with me before they left. A carrot-on-a-stick approach could only strengthen the case for seeing her on her birthday. Lucy didn't reply. It was during times like these I missed having someone to talk to. Janet and Bob were away, I'd miss them, and my mother was no longer there for me. Yet I had to move on, to keep all the plates spinning in the air, yet it was so hard at times.

Dear Laura,

I'm thirty years old and married with two children. My mother died suddenly as the result of an accident two months ago. We were always close, and I feel bereft without her. She called to see us at least twice a week, and we spoke daily on the phone. I've been so depressed since she died, but my husband keeps telling me to pull myself together. He says it's the natural order of things for our parents to die and I should get over it, but Mum was only sixty-one! He isn't close to his parents, so he doesn't understand how I feel. Is he right, Laura? Should I be over it by now?

June

Dear June,

Two months is hardly any time at all, and as you and your mum were so close, I don't find this in any way strange. We never really 'get over' the loss of a loved one, as your husband seems to think. The pain will always be there but will become manageable in time. Your mum was very young, and although it is the natural order of things for our parents to die first, this was an accident, a huge shock and her life ended far too soon. It will take more than a couple of months to come to terms with your loss.

Try to explain to your husband exactly how you feel. If, as you say, he is not close to his parents, he will find it difficult to understand the enormity of your grief. Perhaps you could show him this letter if you find verbalising your feelings hard to do.

I would also suggest you seek professional help, a bereavement counsellor, perhaps? Your GP should be able to refer you to someone locally.

Whatever you decide to do, don't be hard on yourself. We all process things at our own pace, and you should not feel pressurised to 'be over' your mother's death. I think it is wonderful how you were so close, and you'll always have happy memories to remember her by.

Laura

I would give anything for my mother to be here with me today, not the mother whose funeral we've just attended but my real mum, as she was before Alzheimer's stole her away from me. June's letter was very typical of many which 'Ask Laura' receives. Sadly her problem wasn't only the loss of her mum but the expectations of her husband. There isn't a magic formula for solving the problems which fall across our path in life. We are all individuals, and as such, what works for one, might not for another.

Paul and I are a case in point here. We both want to win our daughter back, but he feels being firm and pulling rank will win the day. I'm more inclined to the softly, softly approach. We could so easily lose Lucy, and I'd rather win her back with love and kindness than playing the role of strict parent. It's vital we keep communicating, even if it is only through short, impersonal text messages. It's the way of young people today, and I'm happy to try anything which might win through and bring my child back to me. So, who is right and who is wrong? Perhaps the answer is neither. It may be a two-pronged campaign will win the day. Paul with his discipline and me with my coaxing, who knows?

My reply to June told her not to be hard on herself, but if I'm honest, I'm guilty of the very same thing at the moment. As I lie awake at night, my mind aches with the effort of going back in time to find out where I went wrong. Dredging up old memories, good and bad, have brought me nothing but a headache, coupled with complete and utter exhaustion. It was true Paul and I married hastily, and the unplanned pregnancy was a shock rather than a surprise, but there was no doubting the happiness Lucy brought to us when she came into the world! We couldn't have loved her more, and we both spent hours simply watching her, asleep or awake. She was our little miracle, and our love for her was all-encompassing.

The joy Lucy brought united us, and although we were both young and inexperienced, we were a happy family unit. With very few possessions, we had each other and our baby daughter and wished for nothing more. We rented a flat close to my parents' home in those early days, which was small, but the rent was reasonable, and Paul worked long hours to provide for us.

When Lucy was three, we decided I should seek a job to help make ends meet. I was excited at the prospect, and Lucy loved to be among other children at toddler groups and other social activities, so we knew she would enjoy nursery. I began to research my options. My interests lay in writing, and my degree in psychology could potentially open up all sorts of exciting opportunities. But then I fell pregnant again. You would think, once bitten – but no, another unplanned pregnancy came along to change the course of our lives once again. When we discovered it was twins, there was no chance of embarking on a career. Childcare for one was expensive – for three, it was impossible. However, the joy Sam and Jake brought to us was no less than we experienced with Lucy. I only occasionally thought about all my old friends from university who were living the dream of following their chosen careers. Paul and I never talked about such things, 'what might have been' was, and remains, taboo.

The burden on Paul increased with the addition of another two mouths to feed, but then out of the blue, his maiden aunt died, leaving her house and estate to him. It was wonderful – not that the poor woman had died, but the unexpected gift of a house – a family-sized house! We were ecstatic, and the future became less of a worry. I loved this house from the moment we saw it, and over the years, we improved it as and when we could afford to. Perhaps it is now in need of improving the improvements, but in my current situation, it remains impossible.

I hoped a foray into the past would answer my present predicament with Lucy, but sadly the reminiscing proved to be of no help whatsoever. If anything, it made me maudlin. My memories were of being almost permanently exhausted after the boys were born, and perhaps Lucy was overlooked for a while. Being a placid, easy-going child, I relied on her to be good, which she was, and she learned to occupy herself for hours while my attention was given to the twins. Was this where I went wrong? Could Lucy have felt pushed out? I didn't pick up on it at the time, but with hindsight, it now seems possible, even likely. Children are so amazingly resilient, and my little girl seemed to be happy and delighted with her new brothers, or was my imagination a convenient peg on which to hang my guilt?

In my mind, I attempted to build a timeline, dredging up old memories, some of which were incredibly happy and some almost too painful to remember. Lucy was five when the twins were born and would probably (although unintentionally) have received very little attention from her father or me. It was exhausting looking after the boys. When one settled, the other began demanding attention, and my memories of Lucy from then onwards are of her standing on the sidelines, watching and waiting – but waiting for what? Perhaps if she'd been a more outgoing child, she would have demanded my attention, but she wasn't like that. Lucy was quiet, a little girl who appeared to be self-sufficient, and we assumed she was happy to amuse herself. At the time, I was so grateful for that quality, but had I in some way neglected her? Were our present problems rooted in the past and caused by my being remiss in the care of Lucy?

Looking back, I can see now how so much happened in Lucy's formative years. Her early memories must be of being pushed aside for her two demanding brothers, and then less than a couple of years after they came along, her father left us. We tried to be civilised and adult about it, but looking back, it was another major upheaval in Lucy's life. In trying to pinpoint something from the past which might explain my daughter's irrational behaviour in the present, I can see so many negative experiences for such a young child to understand. In retrospect, I don't think we handled it well, and it's incredible Lucy hasn't turned to a life of crime, or worse!

Tomorrow will be Lucy's seventeenth birthday. I want to spend time with her, to spoil her, but am I too late? Perhaps we should have paid more attention to her in years gone by, years which we can never live again. We only have today and the future to live, a future which quite honestly, totally, utterly scares me!

Chapter Twenty-Nine

L ucy came for tea, alone. This morning, I'd sent another text which simply said, *'Happy birthday'* with lots of smiley faces and kisses. Not receiving a response prompted a few restless hours whilst I wondered if she would turn up as she'd said.

Sam and Jake were beginning to ask awkward questions about their sister now, and it was difficult to fudge the issue any longer. I didn't want them to know, however, that she was living with her boyfriend. I hoped today Lucy would see what she was missing and decide to come home. I'd baked a cake and prepared her favourite meal, lasagne. She hadn't given a time for when she would arrive, so I assumed it would be the usual time we ate, around 5.30. I was right; she didn't come a moment earlier, which left me in no doubt that very little had changed between us.

The three of us had gifts which she opened without enthusiasm and thanked us briefly without much comment. Even the earrings from Janet and Bob didn't raise much of a smile. The boys exchanged a look which I couldn't quite read, but they must have been wondering what was going on. Lucy certainly hadn't made an effort with her appearance and wore an old black sweater, probably one of Brad's, which was two sizes too big, and her hands were hidden beneath the sleeves which were pulled down like mittens.

Our meal was eaten in an unnaturally quiet atmosphere, even though I tried my best to get Lucy to talk. The boys too asked questions about the 'friend' she was living with, but her answer was to tell them to mind their own business.

My gift had been a token box of chocolates, her favourites, and after we'd eaten, I gave her a cheque for a hundred pounds. The amount was more than I would usually give and a look of surprise crossed Lucy's face when she saw it. But her thank you was brief, and she waited only as long as she could without being rude and left, refusing my offer of a lift back.

'She's weird!' Sam said after Lucy left.

'Yeah,' Jake agreed. I remained silent, unable to defend her actions and disappointed the evening hadn't been more of a success. At least I now knew my daughter had some money but I was convinced it wouldn't last long. The amount would barely cover a couple of week's grocery shopping, and I only hoped Lucy wouldn't waste it.

After the twins had gone up to bed, a heavy feeling of loneliness descended once again. Paul hadn't been in touch since Monday, and Lucy didn't say whether she'd seen or heard from him either. Channel-hopping on the television for a while failed to find anything to capture my interest, so I decided on an early night with my book, although it was only 9.30. But the doorbell rang before I even reached the stairs. I couldn't imagine who it would be and froze for a few moments, trying to decide whether or not to answer it. It rang again, more urgently as if someone was keeping their finger on the bell. Afraid it might wake the boys, I moved towards the door, fearful of what such a late call might herald. Keeping the chain on, I opened the door a few inches, and the sight which greeted me made me want to laugh and cry at the same time. There on my doorstep on such a cold, drizzly night was Holly!

Fumbling with the chain, I opened the door wide, and as she stepped inside, she opened her arms and I all but fell into them, sobbing like a baby. Being enfolded in one of Holly's hugs is like being wrapped in a warm, comforting duvet, and I remained there for several moments until able to speak coherently again.

'What on earth are you doing here?'

'Visiting, of course, but if it's not convenient...' Holly turned back towards the door, but I dragged her by the arm into the warmth of the lounge. It was only in the brightness of the room I took in her appearance. My friend was wrapped up in a brightly coloured, long patchwork coat, teamed with fluorescent-green trainers.

'What on earth are you wearing? It looks like a dressing gown!' I laughed.

'That's because it is a dressing gown, silly.' She untied the belt to reveal black-and-white-striped pyjamas.

'My goodness, you haven't driven all the way from Carlisle like that, have you?' Nothing like asking the obvious, is there?

'Of course. I only needed to stop once at a service station for a pee and a cup of coffee. It seemed stupid wearing good clothes to travel in when it would be almost bedtime when I arrived.' My friend stood in front of me and looked me over, holding my shoulders as my mother used to when I was a child.

'Laura Green, you look bloody awful!'

I could only nod in agreement; I'd accidentally caught sight of my reflection in the mirror earlier in the evening, and my friend spoke the very same words which had gone through my mind. Naturally, the tears hadn't helped to improve my looks either.

'Is the kettle on? And where are those two adorable little rascals?' Holly made for the kitchen.

'The boys are asleep, it's school tomorrow, and we can soon get the kettle on, although I'd better stick to decaf.'

'Forget the decaf – it's going to be a late night. I want to know everything that's happened of late. I can't bear you having all this excitement in life and me being left in the dark!'

'Excitement isn't quite the way I'd describe recent events. You're lucky I opened the door. I live in perpetual fear of what might happen next.' As the words came out of my mouth, I realised how true they were. What else could possibly go wrong in my life? We brewed coffee and settled down in the lounge where Holly insisted I tell her everything again, even what I'd already shared via Skype.

I began with the short shorts, which seemed so long ago now and really had nothing to do with anything else. But it was the reason why Lucy wasn't speaking to me, although even I knew the real reason was something which lay much deeper inside my daughter's mind, something which even she probably didn't understand. As I tried to explain it all to Holly, she waved her hand in dismissal.

'Forget the psychobabble, Laura – it's lost on me. Just tell me the facts.' So I did, moving on to relate how I found the birth control pills in Lucy's room and then describing how Paul and I hadn't been able to get through to our daughter and disagreed on how to handle the situation. I told her about Richard and watched Holly's face contort as I described his ugly attempts at seducing me. Next were those abhorrent letters. It was easy to be honest with Holly, she didn't need protection from the horror and fear the letters had brought into my life, and it was a relief to describe precisely how badly they had affected me. She asked several questions, and I told her about my visit to London and the magazine's suspension of '*Ask Laura*', and their insistence the police should be involved.

Holly interrupted at that point to ask about Steve and wouldn't be persuaded he was simply a good policeman, going the extra mile. (Even as I insisted this was all there was to our relationship, I was hoping it meant more to Steve, as it did to me.) My mother's death was the next thing to be laid before my friend for her scrutiny, and finally, I described the abject horror of finding Lucy's letter. An awful cold feeling clutched me again, and as I brought Holly up to date on the situation with Lucy as from today, I realised having my daughter living with Brad was preferable to not having found her.

As I finished the saga, Holly sighed. She'd heard some of it during our conversations on Skype, but now she had all the facts.

'Well, you've been too busy to miss me then?' She grinned.

'Absolutely! But it is so good to see you, Holly. How long can you stay?'

'Oh yes, you want me out before I've even slept a night here, do you?' I laughed; we knew each other better than that. Even as I said how good it was to see her, I thought about my in-laws and went on to tell her how great Janet and Bob had been.

'They're such lovely people. I'll never understand how such an amazing couple could produce such an idiot as Paul.' She pulled a face as she passed judgement.

'Don't be so hard on him, Holly. Paul's trying his best but has so much going on in his life too.' I spoke up for my ex. After all, I had loved him once.

'What could possibly be going on in his life which is more important than his children?' Holly huffed.

'Ah, well, there's another thing. Paul's going to become a daddy again, and soon. Zoe's pregnant.'

'What? Surely it must be an accident! I can't imagine Zoe coping with a new baby and all the stuff which comes out of one end or the other!'

I had to smile at the image. Zoe did seem an unlikely candidate for 'Earth Mother of the Year'.

'You never know, she might surprise us. Baby's due in a couple of weeks or so. It was only through Janet I found out. Paul didn't seem to think we needed to know, but I've left it up to him to tell our three about it.'

'Oh, to be a fly on the wall during that particular conversation!' Holly laughed and I had to agree with her. It was a slightly lighter subject to end our evening, and as it was getting late, we made up Lucy's bed for Holly and eventually attempted to get some sleep at almost two in the morning.

Chapter Thirty

I awoke the following day with a weighty feeling of dread which now seemed to accompany all of my waking hours. However, remembering Holly's arrival last night brought a smile to my face. She was precisely the kind of friend you could turn to in a crisis, and I couldn't be happier she was here. It was early, surprisingly early after such a late night, and I went downstairs feeling grateful we'd stuck to drinking coffee rather than the wine, which often accompanied our friendship.

Moving quietly, I began the morning routine but soon became aware of noises upstairs. Squeals were coming from the boys' room; Holly had woken them up, and as always, they were delighted to see her. A few minutes later, they trooped down together, declaring hunger and demanding food. As I worked, watching and listening to the interaction between my sons and Holly, it struck me how little merriment had filled our home over the last few weeks.

'How long are you staying, Auntie Holly?' Sam asked.

'That's just what your mum asked. Do you want to be rid of me already?'

'No!' Sam replied with horror. Holly ruffled his hair and laughed.

'Well, if it's okay with your mum, I've got a whole week free and thought I might spend it with you guys.' Holly's words brought smiles all around, especially to me. It was such a relief to have another adult in the house and one with whom I could share my thoughts and feelings. It's not only the problems, which are enough in themselves, but also the little daily decisions, like what to eat for dinner and whether my new red jumper would run in the wash. Usually, I coped well with being an only parent, but Holly's presence had come at just the right time to help me retain any sanity I still had left, and I loved her for it. Her very presence spoke volumes about her generosity of spirit, and it was so clear now just how much I'd missed having her around. We hadn't made any plans last night, simply enjoyed each other's company, and I didn't know what to suggest we might do today. Holly, however, was one step ahead.

'I thought I might go to see Lucy this morning,' she announced. 'I missed her birthday yesterday and have a little gift for her.'

All three of us were surprised by this, but why should we be? Lucy had always loved Holly. Perhaps Holly's bohemian ways appealed to young people, and maybe she could reach Lucy where I couldn't.

'What a great idea. We could see if she'd like to come with us for a coffee?' I felt sure Lucy would be much more talkative and open if Holly was with me. There'd always been a connection between them, something I certainly didn't have with my daughter these days.

'Who said you were invited?' Holly threw the remark at me. 'I don't need you to show me the way, you know. I've got a satnav.'

So I was put in my place. As I thought about it, it seemed a good idea – Lucy might respond better to Holly without my presence – all my efforts only served to drive her further away.

The doorbell rang.

'I'll get it!' Sam was off his chair like lightning while I wondered who could be calling so early. He returned with Steve behind him, and I felt my face begin to glow.

'Sorry to call so early,' Steve began. Holly was openly gawping at him and then swivelled her head to look at me, grinning at my discomfort. Naturally, I had to introduce them, and Steve again apologised for arriving unannounced.

'Don't worry on my account. It's nice to meet you. Laura speaks very highly of you.' Holly shook hands with Steve. 'Would you like a coffee or tea perhaps?' Had my friend just taken over my role of hostess here? She was spooning coffee into the cup before Steve had a chance to reply.

'Here, Laura,' she instructed, pushing two mugs into my hands. 'Take Steve into the lounge. The boys and I will be fine here.' The exaggerated smile on her face was such a giveaway to what she was trying to do, but we dutifully obeyed, and as soon as we were out of hearing, I apologised to Steve.

'Holly's one of my closest friends, but she does tend to be rather bossy. She used to live next door until they moved to Carlisle. Her visit's a complete surprise, I didn't know she was coming, but it's great to have her here.'

Steve smiled and sat down.

'I only called to see how you were holding up but having a friend here will help, won't it?'

'It will, even if she is a rather acquired taste!' Holly would kill me if she thought I was making excuses for her. Steve laughed.

'Actually, I find directness rather refreshing. I spend my days listening to people, at least fifty per cent of whom are usually lying to me. So, how are things with Lucy?'

I told him about her birthday and the brief visit home. He

nodded, recognising it as good news, and he was such a good listener – I found myself explaining the dilemma about giving her money too.

'Yes, I can see it's a tricky one. What does her father think?'

'Oh, Paul's set against giving her money. He'd still like to go round and drag her home kicking and screaming.'

'Maybe he'll come to terms with it in time.' Steve's concern was genuine; he was so easy to talk to.

'I think we're both hoping it will only be very temporary. Quite honestly, I hate the idea of my daughter living in such an awful flat and with Brad. He must be so much older than she is too.'

'He's twenty-nine; I did a bit of digging around on the internet and found him on Facebook.'

'Twenty-nine, but she's only just seventeen!' Brad looked to be in his twenties, yet I'd never have guessed at twenty-nine. And why hadn't I thought of looking on Facebook?

'Legally, there's nothing wrong with his age. In another ten years the age difference will seem nothing at all.'

Steve saw the look of horror on my face.

'Laura, I'm not saying they'll still be together in ten years. Age gaps between partners are relative, that's all I meant.'

'Yes, of course, sorry. You must think I'm awfully bigoted about Brad when I don't even know him, but he appears to want nothing to do with our family. I invited him to come yesterday, but he didn't. Anyway, Holly's planning to visit Lucy this morning, and she doesn't want me there either.'

Steve grinned. 'Probably an excellent idea. Sometimes someone neutral can act as a mediator. Does Lucy like Holly?'

'Yes, very much. My friend is rather unconventional in many ways, and all the children adore her. I wish I knew her secret.'

Steve laughed. 'It's easy for an outsider to breeze in and out again. It's the parents who have to be there in the long term.

They're the ones to make the difficult decisions and aren't always popular for doing so.' How wise he was, I couldn't help thinking he'd make a brilliant dad one day.

'Well, there's nothing new to report on the letter front, I'm afraid, and as there haven't been any more, perhaps this mysterious letter writer has given up, let's hope so.'

'Does this mean you'll be closing the case?' Sad person that I was, I was looking for a reason to keep in touch with Steve, even if it meant receiving more horrible letters.

'Not exactly. We never entirely close an unsolved case, but honestly, unless there are more letters or some other evidence turns up, there's little more we can do. It's been a difficult time for you, Laura, with your mum and Lucy as well as the letters. Try not to worry about them. As we said before, whoever is writing them doesn't know where you live, or if he does, he can't mean you any physical harm. He would almost certainly have acted by now. Cold comfort, I know, but please feel free to ring me anytime if you're worried. We'll leave the camera up a little while longer to give you an extra bit of security.' Steve smiled at me, and my heart missed a beat.

'I was just on my way into work, so I thought I'd see how things were. I'm glad you have a friend staying.' He rose to leave.

'Thanks, Steve, I appreciate everything you've done, really.' I wanted to say more but couldn't think of anything. It sounded as if Steve was saying goodbye. The letters, or lack of them now, didn't merit a detective sergeant's attention, even I could see that.

Holly was right behind me as I closed the front door when Steve left, and I almost tripped over her.

'Very nice!' she said rather too loudly and with a massive grin on her face.

'Shh... the boys!' But she laughed and ran upstairs to get into the bathroom before me.

Chapter Thirty-One

Dear Laura,

My only son was murdered seven months ago. He was only twenty-one and stabbed outside a nightclub. I was devastated; he died in the ambulance on the way to hospital. Christopher was my world, but I keep thinking of all the things I should have told him. I can't remember the last time I told him I loved him or how proud I was of him. I feel guilty about the petty arguments we had and all the times I grumbled at him for silly little reasons. As his mother, I should have protected him, but I didn't, so it seems to me that it's somehow my fault he's dead. Will these feelings ever go away?

Susan

Dear Susan,

I am so sorry for your loss; it's always tragic to lose a child even though he was an adult. For these negative feelings to go away, you need to remember the happy times you shared with Christopher and not dwell on the unhappy ones. Thinking of what might have been is very debilitating. We all have regrets about things in our past but cannot go back in time to change them. As for the guilt you are experiencing, the only guilty party here is the person whose vile act killed your son. You could have done nothing to protect him; none of us can wrap our children up in cotton wool, no matter how much we long to do so. They need to make their own way in the world, which, at twenty-one, is what Christopher was doing.

You loved your son, and I'm sure he knew it, so try to concentrate on the many happy memories you have of him, which is what he would have wanted. You may not think you will ever cope with this, and although your grief will always be there, it will become easier to bear as time goes on.

Laura

I was filling in time and trying not to worry about how Holly's visit to Lucy was going, but I really must stop reading all these old letters. I often draw inspiration from them, but the way things were at the moment, they seemed to depress me. Susan's letter was one Madeline didn't want to publish. She reasoned it would be too upsetting for the readers, whom she thought simply wanted to read about everyday problems and topics to which they could relate. After much discussion, I said if it wasn't published, I would like Susan's address to reply in person, such was my empathy with her. It was published, and I'm certainly one 'reader' who can relate to Susan's problem. Not that my child is dead, but in leaving home, Lucy had given me cause to reflect on our relationship, and I am also experiencing guilt for the many times I've failed as a mother. Fortunately, I have the opportunity to attempt to make things up to my child; Susan didn't.

My restlessness was interrupted by the telephone. It was Paul.

'Laura? I'm not going to manage to take the boys next week...' he began.

'Why ever not?' Sam and Jake would be devastated. Paul was due to have them stay over for a few days while they were on half-term break. They'd made all sorts of plans, and I knew they were looking forward to it. It would also probably be the last time they would see Paul before he became a father again.

'There's a conference I have to attend. Sorry, but I can't get out of it. Will you tell them for me?'

'And how does Zoe feel about this conference?' I asked.

'She's not too happy, naturally... but it's none of your business.' That put me in my place then, didn't it?

'No, you're right, it's not. Maybe you should try to see the boys before you go to make up for their disappointment?'

'Look, I'll pick them up from school tomorrow night and take them out for pizza or something. Will that do?' He always made it sound like I was annoyed because I didn't want the boys around, but it wasn't that at all. My annoyance was how he seemed to be letting them down more and more often.

'I'm sure they'll be up for it, and maybe you could prepare them for the birth of their new sibling as well?' I had told the children, but the boys didn't seem to take it in. To them, it was something happening to Zoe and didn't affect them. Lucy didn't offer a comment on the news, just a loud 'tut' and her increasingly familiar roll of her eyes. Spending time with their father during the half-term would, I'd hoped, enable the boys to get used to the idea of a baby and allow them to ask any questions they might have. Sadly, it now wasn't to be. Trying not to sound too judgemental, I asked how Zoe was.

'She's not had an easy time of it and will be glad when it's all over,' he answered with a concerned tone in his voice. 'So, tell Sam and Jake I'll see them tomorrow. I don't suppose there's much chance of seeing Lucy?'

'You could ring her; she still has her mobile phone, the same number. Actually, Holly turned up last night, she's staying for a few days, and she's gone to see Lucy this morning.'

'That's good of her. I hope she can make her see sense.'

I wished the same thing. We said goodbye, and I went to begin lunch, needing something to do to keep my mind off Lucy.

Holly was out for two hours during the morning, and I could hardly wait to hear every detail of what happened. When she eventually returned, I practically grabbed her at the door, anxious to know how she'd got on with Lucy.

'Let me at least get my coat off, will you?' She laughed. Holly was quite animated and deemed the visit a success – not in having persuaded Lucy to come home, but in gaining her trust and engaging my daughter in conversation, something I seemed unable to do these days. When Holly realised I was preparing lunch, she stopped me.

'Oh, don't bother making anything for lunch. I thought we'd go out, you know, ladies who lunch, like we used to?'

'Why not?' The idea appealed to me. I rarely went out to eat; it was no fun on my own. 'But tell me more about how you got on first.'

'Well, her new abode is a bit of a comedown, but there were a few pots of paint around, so presumably, they're decorating. She was certainly surprised to see me, but in a good way, I think. It was Brad who answered the door. He's a bundle of laughs, isn't he? Anyway, he let me in, and Lucy was still in her pyjamas. But hey, who am I to talk? We had a good chat about general stuff, and I asked if she was happy living with Brad. Her answer was yes, but the body language and lack of enthusiasm told me otherwise.'

I wasn't sure if I wanted to know this or not. Naturally, I wanted Lucy to be happy, but it sounded as if she maybe wasn't so sure herself. Was this a good thing?

'Don't look so worried!' Holly chided me. 'Seeing the place she's living in and the nerd she's living with, I'd say you have a pretty good chance of getting your daughter back home, and soon too.'

'But she's so stubborn. It feels as if I can't reach her anymore, and I haven't a clue what to do!'

'There's not much you can do except wait. I asked about her birthday visit home and why Brad didn't come with her. All she could say was he wasn't big into family stuff. Most of the time I was there, Brad was in the bedroom, but I tried to draw him into the conversation when he came out to go into the kitchen. I asked how long they'd known each other, which is only about eight weeks. He doesn't appear to have a job, and when I asked him what he did, he said he used to work in an off-licence which seems the extent of his professional career. I did tell him you and the boys had been disappointed when he didn't come with Lucy, but a shrug of the shoulders was the only answer he could muster for that one.'

'How did they seem together? You know, were they affectionate, happy to be with each other, or not?'

'Not, I would say. I'm rather confident Lucy won't stay long-term with Brad. He's colourless and a bit lacking in the brains department too. Lucy's such a bright girl. She'll get tired of him soon, I'm fairly certain.'

'What I don't understand is why. Why is living there preferable to being here? I've racked my brains to find a reason and simply can't. Yes, we've had rows, but just the usual mother-daughter sort of thing. To suddenly leave school and home, there must be a reason, surely?'

'Not being a mother myself, I can't comment, but I remember being a teenager, and quite honestly, it didn't take much for me to fall out with my parents. Sometimes it was over such trivial things, which in retrospect makes me feel quite ashamed. It's an age when parents are the enemy, it's them and us, and there's often no common ground. But Lucy's an intelligent girl, she'll come round sooner or later, I'm certain.'

Holly was probably right, but I fervently wished it would be sooner.

'I don't trust Brad. If he's genuine, then surely he'd want to get to know Lucy's family?' I moaned.

'Don't forget, they're a different species, Laura. And as I say, he's not the sharpest knife in the block, and I don't think he's capable of even the most basic conversation.'

'But what if she gets pregnant or he persuades her to take drugs? Did you smell anything funny in the flat?' It was a serious question, but my friend burst out laughing.

'Oh, I'm sorry, Laura, but your face is a picture! Look, the flat smelled of paint, nothing else. Lucy seems to be leading a very confined sort of life. I don't know if they ever go out, and she'll soon tire of that. I don't mean to belittle your concerns, Laura, but let's try not to anticipate tomorrow's problems today, all right?'

'Okay, I'll try. Come on then, let's do lunch!'

An hour or so later, when we were seated in our favourite café with the paninis ordered, I told Holly about Paul's phone call.

'Sam and Jake will be so disappointed. Staying at Paul's is quite an adventure for them, and they'd been planning what they would do for ages.'

Holly's face lit up. 'Why don't they come back with me for a few days? I'd love to have them, and we'll find loads of things to do.'

'But I thought you were staying here a while longer?' I didn't want her to go.

'I am. If I stay here until Tuesday and we leave then, I'll be able to bring them back the following Friday, in good time for school reopening on Monday.' The idea seemed to enthuse Holly. It was obviously a genuine offer, so who was I to stand in their way? It was tempting to go with them, but there was just so much going on in my life and I didn't want to be away.

'Holly, you are a star! I know the boys will love the idea, and it'll certainly help them get over their disappointment.' At least I would have her company over the weekend and into next week. I'd just have to make the most of my friend while she was here.

Chapter Thirty-Two

The days of Holly's visit proved to be some of the most relaxing I'd enjoyed for ages. We laughed at nothing in particular, ate out far too often and managed to cram every hour with fun. There were long games of Monopoly with the boys and too many late nights for us all, but it was so refreshing. At times, feelings of guilt danced through my mind. Should I still be grieving for my mother – and perhaps doing something proactive to win back my daughter? Yet if I mentioned any of this to Holly, she simply refilled my wine glass and listed valid reasons why I should not in the slightest way feel guilty. Generally, she was right, and her presence was a tonic. I so wished she still lived next door.

But Tuesday arrived, and very early in the morning, she loaded her little Micra with my sons and their luggage and headed off to Carlisle. Sam and Jake had never been so far north before and were delighted to be staying so close to the Scottish border. Holly promised them a trip into Scotland on a train, maybe to Edinburgh, which they declared awesome. They were also impressed to learn that Carlisle had a real castle, and they added seeing this to their growing list of things to do. There was no doubt I would miss them. It was often only the boys who kept me going, but, as Holly pointed out, I could do with some time to myself, and I dutifully promised to make the most of it. There were still some of Mum's things to sort through, mainly paperwork, old correspondence and cards I'd like to look at again before disposing of them. It was also an unexpected opportunity to do some work on the house and catch up on those jobs which were always so easy to put off. Holly also suggested, quite emphatically, that I should ask Steve Radcliffe round for a meal one night. The jury was still out on that one.

My '*me*' days, however, didn't get off to a good start. Madeline rang a couple of hours after the boys and Holly left.

'I'm sorry, Laura, but it's not good news.' Her voice had a sympathetic quality to it, and I instinctively knew what was coming. 'We've decided to suspend the '*Ask Laura*' page indefinitely.'

'But why? There haven't been any more letters recently, so surely it's time to reinstate the page?' I wished I didn't sound so needy.

'That's precisely the point, Laura. He's stopped because he's got what he wanted. If we introduce the page again, goodness knows what will happen. He may take it a step further!'

'So are you telling me I no longer have a job?'

'I'm so sorry. If the police had found out who was doing this, it might have been different and dealt with appropriately. The fact that they haven't found him leaves us in a tricky position. It's an unfinished scenario, but, of course, we'll pay you until the end of the month, and we'd still like to commission regular feature articles from you, Laura. Your writing is always popular with our readers.'

'Is it only the letters, Madeline? If we do find out who is

sending them, will the page be reinstated?' There was a moment of silence.

'Okay, I'll be honest with you. The board would be finishing the page shortly anyway as one of their "cutbacks". I tried to speak up for you, your page is always excellent, but these letters have made them think again. The feeling is that "agony aunts" are old hat, and they want to introduce something new. They're considering a page for readers' true-life stories, something gritty and contemporary.'

I knew the sort of thing she meant. So many magazines were full of those kinds of stories with sensational headlines on their covers. I'd rather hoped the board wouldn't want to go down that particular route, but it seemed they did. I knew it wasn't entirely Madeline's decision, and there would have been pressure on her to agree, so it seemed there was nothing else for me to do but accept their decision. I thanked Madeline for her understanding, and we finished the call.

It has seriously crossed my mind to get rid of my telephone – each time it rings, something else seems to have gone wrong, really wrong! So, now I was officially unemployed. It was time to start pitching articles to other magazines to put food on the table. No, it wasn't so bad. The regular income from '*Ask Laura*' had been tremendous but hardly the best paying job in the world. I'd survived before on freelance writing but didn't relish the thought of going through the process again, sending ideas out to editors and waiting for aeons until they decided whether or not they liked them. But, needs must, so I'll begin again, and there's always the *one-day* novel.

The need to do something physical, to expend the negative energy I was feeling, sent me upstairs to blitz the bedrooms. By lunchtime, the curtains were in the washing machine and the rooms cleaned thoroughly. I intended redecorating Lucy's room soon, so it would be fresh for when she came home. After eating some leftover spaghetti bolognaise, I changed all the bed linen and tidied some more. My thinking was that physical exhaustion would make me sleep well, despite already missing the boys like crazy. When I eventually stopped cleaning, I decided to Skype them.

They were both excited, having enjoyed the journey, especially the stop at Burger King to eat. They were also seriously impressed with Holly and Brian's 'wicked' house! Brian was in the background and stepped forward to say hello. Sam and Jake had offered to help him work on the house the next day, so I wished him luck. He would need it. After a few more minutes with the boys, Holly came onto the screen. She looked remarkably fresh considering the long journey and her demanding travelling companions, but she insisted they'd been perfectly well behaved, which is when I asked her to check if it really was my sons she had there and not a couple of imposters. I told her about the call from Madeline and my page being dropped from the magazine. She was sympathetic and asked a few questions about any plans I might have.

'Nothing's staring me in the face,' I told her. 'I'll have to write a few articles and pitch to other magazines. It's frustrating work, though, as it can be months before an editor decides to accept or reject an article, and by then it could be out of date and no longer saleable. But there's always the novel!' I said, tongue-in-cheek. Holly had always teased me about my *one-day* novel asking if she could read it, which I steadfastly refused. Now she became serious.

'Yes, why don't you finish it? You could look upon this situation as a window of opportunity; this could be your moment, Laura!'

'It's just a dream. I probably haven't got it in me to even finish it, never mind find a publisher.' My confidence was low.

'Nonsense, you're a brilliant writer. By all means, send off a few articles to keep the wolf from the door but get the novel out – take this chance! It could be the best thing you ever did.'

I loved her enthusiasm, and chatting some more made me feel so much better. The boys came back into view to say goodbye and I promised to Skype them again the following evening.

I felt restless, and it wasn't even 8pm, far too early to go to bed. I browsed the books on the shelves, but nothing caught my eye. Should I ring Steve? Holly had asked if I had when we spoke, nudging me into doing so. There was a reason to ring now too – well, sort of, to tell him the '*Ask Laura*' page was finished. As for inviting him round for a meal, I was still uncertain and didn't want to come over as pushy. I decided to go for it. Dialling his number, my hand trembled. Holly insisted she'd seen interest in Steve's eyes when he looked at me, but what kind of interest? I did not doubt he was an excellent police officer and a very caring person, but did he have feelings for me? Having already admitted I was interested in him, there was perhaps only one way to find out.

'Hello?' Steve's voice made me nervous, and for a moment, I didn't know what to say.

'Hi, it's Laura. Laura Green?' How many Laura's did he know for heaven's sake!

'Oh hi, Laura, how are you?' He sounded pleased to hear from me, or was it a projection of my imagination?

'Okay, well, not really. I wanted to tell you that the magazine has decided to stop my page permanently.' I wanted to tell him so much more, but was too afraid of embarrassing myself.

'That's so unfair. I'm really sorry, Laura, this isn't the result we wanted with your case.'

'It's hardly your fault. You've done a great job, and I wanted to thank you – and Amy too, you've both been very kind.'

'It's been a pleasure, no problem at all. So how are things with Lucy? Have you seen anything of her?'

'Sadly not since her birthday. Holly visited her and thinks

Lucy will soon get bored with Brad and come home. I'm trying to keep in touch, but she doesn't answer my calls. We've exchanged a few texts, though, which is better than nothing.'

'Ah yes, texting is the preferred method of communication for our younger generation. Not something I'm keen on, but it can be useful. And the twins, how are they?'

'Actually, they've gone back with Holly. It's half-term, and they were supposed to be staying with Paul for a few nights but he cancelled and Holly stepped in. They didn't need asking twice.'

'So, you've got a few days to yourself? Will you manage to fill your time?'

'Well, there's a list as long as my arm. I've been sorting out the bedrooms today...'

'What, you've nothing more exciting to do than housework? We'll have to do something about that! How about I take you out to dinner tomorrow evening? Do you like Italian?'

'I, er... yes, it's very kind of you, thanks.' How stupid did I sound? The invitation completely wrong-footed me. I was supposed to invite him for a meal.

'Great, I'll make a reservation and pick you up about seven tomorrow evening, all right?'

'Thank you, yes. That'll be lovely, Steve.' We chatted a little more and I felt giddy with excitement and probably sounded like a bashful teenager – I certainly felt like one! After putting the phone down, I immediately picked it up again and dialled Holly's number. After listening to my description of the conversation with Steve, she gave a little shriek.

'Good for you, I told you he was interested! You'll have to let me know how it goes, a blow-by-blow account, no less!' She didn't need to ask. I'd be bursting to talk to her about it, whether it went well or was a complete disaster. Either way, Holly would be the first to know.

Chapter Thirty-Three

It was dark outside, and I wanted to drift back into sleep, but something was demanding my attention. It took more than a few seconds to realise the telephone was ringing. As I struggled to open my eyes, the luminous face of the clock told me it was not quite 5am. A sense of panic jolted me from sleep. Suddenly I was fully awake and grasping at the telephone, simultaneously dreading and needing to know who was ringing.

'Hello?' My voice was thick with sleep.

'Laura?' I didn't recognise the voice, which was a bad sign, wasn't it?

'Yes... who is this, please?'

'It's Zoe, I'm sorry to ring so early, but I didn't know who else to call.' Her voice was quiet, and it sounded as if she'd been crying. Why on earth would she be ringing me – and so early?

'What's wrong, Zoe?' A cold fear came over me as the thought of Paul came into my mind; something must have happened to Paul.

'The baby's coming... and I don't know what to do.' Relief

that it wasn't anything to do with Paul washed over me. I needed to shake my brain into action and offer some kind of advice.

'Have your waters broken?'

'Yes, and the pains have started. It's awful!' She was crying now.

'Are they regular? If they are, then perhaps you should call for an ambulance?'

'I can't do this alone, Laura, and Paul's away. Could you come round and take me to the hospital?' Her voice was barely a whisper – she sounded so very young. Why on earth would she want me there? Then I remembered – her parents lived in Cornwall and Janet and Bob were away too.

'Is there not a friend or someone you'd rather ask?'

Her reply was a sob.

'Okay; I'll be round in about thirty minutes. If you haven't already packed your bag, you should do it now.' She needed something to do other than think about how awful the pain was. I remember cleaning the kitchen floor when labour started with Lucy, not wanting to go into hospital a minute sooner than necessary and needing something practical to stop me thinking of the pain.

Quickly I pulled on some clothes then splashed my face with cold water. Driving to Paul and Zoe's house usually took the best part of an hour, but at this time in the morning, with little to no traffic, the journey would probably take only half the time.

As I pulled the car out of the drive, it occurred to me how surreal this situation was. I was on a mission of mercy to help the woman who had stolen my husband and was now having his baby. Perhaps I should weave this into the plot of my *one-day* novel, but who would believe such a storyline?

Fortunately, the traffic was light as expected at this time of day, and my half-hour estimate was spot on. Zoe's house was a new build, on three levels and fitted out with every modern convenience. Well, perhaps I hadn't seen the upstairs, but the kitchen was definitely space-age, sleek and elegant. The lounge was pristine, with blond wood floors and fluffy white rugs. They'd look great with baby sick on them. (Excuse my bitching.) The front door was ajar, so I pushed through it, calling out hello. Zoe stood on the turn of the stairs, leaning on the bannister, holding her bump as if trying her very best to stop nature from taking its course. An overnight bag was at her feet.

Although her face was pale and tear-streaked, she still looked amazing, with a certain fragility enhancing her beauty. As I climbed the few stairs towards her, it was impossible not to notice her ankles. They were slim, fine-boned like the rest of her. I might have known. My legs resembled an elephant's when I was pregnant. They were so badly swollen I resorted to flopping around in Paul's slippers for the last three weeks. Zoe was simply one of those women who always looked elegant, even at eight and a half months pregnant. But clearly, although a vision of loveliness on the outside, she was a helpless wreck of a little girl on the inside.

I hate to admit it, but my motherly instinct took over. I smiled at my husband's wife and reassured her all would be well. Then, with me holding her arm with one hand and clutching her bag in the other, we made it to the car. I ran back to lock the door, then climbed into the driving seat and turned on the engine, aware of Zoe stealing quick little glances at me as I drove. It occurred to me then how this situation must be as strange to her as it was to me.

'Hang in there, Zoe, the traffic's good so we'll be at the hospital in just a few minutes.'

'Thank you,' she whispered. 'I'm so sorry to call you out so early but I didn't know who else to turn to.'

'Did you ring Paul to tell him the baby's on the way?' I asked.

'Yes, but his phone was on messaging service and I couldn't remember the name of the hotel he's staying in.'

'Where is the conference?' I hadn't asked Paul exactly where he was going.

'Somewhere in Norfolk. He said the drive up there was horrendous; the roads aren't very good apparently.' Suddenly Zoe doubled up in pain and let out a long moan.

'How often are they coming?'

'Every fifteen or twenty minutes. It hurts so much.'

I swallowed the witty remark which was on my tongue and made sympathetic noises instead.

'It looks like this baby's in a hurry. Don't you have another couple of weeks left?'

'Yes, by my reckoning, but the midwife thought I was further on or that the baby's very large.' We were both silent then until we turned into the hospital car park.

'Can you walk if we leave the car here, or shall I drop you at the entrance?'

'Please stay with me. I think I can manage to walk.' Zoe was seriously scared; she must be to turn to her husband's ex, whom she'd never particularly liked.

'It'll be fine, and I'll stay as long as you need me to.'

Zoe let out a sigh. Whether it was with relief that I'd agreed to stay or the contraction being over, it was impossible to tell. After pulling the car into a vacant spot, and there were plenty so early in the morning, we got out and made our way towards the entrance.

The lady yawning on the reception desk looked at us and pointed toward the lifts.

'Straight up to floor six, maternity,' she said, and we dutifully obeyed.

Zoe was leaning heavily on me by then and I would be as glad to sit down as she was. As we opened the swing doors to the darkened corridor, new-baby noises could be heard at the far end of the ward. A shivering cry, akin to a cat, made me smile. I loved the tiny baby stage – everything is so uncomplicated and exciting. A smiling nurse led us to a side room and asked Zoe to undress before telling us she'd be back in a minute. I turned away and began to fuss over the bag I'd carried in.

'Do you want a nightdress from in here?' I asked. Zoe was down to her bra and knickers then, and as she nodded, I pulled out an unsuitable, chiffon-layered, short nightdress. It was going to be hot and uncomfortable during labour; cotton would have been much better. I was surprised she hadn't been advised about it at antenatal classes. The first spots of breast milk and baby sick would soon have her sending Paul shopping for something more appropriate. For someone so close to her time, Zoe seemed quite unprepared.

'Now what should I do?' she asked as if I was the oracle.

'Hop up on the bed. They'll probably want to examine you.' It was eleven years since the twins were born; things would have changed considerably. Zoe cast a puzzled look at the stirrups at the end of the bed but said nothing. What delights awaited the poor girl! The nurse came back in just as another contraction made Zoe groan.

'How regular?' the nurse asked.

'Fifteen minutes or so, I'm not sure.'

'Well, let's take a few details, and then we'll have a look, shall we?'

I always love the way people phrase such statements, as if 'we' really have a choice.

'Shall I wait outside?' My question was directed at Zoe, whose doe eyes suddenly widened with fear.

'The birthing partner, are you?' asked the nurse.

'No, just a... a friend.' We could hardly go into complicated details, could we? And at least she didn't take me for Zoe's mother.

'You can stay if you like,' she offered.

'Please!' Zoe pleaded. So I took the seat by the window at the top of the bed, not wishing to be at the business end of things. Answers to the nurse's questions were recorded in a file, and then it was time for the examination. I busied myself searching in my bag for nothing in particular, catching only a brief glimpse of Zoe's bewildered expression as her legs were raised into the stirrups.

'Yes, baby's head is well down, just as it should be, and dilation's about eight centimetres.' The nurse spoke kindly and explained what would happen next.

'I'm just going to have a little feel of your abdomen to make sure everything's okay there, and then I'll listen to baby's heartbeat and check your pulse and blood pressure if it's all right with you?' Zoe nodded, looking more and more like a frightened rabbit.

'I think you'll be heading for the delivery room pretty soon.' The nurse chatted as she worked, while I wondered why Zoe seemed to know nothing about what was happening. *Still, she's young*, I thought, *but not as young as I was when Lucy came along.*

The nurse left after the routine examinations and I checked my watch. It was almost seven. A sudden thought crossed my mind, what if this took all day? What about my date with Steve? It was such a selfish thought – Zoe's need was far more important than a meal out, even if it was a first date.

'Can I get you anything?' I hadn't a clue what; perhaps a coffee, then I could escape to the vending machine we'd passed on the way in.

'No, nothing, thanks, but could you try to phone Paul again for me? I forgot to bring my phone.'

I took out my phone and scrolled through the contacts to

find Paul's number, wondering if he'd even be out of bed. Surprisingly he answered after three rings.

'Laura, whatever it is, can it wait? Zoe's started with the baby, and I'm driving back.'

'I know, I'm at the hospital with her.'

'What? You, but why?' His shock made me smile, I could picture the astonished look on his face.

'It could be because you are away, at the same time as your parents? I'll pass the phone to Zoe.' Trying to be tactful, I went outside to give them privacy to talk. It was warm in the hospital and stuffy. I felt relieved it wasn't me who was giving birth, yet strangely I envied Zoe. If Paul and I had stayed together, would we have had more children? It was academic and a waste of time and energy even thinking about it. I took a walk to the end of the corridor and back, then knocked on the door and went back in to resume my undefined role with Zoe.

'So, he's on his way?'

'Yes, he was up early and found my message. The conference was due to finish later today, so he won't miss much.'

'Any idea of when he'll arrive?' The answer was delayed as another contraction came. The nurse returned and told us the delivery room would be ready shortly and she immediately turned to leave. When the contraction eased, Zoe asked me how much longer it would be, hoping the baby would be here soon.

'It can take longer than a few hours, Zoe, especially for a first baby. With a bit of luck, Paul will be here in time for the birth.' I poured water from the jug the nurse had left. Zoe was warm and uncomfortable, but I couldn't think of much to say which would be helpful. Talking about my own childbirth experiences was hardly appropriate, so I smiled and sat quietly until the next contraction. It was a bad one, or a good one depending on your point of view. I moved to Zoe's side, and she gripped my hand, her beautifully manicured nails digging into my palms, generously sharing the pain.

After it eased, Zoe confided, 'I skipped most of the antenatal classes. I've been depressed, and being pregnant isn't what I thought it would be. I'm an only child and haven't had much to do with children, but I so want Paul's baby.'

I hoped she wasn't going to stray into topics about which I'd rather not know. Time to change the subject, perhaps?

'After the baby is born you'll forget all about this. It's worth all the pain just to hold your child close and marvel at such an amazing miracle. I take it you don't know what sex it is?'

'No, we wanted it to be a surprise...' We were interrupted by the midwife and a porter who came to move Zoe to the delivery room. A look of panic crossed her face again, and I stayed close by the bed as the porter moved it, assuring her I would still be there. Strangely I was warming to Zoe, we'd never exchanged more than a single sentence to each other before, but I was seeing her in another light. We all have different facets to our personalities, and I'd never before attempted to view her from any other angle except one of home-wrecker.

Chapter Thirty-Four

I would not have recognised the room Zoe was trundled into as a delivery room, so different was it from my pregnancies. An oscillating fan cooled the air, and music played from a small unit in the far corner. The blinds were discreetly drawn, unnecessary perhaps as we were on the sixth floor, but they presented a more homely feel than the clinical room I remembered giving birth in. A sofa was against one side wall with a couple of beanbags sagging beside it. There was even a water cooler with a stack of those little conical paper cups to help ourselves, presumably.

The midwife repeated the examination performed earlier by the nurse and pronounced baby to be coming along nicely. She put me in mind of a television chef, checking the sponge cake in the oven.

'We'll leave you for now, but there's the buzzer if you need anything. You seem to have started a rush, Mrs Green – four more mothers-to-be have come in since you.' She smiled reassuringly and left the room. I filled two cups with ice-cold water and took one over to Zoe.

'You don't have to stay on the bed, you know. I think these

days you can choose whatever position is most comfortable to give birth, hence the beanbags.'

Zoe swung her legs off the bed. I had noticed a clean hospital gown folded on a trolley and picked it up.

'Why don't you change into this? Cotton will be much cooler than what you're wearing and more practical too.'

'Do you think I should?' She looked like a frightened little girl.

I nodded and turned away while she changed. Another contraction made her squeal, they were coming quickly, and it probably wouldn't be too much longer. Zoe bent forward over the bed until the pain eased.

'It's more comfortable leaning forward; it doesn't seem to hurt my back as much.'

'Good, well, if you want to deliver baby that way, then say so. It's your baby and your labour, and the midwife will want you to be as comfortable as possible.' I remembered my first pregnancy. Being so timid, I did exactly as I was told, even as to when Lucy could be lifted from her crib. By the time the boys came along, I'd decided to take charge. They were my babies and I would do what I thought was best. Zoe, at twenty-seven, was older than I'd been with Lucy, but she seemed so young. Perhaps it was just me getting old. As if to confirm my thoughts, a doctor came into the delivery room who looked no older than seventeen! The midwife hurried in to stand beside him as he looked at the notes. She told him about Zoe's blood pressure and dilation. He smiled at his patient, saying it was looking good, then they left us alone again.

'What time is it?' Zoe's look was pleading.

'It's 10.30,' I replied, assuming she was counting the hours until Paul arrived. In a way, I was too. A shower or perhaps a long soak in the bath seemed so appealing. I'd intended to spend time on my appearance in readiness for going out with Steve. But all was going well, so hopefully, the baby should arrive soon, and when Paul came, I would be able to take my leave. It wasn't turning out to be the kind of day I'd anticipated.

Zoe was half lying on the sofa now, looking tired and worried.

'He's not going to make it for the birth, is he?' Her eyes were moist.

'Sorry, but it doesn't look like it.' I sat down beside her. 'Why don't you close your eyes for a few minutes and rest? You should take every opportunity; you'll need all your strength for the birth.'

'Is it very awful?' Her brow was furrowed.

'Well, they don't call it labour for nothing.' I smiled. Zoe returned my smile.

'I've always envied you, Laura...' she began.

'Me? Why on earth would you?' Now, this was a surprise.

'You're such a natural mother, whereas domesticity doesn't come easy to me. You cope so well with three children, and I'm petrified about looking after just one. And you have such a glamorous job too. It must be so exciting working for a magazine. I've always felt I could never match up to you as Paul's wife.' The last sentence was spoken with such sadness – where on earth did she get such ideas?

'Zoe, can you hear what you're saying? You are the one who Paul is with now, not me. And I don't still blame you, it's history now. You're the one he chose, the one who makes him happy, which I obviously couldn't do. As for managing the children, you know the situation with Lucy, so I'm certainly no great mother figure. And the job, well, I don't have one anymore but it wasn't a particularly glamorous job, even though I loved it.' It was hard to believe she'd been envious of my life. Zoe opened her mouth to speak but another pain gripped her, only about five minutes after the last one. I rang the buzzer then took her hand.

'I think baby's ready now, even if Paul isn't.'

The midwife arrived with a different nurse and asked Zoe to get on the bed for another examination, after which she sent the nurse away to get something and told us it was almost time.

'Are you happy to stay there, or would you like to walk about?' the midwife asked.

'I'm okay here, perhaps on my side?' She rolled over to get comfortable, and the delivery began.

I knew how frightened Zoe was, but she did remarkably well and I felt a strange empathy with her. I was almost proud of the way she got on with things when I'd assumed she'd be a wimp.

During the worst contractions, she gripped my hand so hard I thought my fingers would break, but it didn't matter, and I found myself encouraging her and praising her efforts. Having dampened a face-cloth from her bag, I cooled her face with it and offered sips of water to moisten her lips. I rubbed her back in between contractions, trying to make her as comfortable as possible.

Time passed quickly, for me at least, and then, almost suddenly, Zoe's baby was born.

'It's a girl!' the midwife announced, lifting the squirming, mewing infant so the new mother could see her beautiful daughter. After cutting the cord, the baby's face was quickly cleaned, and she was laid on her mother's breast, skin to skin.

Zoe looked at me with tears in her eyes and whispered, 'Thank you.' I could hardly speak. It had been an incredibly emotional experience. Instinctively I leaned over to kiss Zoe's cheek and gently touch her daughter's tiny fingers.

'Well done!' was about all I could manage.

The nurses were content to leave the baby, now swaddled in a blanket, bonding with Zoe while they cleared the trolley away, presumably to reset for the next delivery. It was a busy day. The porter appeared again to whisk mother and baby on to the ward. By now, it was almost midday, and the smell of food made me realise how hungry I was. Zoe too must be starving after all her effort. She still held her daughter. I didn't like to ask if they'd chosen a name yet. It was none of my business. All in all, it had been a swift delivery without complication, which is all any mother can ask.

We were now in a small, six-bed ward with a bathroom at one end. I sank into the easy chair next to the bed, glad to sit down.

'Would you like to hold her?' Zoe asked. Naturally, I wanted to but was uncertain. What would Paul say if I held his new daughter before him?

'Yes, please.' Why worry about Paul? – new babies are irresistible. I took the little bundle, breathing in the distinctive baby smell which turns adults into malleable putty.

'She's so beautiful.' Tears threatened to fall, but then I lifted my head and saw Paul walking through the ward doors, a massive bunch of flowers in his arms and a somewhat ambiguous expression on his face. Zoe's face lit up as she reached out for him, everything was forgotten except the happiness she was experiencing. I felt like a child caught with their hand in the sweetie jar and gently passed the baby back to Zoe.

'Congratulations, Paul, she's beautiful. I'll leave you now. I'm very pleased for you both.' With one last smile at Zoe, I left.

It was a relief to get out into the chill air. Hospitals seem to have their own microclimate, and you could almost forget what season it is once inside its walls. The car park was full by then, outpatients, staff and visitors all scurrying around like ants. I yawned, opened the car door and climbed in to head home.

Chapter Thirty-Five

O nce home, I took two fruit teacakes out of the freezer, defrosted them in the microwave and put them in the toaster. I wanted something fast and comforting to eat, and a toasted teacake fitted the bill nicely. A proper meal would come later, with Steve. I turned the gas fire on in the lounge and put my feet up with a huge mug of tea and my teacakes beside me. So far, the day had been totally unpredictable, and I wondered how the evening would turn out. I closed my eyes; my body clock was out of sync and tiredness was overtaking me. It wouldn't hurt to sleep for a while to catch up. It would be embarrassing if I fell asleep over dinner tonight.

The next thing I knew, it was four o'clock, still plenty of time to Skype Holly and the twins before getting ready for this evening.

'Hey!' Holly's beaming face came into view on my laptop. 'I was expecting to hear from you later, after the date! You're not going dressed like that, are you?'

'Of course not. I thought I'd wear a smart navy business suit.' I grinned.

'Don't you dare!' my friend growled.

'Are the boys about?'

'They're helping Brian in the garage. Shall I get them?'

'No, not yet, I want to tell you about my day first, but I think it will be better for them if they hear it from Paul himself.'

'Sounds intriguing; tell me more.'

'I got an early morning call from Zoe; labour had started, and she wanted me to take her to hospital.'

'No, the bloody cheek of it!' Holly laughed. 'Did you give her the number of a taxi firm?'

'Actually, I went. She was frightened and alone, Paul was still away, and Janet and Bob are on holiday. It's rather sad, don't you think – she only had me to call on for help?'

'So, what happened? Has she had the baby?'

'Yes, a beautiful little girl. But it's only right that Paul should tell the boys when they get back home. Paul missed the birth by an hour, so it was left to me to hold Zoe's hand.'

'You didn't, seriously?' Holly's mouth was open.

'Yes, seriously! It was a bit strained at first, but she was so frightened I couldn't leave her. It was an amazing experience, and now, when I have the time to think about it, I'm glad I was there.'

'So what did Paul say when he arrived?'

'It was a bit embarrassing really. I was holding the baby when he walked through the door! I left pretty soon, though, so Zoe would be able to update him on why his ex was there.'

'Laura, you're great, you really are. I don't know of anyone else who would go to such extremes to help the woman who stole her husband.'

'I wasn't that great, but admittedly as the time went on, Zoe and I got on quite well. She's not so bad, I've just never had the chance to get to know her before.'

'So now you'll be the best of friends?' Holly asked, one eyebrow raised.

'I don't think so, but maybe we'll have a more civilised relationship in the future. Anyway, tell me how the boys are. Are they driving you nuts yet?'

'Not at all, you know I love having them. Even Brian's enjoying having children in the house, and they're so enthusiastic about his plans and the renovations he's doing. We're all having fun! Now I hope this call isn't instead of later. I still want all the details of your date.'

'Is it a date, Holly? Steve just sort of asked me, knowing I'd be at a loose end without the boys, and I'm beginning to wonder if I'm building this up into something it isn't. Perhaps he was just considerate?'

'Rubbish, it's a date, so you need to get yourself ready, dress to wow him and see how the evening goes, okay?'

'Okay. I'm off to the shower now, and then the difficult thing will be deciding what to wear.'

'Make it something to show off your curves. Don't hide behind those sloppy tops you wear,' Holly instructed.

'Those sloppy tops are to hide the flab, not curves! But I'll see if I can find something to meet your approval.' I promised to let Holly know how the evening went, then she called the boys and we chatted for a few minutes before saying goodbye. It was strange in the house without my children, almost as if the colour had been wrung out of every room, and laughter was noticeably absent. I missed them so much but wondered if I would ever have all three of them together with me again. Before getting ready, I sent a quick text to Lucy:

> Missing you, hope to see you soon. I love you,
> Mum xx

It took almost as long to decide what to wear as it took to shower and wash my hair. There were several clothes which I hadn't worn for years, simply because I rarely went anywhere to wear them. Whittling the selection down to three possibilities, I tried them all on, studying each outfit in the mirror, eventually settling for a bias-cut skirt which fell well below the knee and would look good with my boots. I teamed it with a soft cashmere, cream-coloured jumper, an extravagant buy from last winter. For once, my hair behaved itself and fell in soft curls onto my shoulders, rather like Lucy's used to before she began dyeing it. As the time neared seven o'clock, I became increasingly jittery, silly really, as Steve was such easy company and a great listener. He always had something funny to say, and if we'd managed to be in each other's company before without embarrassing silences, why should this evening be any different?

The doorbell rang precisely on time, and Steve greeted me with a gift of flowers – roses – which he gave to me as he leaned down to kiss my cheek. Okay, so it was an actual date! He helped me with my jacket and told me I looked good.

'You don't scrub up too badly yourself,' I replied.

Now he was here, the tension left my body. Steve was the kind of man who made you feel special, and the evening ahead suddenly looked exciting. The restaurant he'd chosen was new to me, and although the food was good, it was Steve himself who made the evening. He asked about my day, and I was suddenly grateful to have something interesting to tell him rather than the mundane stuff my days usually consist of. Steve saw the funny side of being called out to assist Zoe, and very soon, we were both laughing at the absurdity of the situation. It seemed to be an unspoken agreement not to discuss the letters, or Lucy's current situation, for which I was grateful. I didn't want Steve to become simply someone to unburden myself to each time we met, so we kept the conversation light. '*Ask Laura*', however, did crop up in the conversation and Steve confessed to being a closet reader of my page.

'Never!' I laughed. 'So, do you buy the magazine?'

'No, I'm not much of a fan, but my mother is a regular subscriber, and whenever I visit her and Dad, I have a sneaky peek. When we first met, I thought you were familiar, but it was only when you explained your role at the magazine that I connected you to your photograph. Although I have to say you are certainly much prettier in real life!'

Blushing at the compliment, I asked if he'd ever written to me. Men occasionally did; women don't have the monopoly on problems.

'No!' He laughed. 'But I might have done if I'd had a problem with which you could have helped. I particularly enjoy reading your answers; you seem to combine empathy with reality and a liberal dose of common sense. Your readers might not get the answer they want, but you seem to have a knack for knowing what to do in a given situation.'

For a moment, tears stung my eyes.

'Sorry, Laura, have I said something wrong?'

I waved my hand in a gesture of dismissal.

'No, it's just… I clearly don't get it right in my own life, do I?'

'Oh, I don't know. You're out with a handsome man who admires you; which is something, isn't it?' He grinned at me, making me laugh. Steve was great company.

'This is good for me, Laura. Being able to ask you out, I mean. I'd have done so earlier, but it didn't seem appropriate with the case and everything. I'm glad you came, thank you.'

'If this is confession time, then I have to say I liked you from the beginning, and am more than happy to be here. The only thing which worries me a bit is the fact that I'm so much older than you.' There, it was out in the open and hovered over the table between us. Steve looked puzzled and smiled.

'So, how old are you then?' He grinned. 'No, let me guess, fifty, sixty?'

'What a cheek!' I feigned annoyance. 'I'm thirty-eight, but I also have three children and a bagful of problems.'

'And how old do you think I am, Laura Green, mother of three children and a bagful of problems?'

'I don't know, thirty-one, thirty-two maybe?' I hated being asked to guess people's age and nearly always got it wrong.

'Well, thank you, I'll take my youthful looks as a compliment, but I'm actually thirty-five, thirty-six at the end of March.' He was smiling again and took my hand across the table. 'So, you may be good at problem-solving, but you're rubbish at guessing ages. And as for your children, I love kids, and yours are.... interesting to say the least! Laura, I'm not declaring undying love here or asking you to marry me, but I've grown very fond of you in such a short time. I'd like to see you again, to see how it works out. Would that be okay with you?'

'Absolutely!' I said. Yes, it was a proper date, and I was ecstatic. Steve did have feelings for me, and I wanted to get to know him better too!

For the rest of the evening, Steve talked about his family, his mother, who I already knew had excellent taste in her reading choices, his father and younger brother. They were evidently close, which was great, and Steve spent as much time as he could with them. We discussed films; he was more into action films than I was, and music and books we'd read which impacted our lives. We found plenty of shared interests and others that weren't, but there's nothing wrong with a few differences. A Jason Bourne film was showing and we decided to see it together. We both liked the series, and if we went soon before the boys were home, I wouldn't need babysitters.

The evening turned out to be everything I'd hoped for and more. We sat talking for ages in the restaurant until the waiter began hovering, hinting it was time to leave. When we arrived home, it seemed natural to invite Steve in for coffee, and we spent another hour getting to know each other. I didn't want it to end, but eventually, Steve stood to go. He came towards me, took me in his arms and kissed me, slowly and gently, his lips warm and searching, sending shivers running through my body. As we pulled apart, he smiled.

'I'm going to enjoy getting to know you, Laura. Thank you for a lovely evening.'

'Thank you. I've loved every minute.'

'Every minute?' he asked playfully and kissed me again before he left.

Chapter Thirty-Six

The morning following my date with Steve began quietly enough. Without anything to get up for, I lay in bed with my eyes closed, reliving each moment of the previous evening. The strength of my hope surprised me, but while my thoughts lingered on the positive aspects of the evening, a niggling doubt hovered at the back of my mind. Steve had been open and honest, which I certainly appreciated. But was I prepared to allow myself to fall unreservedly in love with him, only to have him decide against continuing our relationship at some point further down the line? It would be understandable. I come as a package, and three children are not to be taken on lightly. I was not in the market for a casual relationship but realised Steve couldn't possibly commit without being sure of his feelings, and I wouldn't expect him to either.

Dear Laura,

I've recently met a man who seems kind, generous and loving. He's talking about us moving in together, but I'm afraid it might go wrong.

I've been married and divorced twice and don't think I could bear to be hurt again. My judgement of both of my husbands was proved wrong, and I'm scared this relationship will go the same way. I really can't decide what to do, yet I enjoy his company and would miss him if he wasn't around. Should I trust him and risk being hurt again?

Gemma

Dear Gemma,

Life is all about taking risks. Each day we make decisions which affect our future in small or greater ways. You could steer clear of men for the rest of your life, which is a choice some women make, but would it make you happy?

You say your new man is kind, generous and loving, so he's surely worth considering as a long-term partner. Do you have any mutual friends who could offer an opinion of his character or someone who has known him for a long time? You say you would miss him if he wasn't around, which perhaps indicates which way you are leaning. No one can guarantee you won't be hurt again. You can, however, ask him to wait a while longer until you are sure, and if he loves you, he will do this. Yes, it is a risk, all relationships are, but it could just as easily turn out well as not, and I wish you happiness with whatever you decide,

Laura

Gemma's letter was typical of many in my postbag. Relationships can be fraught with difficulties but can also bring us some of the happiest times of our lives. But for me, there was no way of knowing how things would progress with Steve, yet I did know I wanted to take the risk. Having been alone for so long, the thought of someone to share my life with was at the same time both exciting and scary. Yes, I would be opening my life to let in love or hurt, we cannot predict the future, and I decided then and there I would take the risk, no matter what the outcome and only hoped Steve would do the same.

After a leisurely shower (when I even found myself singing), I dressed and went in search of breakfast. The bread was stale, and the milk off – I would need to shop before the boys came home. Fruit and yoghurt sufficed, and I congratulated myself for choosing the healthy option, even though there'd been no choice at all. As I was finishing, I heard the key in the door and was surprised to see Lucy coming in.

'Hello!' I almost ran to meet her, but she moved back, an invisible aura around her warning me to keep my distance.

'I need some more clothes.' My heart sank; momentarily, I'd hoped Lucy had come home to stay.

'Of course, do you want any help?' I forced my face into a smile which nowhere near matched my feelings.

'No thanks.' Lucy ran upstairs, and I listened as drawers opened and closed as she moved about her room, comforting noises which had been missing of late. Hopefully, I put the kettle on, praying she could be persuaded to stay for a coffee with me. Ten minutes later, when she came downstairs, she carried two sports bags, both crammed full of clothes.

'Would you like a coffee, Lucy, then perhaps I can give you a lift? They look heavy.'

My daughter hesitated.

'Okay,' she said. Only one word, but it gave me such hope and felt like progress. We sat at the kitchen table.

'How's the decorating going?' I asked.

'We've finished the lounge.'

'Oh, good. Are you pleased with it?'

'Yeah, suppose so.' She turned her attention to the coffee at the same time as the doorbell rang. I sighed angrily; why now, just when I had Lucy to myself with an opportunity to talk? The guilty party at the door was Paul. He entered with a bunch of lilies and an apologetic expression on his face.

Puzzled, I took the flowers and told him Lucy was in the kitchen. He headed there before I had chance to give him instructions not to upset her as I was making progress.

'Hello, Lucy, I was going to phone you today.' Paul took in her blank expression but ploughed ahead anyway. 'You have a new baby sister!' He waited for a reaction which was slow in coming.

'Congratulations.' Her tone was monotonous, giving nothing away.

'Yes, thanks... we're calling her Imogen, and we'd love you to come and see her. Brad too if he likes?'

'Yeah? We'll let you know. I'd better be off now; I can catch the bus.' Lucy stood and headed for the door.

'Hey, I can still give you a lift; your dad won't be staying long.' Oh, how needy that sounded!

'It's okay – I'll get the bus.' Our daughter was gone. Instinctively I wanted to blame Paul, he'd called at an inopportune moment, but he couldn't have known. I then began to wonder why he'd called and why the flowers.

'We wanted to say thank you, Zoe says she wouldn't have got through it all without you, and I'm grateful for your help.' He actually managed to maintain eye contact throughout his little speech.

'It's fine; anyone would have done the same but thanks for the flowers. When are you going to tell the boys?'

'Well, now Lucy knows it'll have to be soon. She didn't seem too happy about it, did she?' He looked wistfully at the door.

'It'll take time, she's coping with a lot of change at the moment, but she'll work her way through it. I was just about to Skype the boys at Holly's. Do you want to tell them now?'

'Yes, that's probably a good idea. When are they coming home?'

'Friday, if Holly can drag them away. They're having a

great time.' I logged onto my laptop and pressed the Skype app. In less than a minute, my friend appeared on the screen.

'About time too, Laura. I've been waiting to hear all about last night!' Holly blurted out. I quickly swivelled the screen so she could see Paul was with me.

'Hey, I'm here now!' I almost shouted to drown her out. 'Are the boys up and about?'

Holly scurried away in search of our sons, and fortunately, Paul didn't seem to cotton on to what she'd said, or if he did, he wasn't saying.

'Hi, Mum, hi, Dad!' Sam and Jake chorused. Paul asked if they were having fun, and Sam waved his spoon at us. They were eating chocolate-coated cereal, something they were only allowed very occasionally. My sons would never want to come home if Holly kept spoiling them.

'I wanted to tell you my news.' Paul was grinning. 'Zoe had the baby yesterday, a little girl! We're calling her Imogen.' The boys seemed unsure as to what was expected of them.

'Great news, Dad,' said Jake.

'Yeah, great,' Sam echoed, his mouth full of cereal. Paul said they must meet their new baby sister when they came home; he sounded almost as embarrassed as they were. After a few minutes of strained conversation, we said goodbye, and I promised Holly I would Skype again later. Paul thanked me again and asked if I'd like to visit them with the twins when they came home. It wasn't easy for him to ask – presumably, this was his wife's idea.

'Yes, I'd like to, but only when Zoe feels up to it, visitors can be tiring.'

'Zoe told me you're not working for the magazine anymore, is she right?' Paul looked concerned.

'Yes, I'm afraid so, they've axed the '*Ask Laura*' page completely. Those letters didn't help, but they've decided problem pages are old-fashioned.' Talking about it brought back the hollow feeling of despair. I hadn't realised just how much my page meant to me. In a way, it was another bereavement; I'd lost something precious to me, my identity perhaps? Life was certainly a rollercoaster at the moment.

'I'm sorry, Laura, you were really good at your job. Have you anything else in mind?'

'Well, they said they'll still commission regular features, but I'll have to go back to pitching to other sources. We'll be okay; worse things happen, but thanks for asking.'

Paul nodded, then left soon afterwards to go home to his wife and new baby daughter, leaving me alone again with my mug of cold coffee.

Chapter Thirty-Seven

Perhaps I didn't make the most of my days alone. True, the house was somewhat cleaner and tidier, but there was no earth-shattering writing, either features or my novel, to show for my time alone. It was difficult to concentrate, with my mind frequently wandering to good things and bad. When the boys finally came back, I was so glad to see them I could have cried but didn't. It would have embarrassed us all. They did both hug me for longer than the token squeeze I usually have to make do with, so presumably, they'd missed me too.

Holly stayed overnight, ostensibly to break the journey, but in reality, to pressurise me into spilling all the beans about my budding relationship with Steve. I was happy to oblige; it wasn't a subject I could discuss with my children. Holly had always been my confidante and quickly fell back into the role. She already knew about our first date but wanted to hear it all again, so she could squeal and giggle in all the right places. Since our meal together, Steve had taken me to the cinema and we'd spoken every day on the telephone. It didn't take long to tell her everything. With Steve's shifts, our dates would be pretty irregular, but hey, routine's overrated anyway.

Steve was coming for Sunday lunch, so I needed to prepare the boys. We'd discussed telling them about 'us' and decided to play it low key initially; the only problem Steve brought up was that he wouldn't be able to kiss me when he wanted, and he wanted to a lot! For a woman who had just lost her job and her mother and whose daughter didn't want to know her, I was feeling remarkably upbeat.

As Holly and I talked late into the night, we finished off a bottle of wine between us and a large box of chocolates. We laughed at things which weren't funny, and all those problems which at times threatened to overwhelm me were pushed to the back of my mind, assisted no doubt by the wine.

Inevitably Holly had to return home. It was Saturday morning, and we enjoyed a lazy breakfast together after I'd dropped the boys off at football practice.

'So when's the next date?' Holly asked.

'Steve's coming for lunch tomorrow, which isn't a date as such, but we want the boys to get used to the idea of him being around. So we'll probably only tell them we're friends and see how things go from there. I'm hoping there won't be any embarrassing questions.'

'They'll probably take it all in their stride; it'll be me asking the embarrassing questions!' She would too, so maybe it was a good thing she'd be going.

When Holly left, I felt a little deflated but turned my thoughts to Sunday lunch. Picking up some groceries before collecting the boys was on my to-do list, so I set off early. It was good to have something positive to concentrate on instead of those recent, more negative events. I shopped quickly and then drove to the playing field to pick up Sam and Jake. They were full of excitement after a good practice game and seeing some of their friends whom they'd missed during half-term week. When their chatter died down, I told them Steve was coming for lunch the following day as casually as I could.

'Is he coming to take the security camera away? Why does he need to stay for lunch?' Sam, always the talker, asked. Jake remained silent, more thoughtful and I guessed he would be the one to arrive at the proper conclusion first.

'I thought it would be nice to invite him for a meal, to say thank you for all the help he's given us.' Sam bought the story; I wasn't so sure about Jake. 'You do like him, don't you?' I asked to which they replied without having to think, a resounding yes. It would dawn on them in time that it was a little more than friendship, but it was better for us all to take things slowly. Sam ran to open the door when we arrived home while Jake helped me carry the shopping.

'You like Steve, don't you, Mum?' he asked perceptively. I smiled.

'Yes, I do. Is it okay with you?'

'Absolutely!' Jake grinned, and nothing more was said.

After lunch, Janet and Bob called round. Having returned from holiday to the news of their new baby granddaughter, they were calling in to see us on the way to visit her. As always, when they'd been away, they arrived with gifts for the boys, and as they were busy regaling a humorous story about their holiday, my phone rang. Glancing at the screen before answering, I saw to my surprise that the caller was Lucy. Trying not to panic, I hoped it was good news but was totally thrown on hearing Brad's voice on the line.

'Is that Mrs Green?' he drawled.

'Yes... is everything all right, Brad?'

'Don't know really, Lucy's not so good – I wondered if you'd come and see her.'

'What's wrong with her? Can you put her on the line?'

'No, she's in bed. I thought it might be flu or something. She's quite hot.'

'I'm on my way. Tell her I'm coming!'

'Okay,' he said nonchalantly and disconnected the phone.

I'd moved into the kitchen to take the call, and now returned to the others.

'Janet, I'm so sorry, but I have to go out. Do you think you could stay a little while longer with the boys?'

'What is it?' Bob asked. 'Is something wrong?'

'It was Brad, Lucy's boyfriend. He says she's not well and he wants me to go round.' I tried to hide my anxiety. It could be something as simple as flu, but I was pretty sure Brad wouldn't ring me unless it was serious.

'Of course you should go. We can take the boys with us to meet their new baby sister.' Janet spoke with enthusiasm, although the boys' expressions certainly didn't match it. I thanked her then ushered us all outside. The boys ran to their grandparents' car; it was beginning to rain and the temperature had dropped almost to zero. I hoped we weren't in for another bout of snow. Janet came to my car window.

'Let us know what's happening with Lucy, but don't worry about the boys. They can always come to ours if need be.'

'Thank you, Janet. I'll let you know as soon as I can.'

The rain was getting heavier and the wipers struggled to clear the windscreen as huge drops drummed onto it. The traffic was terrible too. It was two o'clock on Saturday afternoon with many of the cars heading for football grounds, scarves blowing out of windows, announcing to the world which team they supported. I shivered as I stepped from the car, partly with cold and partly at the sight of the ugly concrete building where my daughter had chosen to live. Then, without even checking to see if the lift was working, I hurried to the stairs, unwilling to risk the lift breaking down with me inside it, alone.

Brad's flat looked every bit as dreary and uninviting as the last time we'd been, except today the door was slightly ajar. Pushing it open, I expected to find Brad waiting for me, but he wasn't, and there was no answer as I called Lucy's name. It was altogether worrying, and I moved quickly towards the bedroom, fearful of what might greet me. Lucy was in bed, her eyes closed and her body restless. I was beside her in seconds and could feel the heat radiating from her body. My daughter was hot to touch, bathed in sweat and thrashing around wildly. I called Brad's name again while fishing in my bag for my phone, but there was no reply. He appeared to have left her alone when she needed him the most. I dialled for an ambulance and was connected to a calm, efficient operator whose clear, gentle voice helped me to be practical and think logically. After giving my daughter's symptoms and the flat's address, she asked me a few questions, some of which I couldn't answer. To my shame, I didn't know how long Lucy had been ill. Assuring me an ambulance was on its way, she then asked me to stay on the line and monitor Lucy's condition, and she would advise if necessary. But my daughter began convulsing, and I dropped the phone.

All I could think to do was hold tightly onto Lucy to stop her from hurting herself until the convulsion passed. Her body was rigid, but her arms twitched and flailed about – it was nothing short of terrifying! When her body eventually relaxed and the fit was over, I ran to the kitchen to fetch cold water and a cloth to try and get her temperature down. Back at Lucy's side, I pulled the covers off the bed and was shocked to see what looked like a huge, weeping graze on her left leg, stretching from just below her hip to her knee. The skin was blistered and badly discoloured, with pus oozing from the open wound. It looked incredibly painful and was obviously the cause of her symptoms, as even I could tell it was infected. I rolled her onto her right side, into the recovery position, avoiding touching the open sore. Wiping Lucy's face with the cold cloth and talking to her all the time, I told her she would be fine and I'd stay to look after her. It was pretty clear she wasn't aware of my presence; Lucy could neither hear me nor respond.

The bed was soaked with sweat and her hair stuck to her scalp and face. I smoothed it back with the cool cloth, feeling so helpless and so terribly afraid. Had Brad done this to my daughter, and how? All kinds of thoughts ran through my mind, and I was so lost in my agony I didn't hear the paramedic enter the flat. He suddenly appeared in the bedroom doorway, dropped his bag to the floor and began to examine Lucy.

'Is she your daughter?' he asked.

'Yes. Will she be all right?'

'We'll know more when we get her to hospital. Can you tell me how long she's been like this?' Again, guilt and shame washed over me as I couldn't answer the question and began to explain how Lucy lived there with her boyfriend, who rang me but had since disappeared.

The sound of an ambulance rose from the street below, this paramedic was the first responder, and his colleagues had arrived to help. Soon Lucy's face was covered with an oxygen mask, and she was being transferred to a stretcher. The paramedic set up a drip, speaking continually to Lucy, positive and upbeat and even making little jokes, as if she was conscious. It almost broke my heart as she still appeared not to be. Finally, one of the crew, a small pretty lady with long hair scraped back into an efficient ponytail, ushered me out of the bedroom.

'Your daughter, is it, love?' she asked. I nodded, unable to find my voice among the sobs which were threatening to choke me.

'How long's she been like this?'

'I don't know.' My shame was overwhelming; Lucy was so seriously ill, and I'd been entirely unaware of it. As I tried to explain, my words sounded jumbled, even to me.

'I should phone her father...' Paul should be here. The paramedic nodded and left me to make the call. While I was trying to explain to my ex what had happened, the ambulance crew carried Lucy down the four flights of stairs and out into the cold afternoon air. Paul said very little. He was as stunned as I was but told me he'd meet me at the hospital. I followed behind Lucy, wanting to hold her hand, to reassure us both that all would be well. After watching them load her inside the ambulance, I was allowed to sit beside her. The woman, who told me her name was Julie, was in the back with us as we set off, sirens whooping and lights flashing. The ride was anything but comfortable, the ambulance seemed to find every pothole in the road, and we were tossed about inside as we rattled along. Even this didn't rouse my little girl into consciousness.

'When did she get the tattoo?' Julie asked.

'Tattoo?' I was puzzled.

'Yes, on her leg? It's badly infected and should have been treated earlier before the infection had the chance to spread. Tattoos often become infected, but if it's caught soon enough, it remains localised. The infection's in Lucy's bloodstream now, hence the fever, and she's very dehydrated.'

'I saw her leg but didn't realise it was a tattoo!' It sounded so stupid, even to me. Julie just smiled and patted my arm.

'She moved in with her boyfriend... we didn't want her to, but I can't believe she got a tattoo!' I felt sick at the thought of it and had a fair idea of what Paul would say.

The A&E at the hospital was busy, but the triage nurse prioritised Lucy, who was wheeled straight into a cubicle where a doctor was with us in minutes. Paul arrived shortly afterwards. The anger I expected was strangely absent. Instead, he appeared shocked and afraid, exactly how I felt. His anger would be directed at Brad – I only hoped he didn't decide to act on it.

After an initial examination, the doctor issued instructions to the nurse then asked to speak to us outside the cubicle.

'Lucy should be okay.' They were the best words I have ever heard! 'The tattoo on her leg is infected and should have been treated immediately.' He spoke kindly, not in the judgemental way I'd expected and thought I deserved, but then I was feeling guilty enough without any outside condemnation of my role as a mother.

'She's on a drip to rehydrate her body and we're giving her intravenous antibiotics. We'll keep her in for a couple of nights until she's over the worst.'

'What about the convulsion? What caused that?' It had really shaken me.

'It was a febrile convulsion, not uncommon with high temperatures, but it shouldn't have any lasting effect. Unfortunately, young people don't always think of the risks when considering tattoos and there can be some severe side effects. We'll test Lucy for hepatitis and HIV before she leaves our care, and she'll need to be tested again after three months. It can take that long for HIV to show up in the blood.' The doctor's words struck me like a physical blow and Paul, too, was visibly shaken. The very thought of HIV sounded like a death sentence! I was terrified but couldn't verbalise the questions which ran rampant through my mind. Paul, however, asked for more detail.

'Isn't HIV fatal?'

'Well, as yet there isn't a cure but these days it's treatable. So please don't expect the worst. With a little luck and the right care, Lucy should make a full recovery. Her leg, however, will probably be badly scarred, the blistering is quite severe, but we can look into solutions when she's better, plastic surgery perhaps?' He smiled as we thanked him and then hurried off to his next patient.

Chapter Thirty-Eight

When the doctor left, Paul and I went back into the cubicle where a nurse was attending Lucy's wound.

'We're taking her to the ward after I've dressed this leg. There's a waiting room down the corridor with a coffee machine, perhaps you'd like to wait in there and I'll come and get you when we're ready to move her.' It wasn't a question, so we left the nurse to get on with her job and headed for the waiting room.

'A bloody tattoo?' Paul said. 'When did she get a tattoo?'

'I know no more than you do, but let's not argue about it now. Getting Lucy well again is the important thing.'

Before helping ourselves to coffee, we needed to make some phone calls. Paul rang Zoe, who told him Janet and Bob had taken the boys home with them. I rang their home number and Bob answered.

'How is she?' He sounded anxious.

'It looks like she'll be okay. Apparently, she'd had a tattoo which became infected. Because she didn't seek help, the infection poisoned her blood, and she was well out of it by the time I arrived. She's on antibiotics now, and they're going to keep her in for a couple of days, but it seems she's over the worst.'

'Thank goodness!' Bob sighed. 'Now don't you worry about the twins, they can stay here tonight and as it's Sunday tomorrow, they don't have school to worry about.'

'Thanks, Bob, you're both brilliant.' I finished my call soon after Paul finished his then we helped ourselves to coffee from the machine.

Once we were seated, Paul asked, 'What did Brad have to say about this?' His voice was stern, with anger seething below the surface.

'Brad was the one who rang me, but when I got to the flat, he'd gone.'

'He left Lucy alone in that state?' The anger was barely disguised now. All I could do was nod. I felt every bit as angry towards Brad as he did.

'I've got a good mind to go round there and find him!'

'Please don't. It won't do any good, and we should both be here for Lucy when she comes round.' Paul losing his temper wouldn't help anyone; we could decide what to do about Brad later, but Lucy was our priority for the time being. My ex nodded and began pacing the tiny room like a caged animal.

Before we'd finished our coffee, the nurse popped her head around the door.

'They've just taken Lucy up to the ward. You can go and see her now if you like?'

We didn't need to be asked twice and went back out into the corridor, which was even more crowded than it had been when we arrived and made our way to the lifts. As we entered the ward, Lucy was being transferred from the trolley to a bed in a side room. She was awake but stared ahead blankly, bewildered and afraid. She looked up when we entered then turned her eyes away. We could see the tears beginning to well in her eyes, and the sight of my daughter, so pale and vulnerable, tore at my heart. I wanted to gather her into my arms, to hold her forever, to protect her and make up for all the pain she had, pain which somehow, I felt I'd caused, yet didn't fully understand how.

There were no words of rebuke from Paul or me. Instead, we both struggled to find the right thing to say, not wanting to upset Lucy but needing to know what had transpired between her and Brad and why he'd left her alone when she most needed him. Yet it wasn't the right time for such a discussion, so we sat, one at each side of the bed, holding our daughter's hands and watching as she drifted in and out of sleep.

The clatter of trolleys outside the room announced the hospital mealtime. An orderly came in and gave Lucy a choice of two meals, apologising and saying she'd have more options the following day.

'I'm not hungry,' Lucy whispered.

'Perhaps you could leave the sandwich; she might have it later?' I said to the orderly, who smiled and left a packed sandwich and an apple on the table. Paul was getting restless.

'Look, I have to go now,' he said. 'Will you ring me later, Laura?'

'Yes, I'll stay a little while longer. Your parents are keeping the boys overnight.'

Paul leaned down to kiss Lucy's cheek. She didn't turn away. As she'd said very little since coming round, it was difficult to read what was going on in her mind. Paul left, and I hoped Lucy would open up a little and tell me what was going on with her and Brad. But perhaps it was too soon – she was exhausted and kept closing her eyes. I so wished I could erase the troubled look from her face and make her life as carefree and happy as it should be, as it used to be.

After an hour or so when she was fully awake, I persuaded Lucy to eat the sandwich, which she did half-heartedly. Making small talk seemed inappropriate, but I was aware any meaningful conversations would be better later; it was too soon for heart-searching questions now. Lucy's temperature had gone down considerably but she still looked very pale and drawn and the blistering on her leg must be painful. I stayed until about 9pm and then left her to get some sleep.

Sam and Jake would probably be asleep at Janet and Bob's by then, but I drove to their house anyway. Paul had telephoned to update them, and he'd spoken to the boys as well to explain what was happening. I was greeted with warm and welcome hugs, and Janet boiled the kettle within a minute of my stepping through the front door. She also offered food; a toasted cheese sandwich followed by a generous slice of her chocolate cake. I accepted readily – it wasn't the time to worry about extra calories – I was starving by then. Finally, after an hour with them, it was time to leave. I intended to get back to the hospital first thing in the morning, so I needed to get some sleep myself. I thanked them both again; they offered to keep the boys on Sunday, which was a real help, it wasn't going to be the Sunday I'd planned, and I'd have to phone Steve to cancel lunch.

It was late, but Steve had rung earlier and left a couple of messages, so I knew he'd be worried if I didn't return the calls.

'Hi, Steve, I haven't woken you have I?' He did sound sleepy.

'No, I was dozing in front of the telly, thinking of you, of course! Is everything okay? Did you get my messages?' I suddenly felt terrible for not ringing him sooner and began to explain.

'Lucy's in hospital, so I've been there most of the day. And Sunday lunch will have to be cancelled too, I need to be with her as much possible.' So I began the long explanation, beginning with the phone call from Brad and the awful events following.

'Shall I come over?' Steve offered when I'd finished my story.

'That would be lovely, but I need some sleep. I'll have to be up early again tomorrow, and you'd be a terrible distraction!'

'Well, I've never been called a distraction before!' Steve laughed. He did, however, understand and wished me goodnight after I promised to keep him in the loop tomorrow. After a hot shower, I climbed into bed, not expecting to sleep, but I did until the alarm woke me at 8am on Sunday.

Chapter Thirty-Nine

The advantage of Lucy being in a side ward was that the nurses were flexible with visiting hours, and no one challenged me when I arrived at the hospital at 9.30am. Lucy was sitting up in bed with the television switched on, yet the sound muted.

'Hi!' I said as cheerfully as possible. My daughter smiled, not a massive grin but more than I'd seen for weeks.

'Have you had any breakfast?' Hospital conversations are always the same; the menu, the staff, the ward, the weather outside; I hoped we could manage better.

'Yes, cereal and toast.' She switched the television off.

'So, how are you feeling? You certainly look much better today.'

'I have a headache, which the nurse said is due to dehydration, so I have to drink as much as possible.'

'Did you get much sleep last night?'

'On and off, it's quite a noisy ward, and each time I turned over my leg was painful.' One of those racks they put under the covers to keep the sheets from touching your legs was beside the bed. It was lucky she'd managed any sleep at all.

Opening the bag I'd brought in with me, I took out some toiletries, a couple of pairs of pyjamas, some clean underclothes and a towel.

'Thanks, Mum. I meant to ask for a few bits last night.'

'Well, I don't think any of us were thinking straight yesterday, but it's good to see you so much better now.'

'The nurses said Dad rang this morning to ask how I was. He'll be in this afternoon.' Lucy seemed pleased at the thought.

'Have you heard anything from Brad?' I asked. He wouldn't have had a chance to visit but he might have rung.

'No, nothing.' Lucy's head dropped almost onto her chest, and tears began to fall.

'Hey, why the tears, love?'

'Oh Mum, it's not working out... with Brad and me. I thought it would be different, but all he wants to do is play computer games. And he expects me to make all the meals and buy the food.' I passed her a tissue – she blew her nose noisily.

'I'm sorry, Lucy, but it's as well to find out sooner rather than later.' There wasn't much else to be said, and I certainly wasn't going to go down the route of 'I told you so'.

'Can I come home?' Lucy asked in such a quiet little voice. I flung my arms around her.

'Of course you can. There's nothing in the world I would like more! I've missed you so much, and so have Sam and Jake.' Lucy looked a little sceptical but said nothing.

'Lucy, I am so proud of you. Admitting you made a mistake is such a hard thing to do. But we can make a fresh start – I love you so much, you know!' Okay, perhaps it was a little over the top but it was how I felt. This was the best thing to happen in what seemed like ages.

'Do you think I'll be able to go back to school?' This, too, was totally unexpected, although it shouldn't have been, the hating school thing was probably all tied into Brad. He had much to answer for.

'I don't see why not. I'll get in touch with Mr Bennett tomorrow and see what he thinks, but I'm sure he'll be delighted.' We were interrupted by the nurse coming in to take Lucy's blood pressure and temperature, and then she asked if she could check her leg. Lucy seemed a little embarrassed with me there, so I offered to go out.

'No... I'd like you to see it.' She was so brave as the nurse removed the overnight dressing. To me, the leg looked worse than the day before, but perhaps this was because I was paying more attention to it now. The whole area was dark red, turning pink at the edges; the blisters were raised and looked extremely painful. Yet it didn't appear as wet as yesterday, a sign the infection was clearing, perhaps? I've never been squeamish, but looking at the raw flesh on my daughter's leg made me feel rather sick. The nurse laid a clean piece of gauze lightly onto the wound and asked Lucy to keep the covers off for a while.

'Being exposed to the air sometimes will help the healing process,' she explained.

When we were alone again, Lucy brought up the subject of the tattoo. I wasn't going to raise it.

'It was Brad's idea to get a tattoo. He's got loads and thinks they're cool. It was supposed to be a garland of roses, but it looked swollen right from the beginning and was very sore. Brad told me not to be a wimp, he'd had them and never complained, but it only seemed to get worse, not better. After a few days, I began to feel hot and sick as well, and then I can't remember anything else.'

I filled in the blanks for her.

'Brad rang me yesterday to say you weren't well, but he didn't mention the tattoo. He suggested I go to the flat, which worried me, knowing he wouldn't want me there if everything was okay. When I arrived, there was no sign of him, but the door was open, so I went in and found you in bed. You were quite delirious and even had a convulsion, which the doctor told me was due to such a high temperature. I called an ambulance and came with you to the hospital. Once the antibiotics got into your system, you began to improve quite quickly, although you probably won't remember much about yesterday at all.'

'I only remember waking up in here and finding you and Dad were with me. I felt so sick and hot, but they gave me some painkillers to help me sleep. When I woke up this morning I thought it had all been a bad dream, but it wasn't, was it?'

'No, but it's over now and we'll soon have you home. Life can then get back to normal. Boring, safe, normal!'

Lucy laughed – it sounded fantastic.

'I don't want to see Brad again, but there's lots of my stuff at the flat. Do you think Dad would go round to pick it up sometime?'

'Why don't I go while Dad's here this afternoon? If we send him, he might just kill Brad, and then we'd be in more trouble than ever!' Lucy smiled again. She looked pale but so very beautiful. 'Give me Brad's number and I'll phone him to make sure he'll be there and tell me exactly what he has of yours.'

'Apart from my clothes, he's got my mobile and laptop. There's not much else of value.' She looked suddenly wistful.

'Don't worry. I'll get it all today, then come in again to see you this evening. Shall I bring the boys?'

'Do you think they'd want to come?'

'I'm sure they would. We've all really missed you – the house hasn't been the same since you left.'

'My leg looks a mess, doesn't it?' Lucy lifted the gauze to view the damage.

'It might not look so bad when it heals,' I said optimistically.

'Can I have it removed?'

'I'm not sure how they can do it, perhaps by laser, but we'll have to make enquiries. Let's not worry about it now – it's in a place where no one will see it. Because of the infection, the doctor says they'll have to test your blood for hepatitis and HIV, just as a precaution, you probably won't have either.'

'I've been really stupid, haven't I?'

'You're not the first girl to make such a mistake, and you'll learn from it. All of life's experiences are learning curves; it's just that some are more painful than others.' It was so good actually to have a conversation with Lucy. I still didn't understand why she'd turned against Paul and me to the extent of wanting to cut us out of her life. Could it simply be adolescence, or was there something else which turned her against us? Things were looking brighter now, but I wish she would talk to me some more and tell me why everything went so badly wrong.

I stayed until Lucy's lunch was brought. She drifted off to sleep for half an hour mid-morning, and I watched her, so peaceful yet so troubled. Things wouldn't change overnight; this was a great start, but I wasn't so naive as to think it was all over. Something had triggered these last few months of change in Lucy, and I'd like to get to the bottom of it before something, or someone, took her back into that dark moodiness of late.

Lucy was still tired, so I suggested she tried to sleep again before her father came in as I left. Armed with Brad's phone number, I headed home to make some calls first. Brad was top of the list, and I hoped he would answer. I wanted to get him out of our lives as soon as possible and that afternoon wasn't soon enough for me. Surprisingly he answered after the first couple of rings.

'Hello.'

'Brad, this is Lucy's mother here.' I paused to give him time to think about Lucy and perhaps ask how she was. He was silent but still on the line.

'I'm coming round in about an hour to pick up my daughter's possessions, including her phone and laptop. Will you get them together for me and make sure you're there when I come?'

I tried to make it more of an instruction than a request, not wanting to find an empty flat like yesterday.

'Okay,' was all he said. Anger boiled up inside me. I was ready to tell him exactly what I thought of him but he disconnected. Two words were all he could manage, no enquiring after Lucy, no questions about why I wanted her things. She could have died, and he probably wouldn't have cared. I cannot recall ever being so angry at another human being as I was with Brad Johnson then.

Chapter Forty

After waiting several minutes to calm down from my rage at Brad, I rang Janet.

'Hi, how's Lucy doing?' Her concern was touching.

'She's so much better, Janet, and more importantly, she wants to come home!' I knew Lucy's grandparents would share my delight.

'Wonderful news. When will they let her out?'

'The doctor's due to review her case tomorrow and he'll decide then. It'll be great to have her back home; it seems some good has come out of all this. Can I ask one more favour?'

Janet was always so willing to help but I didn't want to take advantage of her kindness.

'I'm going round to Brad's flat now to pick up Lucy's things. Can you keep the boys for another couple of hours and I'll come for them when I've finished?'

'Of course, it's no problem, but we'll bring them over to you, shall we? You must be exhausted with all that running about. If we have them back by about four, all right?'

'Thank you, Janet, you're an angel. Could you tell them they can come in to see Lucy with me this evening? It might be better to forewarn them.' My ex-mother-in-law agreed and I thanked her again.

My last phone call was to Steve, whom I'd promised to keep updated on my rollercoaster of a life. As I dialled his number, a thrill of excitement ran through me at the thought of just hearing his voice.

'Hello, Steve speaking.' The words cheered me up immediately.

'Hi, Steve, it's Laura.'

'Laura! How are things today?'

'Much better, thanks. Lucy's quite lucid now and she's asked if she can come home, not just from the hospital but to live here again!' My excitement was evident and Steve was genuinely pleased for me.

'I'm going to Brad's flat now to pick up her things. Paul's visiting Lucy this afternoon, and I'm taking the boys in this evening.'

'Slow down a bit, Laura. Did you say you're going to Brad Johnson's flat?'

'Yes, I'm just about to leave. Paul would probably have gone, but I was afraid he might thump him, or worse!'

'You can't go back there alone, Laura. Wait for me; I'll be round as soon as possible to take you.'

'Steve, you don't have to do this. I'll be fine, honestly.'

'It's no place for you to go alone, especially in the circumstances. Brad's not to be trusted, but he'll be less inclined to start any trouble if I'm with you. I'm coming, Laura, so don't leave without me.' Steve was determined, and as we finished the conversation, a warm glow ran through me. He'd made a decision, concerned for my safety, emphatically telling me not to go. On further reflection, he was right. I'd not given a second thought to any danger, simply wishing to get Brad out of our lives as soon as possible, for my sake as well as Lucy's. But I was pleased Steve would be with me, not only for the protection he could offer but also the chance to see him again. I'd been looking forward to him joining the boys and me for Sunday lunch until we had to cancel, so in a small measure, this made up for it. As I passed the hall mirror, I hardly recognised my reflection as a huge smile was plastered on my face. Could this be the beginning of better times for the children and me? And would Steve figure in our future? I certainly hoped he would.

When we arrived at the flats, which for a while my daughter had called home, I was grateful for Steve's presence. After taking the stairs two at a time, he rapped loudly on the door, with me following behind. It took another couple of tries before we received an answer and when Brad did open the door, he looked as if he'd just woken up. For a few moments he stared at us as if he'd never seen us before.

'We've come for Lucy's things,' Steve said, already moving inside the doorway. Brad stepped back and we entered, hopefully for the last time. A few black binbags were stacked in the corner of the lounge, presumably my daughter's clothes.

'She had a couple of sports bags which she brought her things in?' I looked questioningly at Brad, who in turn glanced from me to Steve before nodding and disappearing into the bedroom. He returned with the empty bags which I took, then began putting Lucy's clothes inside, without taking the time to fold them. They would all go straight in the wash at home anyway.

'Anything else?' Steve asked me.

'Her laptop and mobile phone,' I answered. Brad scowled at me, looked at Steve, then returned to the bedroom and came out with them both. It crossed my mind he might not have given them up so readily had I been alone.

'Are you not even concerned to know how Lucy is?' I couldn't resist asking, even though the answer was evident by the way he had deserted her when she was so ill.

'Oh, yeah, how is she?'

'She'll recover, but no thanks to you!' I was so angry and turned to leave before I decided to punch him myself!

The cold air cooled the anger in my face as I drew in deep gulps to regain my composure. I carried the laptop and phone, and Steve followed with the bags after saying something to Brad once I was out of earshot. It was such a relief to get down those ugly concrete stairs and back into the warm car, knowing I would never have to set foot there or see Brad Johnson again. Steve dropped the bags into the boot and climbed into the driver's seat.

'What did you say to him?' I asked.

'Nothing much. I just wanted him to know I was on his case. He got the message that I'd be looking out for his name in connection with all local crimes in the future.'

'Do you think he is a criminal?'

'Petty stuff probably, yes, but it's the way many criminals start out. He knows now we'll be watching him, so hopefully he'll keep his head down.'

It was so good to have Steve beside me. His physicality was comforting and it was beginning to dawn on me just how lonely I'd been over the past few years. Yes, I've always had the children, but it's not the same as the company of a partner; another person to share everyday routines with and discuss the mundane events which make up the fabric of our existence. It was true I may be leaving myself open to hurt, but at that moment, I knew I wanted Steve to be a permanent part of my world. My only hope was that this wonderful man, who had already helped me through some difficult times, would want me to be in his life too.

Steve helped to carry Lucy's belongings into the house and up to her room.

'I'd intended to decorate in here before she came home, but I'd much rather have her than a freshly painted room.'

'I could come round tomorrow and do it if you like? I'm not at work until late on Tuesday.'

'Sorry, I wasn't hinting. It can wait, and maybe Lucy will help to choose the colour herself.' Steve seemed keen to spend time with me, which was surely a good sign? I put the kettle on for coffee, telling him Janet would be round soon with the children.

'Do you want me to go?'

'No, not at all. I'm just warning you of the chaos about to descend on us! You'll stay for coffee, won't you? The Sunday lunch will have to wait until next week if you can make it?'

'Try stopping me!' he said with a laugh. I cut into a chocolate cake I'd bought as a dessert; we could all do with a bit of a treat, and I cut a large slice for Steve and a somewhat more modest piece for myself. The boys would probably demolish the rest.

As if they'd smelt the cake, they appeared at the door, full of the things they'd been doing since they last saw me. Janet followed them into the kitchen.

'And did you meet Imogen?' I asked.

'Yes,' Jake answered, 'she's sweet, but new babies are a bit boring. It'll be better when she's older and can at least play with us.' Sam didn't pass comment. If she didn't like to play football, his interest in his baby sister would be minimal.

'When are we going to see Lucy?' Jake asked.

'In a couple of hours, but have a drink and a piece of cake to keep you going. We'll call and pick up a pizza on the way home from the hospital.'

'Great!' Pizza was Sam's current favourite.

'Well, I, for one, am sorry to have missed one of your mum's Sunday lunches. It'll have to wait until next Sunday, I suppose,' Steve said.

'You might regret it!' Sam laughed and I pretended to take a swipe at him. Janet had been taking this all in and I could tell

Steve's presence had been noted by the little smile she gave me.

'I haven't told them the good news about Lucy yet, Laura.'

'What good news?' Jake asked.

'She's coming back home when she leaves the hospital, great, isn't it?' I looked from one of my sons to the other to gauge their reaction.

'If that's the good news, I don't want to hear the bad!' Sam laughed and ran off upstairs before I could catch him. It was all light-hearted and was good for my soul. I would soon have all my children together under the same roof, there was a new, gorgeous man in my life and those despicable letters seemed to have stopped, even though it was at the expense of my job.

Steve finished his coffee and left for home. I couldn't thank him enough, and as we stood at the door, he leaned towards me and kissed me slowly and gently. Perhaps I should have pulled back a little in case the boys were watching, but I enjoyed the closeness and the feeling of Steve's lips on mine. We parted, and I went back inside. Janet was still in the kitchen and the boys were upstairs.

'So, is this all official with your lovely policeman then?' She grinned.

'We're taking it slowly, a lot is going on for the boys to take in at the moment, and Lucy will have to be my priority for a while, but I do like him.'

'And judging by the way he looks at you, he feels the same too!'

'I hope so, Janet, I've never felt like this since Paul and I split up.'

'Well, you deserve a little happiness. I hope it works out for you both; he seems like a lovely man. I've heard all about how you helped Zoe and the baby too. Life's anything but dull for you lately. It was good of you, Laura, Zoe is full of your praises, and Paul's a bit gobsmacked, for want of a better word.' We both smiled. From what I'd seen of Paul lately, he was undoubtedly somewhat bemused at the circumstances of Imogen's birth and didn't quite know what to expect next. I told Janet I'd seen another side to Zoe and thought it was time to bury the hatchet. Hopefully, things between us could be on a friendlier basis in the future; after all, she was now the mother of my children's sister.

Janet left soon after, and the twins and I got ready to visit Lucy.

Chapter Forty-One

Lucy seemed genuinely pleased to see the boys, although, as usual, they did most of the talking. The embarrassment and awkward questions I'd anticipated didn't arise. Although I hadn't mentioned the tattoo to Sam and Jake (only telling them she had an infection), surprisingly, Lucy told them herself. Typically, they wanted to see the tattoo, and Lucy obliged! To my eyes, it looked slightly better, but to the twins, it was gross and held a fascination which almost lifted their sister's status to the rank of cool. Hopefully though, the pain Lucy described to them would put them off considering tattoos for themselves in the future.

The visit went well and when we left, I promised Lucy I'd speak to Mr Bennett the following day, for which she seemed pleased. My daughter had grown up considerably during this experience.

I rang the school quite early the next morning, hoping it would be the best time to catch the headmaster before the pupils arrived, which proved right as his secretary put me through straight away. Mr Bennett already knew Lucy had left home but was aware of little else. There seemed no purpose in telling him all the details; he would probably read between the lines anyway, so I got straight to the point. As I hoped, the headmaster was positive about Lucy returning to her studies, enthusiastic even, and asked if I could call in to discuss the details. It was agreed I should go later that morning after he'd had a chance to speak to some of Lucy's teachers, who would be able to provide notes on the work she had missed. Mr Bennett also kindly said there was no reason for her teachers or classmates to know anything other than she'd been in hospital and was returning soon. If all was well and Lucy's leg healed quickly enough, she could begin as early as the following Monday.

Two hours later, I walked down the corridor heading to Mr Bennett's office when Richard Ward stepped out of it. We both seemed to be startled, but I was saved from having to acknowledge him in any way by the headmaster's appearance behind him. Richard set off for the main door while I, somewhat shakily, went into the office, trying to put that awful man out of my mind.

'I'm so pleased Lucy's coming back to us, Mrs Green. She's an intelligent girl and I'm sure she'll soon make up the work she's missed.' He pushed a relatively thick file across his desk. 'Don't look horrified; these are simply recent notes from most of the subjects she's taking. Some of it is set homework which the others will already have done. Lucy might like to study these to catch up. There are also suggestions for reading material and websites for the same purpose. Now then, how are you, Mrs Green? It's been a difficult time for you, I'm sure.' He smiled, and those caterpillar eyebrows almost danced on his face. I liked this kind man.

'I'm doing okay now, thank you. I can't pretend it's not been hard, but Lucy seems to have realised where she belongs and I'm delighted she wants to come home. I appreciate all the help you've given me, and I'm sure Lucy will too.'

'We're here to help, and please tell Lucy my door is always open, as with her tutors. She's a very bright girl; we all want to see her succeed.'

After thanking him again, I picked up the file and made my way out. Lucy was fortunate in having such an understanding headmaster. The school's whole ethos, led by this man, impressed me.

My car was in the visitors' car park, but when I rounded the corner of the school, it was to see Richard Ward leaning on the driver's side door. A wave of panic ran through me but also a determination not to let him intimidate me in any way. I walked steadily towards my car and, once in hearing distance, asked politely for him to move. He didn't and a slow, rather smug smile crept across his face.

'Excuse me!' I said again more forcefully, but he remained still. I considered getting in the other side and climbing over the gear stick and handbrake, but why should I be the one to give way?

'What do you want, Richard?'

'Nothing from you!' was the reply.

'Then please move so I can get in my car.'

'So, like mother, like daughter, eh? Lucy's a little slut, I hear, but what can you expect? You lead a man on, then pretend you don't want it! It's not surprising she's turned out the same as you!' He leered, a superior, self-satisfied expression on his face.

'I never led you on, Richard, and you know it!' Not wishing to engage in any kind of discussion, I refrained from saying more in case I lost my temper. I stepped back a few yards and took my phone out of my bag, making the pretence of dialling. I put the phone to my ear, silently counted to ten, and then said, 'Hello? I'm in West End Academy schoolyard and am being prevented from getting into my car by a man.' I paused, pretending to listen and unsure what to do next. But the bluff worked, and Richard stepped back from my car, turned his back on me and walked away. To end the charade, I said, 'It's okay, sorry to have bothered you, the man has left now.'

If Richard heard me, he didn't turn back, so I quickly scrambled into the car and drove home even though my legs were shaking. But how did Richard Ward know I'd had problems with Lucy? Some of her friends knew she'd gone missing as I'd phoned their houses when looking for her. I suppose children talk, and Lucy's disappearance from school and home was probably common knowledge, which wouldn't make it easy for her to return, yet I couldn't wrap her in cotton wool. It could prove problematic for Lucy to pick up her studies, although I dearly hoped not.

After a quick lunch, I drove to the hospital, arriving on the ward as the doctor left Lucy's room.

'Mrs Green,' he smiled, 'Lucy looks as if she's healing nicely; she's a fortunate girl. We want to keep her another night to complete the course of antibiotics, but then she's free to go home.' I thanked him for his care then went in to see my daughter.

'Hey, how are you feeling?'

'Much better and the doctor says I can go home tomorrow!'

'Yes, I've just seen him. Is your leg any better?'

She lifted the gauze off the wound to show me. It was certainly getting better; the blisters were going down and the skin didn't look so red and angry.

'It's looking good, but we'll have to be careful you don't get another infection in it when we get home.'

'The nurse said they'd give me a pack of dressings so I can change them myself, and a district nurse will call in a couple of days to check on me. They said I'd be ready after lunch tomorrow, so will you pick me up then?'

'You try to stop me!' I was so thankful Lucy wanted to

come home and appeared to be looking forward to it. I began to relate my visit to Mr Bennett and mentioned the pile of homework he'd given me. Perhaps I exaggerated precisely how much there was, but she seemed keen to get started. Lucy must have been bored to tears living with Brad; he certainly wasn't a great conversationalist, and playing computer games most of the day wouldn't appeal to Lucy. Catching up on schoolwork was suddenly an attractive proposition.

There were a couple of magazines at the bottom of the bed, one of them being the one I'd worked for. Lucy saw me looking at it.

'Why isn't the '*Ask Laura*' page in the magazine?' she asked.

'Well, they suspended it while the police were investigating those letters, but they've now decided to finish the page altogether. They can't take the risk that whoever's writing them won't start doing so again. But I also think it's a convenient excuse to make some changes to the magazine anyway.'

'How awful, it's so unfair! What will you do?' Lucy seemed genuinely upset for me.

'Oh, don't worry, there are still the articles which they commission, and I'll just have to do a bit more freelance work. We'll manage somehow.' I hadn't told Sam or Jake yet either, wanting to protect my family from worry. Lucy seemed a little sad, but I made light of it; getting her well was the priority now and I couldn't wait to have her home again.

Chapter Forty-Two

I picked Lucy up from the hospital after lunch on Tuesday as planned and took her home. The prospect of an entire week at home with her both thrilled and scared me. A feeling of being on trial haunted me, and I measured every word I spoke, afraid to say anything which might cause her to take off again. Initially, Lucy was tired, and the first thing she did was go upstairs and lie down for an hour, which gave me the chance to prepare a meal. When the boys came home, they enthusiastically barged into Lucy's room to say hello and woke her up. Sam tried to persuade me to order pizza, declaring it a day of celebration, but I vetoed the idea as it was only two days since we'd last eaten pizza. However, we ate together around the table, and I felt a huge swell of peace and pride in my chest at having all my children safely with me again. Lucy selected a film for us to watch that evening, and we demolished a whole tub of ice cream and a bag of popcorn. Perhaps it wasn't the best choice of film, *My Sister's Keeper*, the adaptation of Jodi Picoult's beautiful but emotional story. The theme running through it was of siblings, and their love for each other, which made up for some of the more emotional scenes.

After the children went to bed, I rang Steve. Hearing his voice brought a strange but pleasant quiver throughout my body. As I told him all about my day, he listened patiently and then asked if we had any plans for the rest of the week. Steve was due some rest days and offered to take us out, but I hesitated as Lucy knew nothing yet about our blossoming relationship.

'I'll talk to her tomorrow and see how it goes; if she's okay with it, then we'll make some plans.' I was acutely aware Steve was the one whose needs were being put on hold in deference to my family. Sadly, this went with the territory – I was the mother of three children – he knew they would always come first. But his being so keen to see me made me feel special!

The following morning, Lucy was downstairs and dressed before the boys left for school.

'I want to make a start on the work I've missed,' she explained, buttering toast and tipping far too much marmalade on it. I said nothing. Pigging out on marmalade was trivial compared to what we'd been through of late. I'd learned to choose my battles with the children carefully, stopping and thinking before making even the slightest comment or decision. It was too easy to say 'no' to something just to make life easier for me.

After breakfast, my daughter commandeered the kitchen table, spreading papers haphazardly and making me wonder how she could possibly work in such clutter. Again, I kept my own counsel and used the time to do the usual round of morning chores.

An hour or so later, I ventured into the kitchen to make coffee and found Lucy slumped over the piles of paper, fast asleep.

'Hey,' I shook her gently, 'if you need more sleep, perhaps you should go back to bed?'

'What?' She rubbed her eyes. 'Oh no, I'm fine. I want to get it finished.'

'Have a break for a coffee, then go back to it later. I don't think your tutors expect you to work through everything they sent. You can always catch up when you start school again, a little bit extra each night, maybe?'

Lucy stretched her arms and stood up, then together we took our coffee to the lounge where I turned the fire up. We sipped in silence for a few moments as I wondered how to tell her about Steve.

'Do you remember Steve Radcliffe, the detective who came with me to Brad's flat?'

'Yes, of course I do. Why?'

'Well, he's been really helpful lately, and we've seen each other on occasions...' Was this the right way to phrase it?

'Do you mean "seen" as in "dating"?' Lucy asked.

'Yes, in a way it is. We've been to the cinema and out for a meal, that's all – but I do like him.'

To my utter horror, Lucy burst into tears.

'What's wrong?' I asked. 'I thought you'd be pleased for me.'

Lucy shook her head.

'It's not that... really, it's not Steve.' But Lucy could say no more and began sobbing her heart out. I moved beside her and put my arms around her, wanting to take all her troubles away. She allowed me to hold her and even laid her head against my shoulder. It had been a long time since Lucy had accepted any affection from me and tears were brimming in my own eyes. We remained still for several minutes until the sobbing died down, and Lucy eventually looked up, although not directly at me.

'What's the matter, love? You can tell me you know, I'm on your side and always have been.'

'Have you, Mum?'

'Of course I have. I love you, Lucy, and nothing will ever change how I feel!'

'But you love the boys more?'

'No, of course not! Why on earth would you think so?' Not only was I shocked at her words, but I was also hurt too.

'Because everything has always revolved around them!' Lucy's tears were flowing again. She dropped her head and turned away, and my heart sank.

'Lucy, you've got it all wrong. Yes, they take up much of my time, but I don't love them any more than I love you. Tell me why you think this, please?' How she could think such a thing was beyond me. I racked my brain to think of anything which could have given her such a ludicrous idea but couldn't come up with a single thing.

'Talk to me, Lucy. If I've made you feel like this, then I need to know what it is I've done.' She shook her head and made to move away. I caught her arm.

'No, Lucy. We need to sort this out. Now. Is this why you took up with Brad because you thought I love Sam and Jake more than I love you?'

'Well you do!' She looked at me directly now. 'Even when they were born, they got all the attention, and I had to look after myself! When I started school and you took me, everyone crowded around the pram to see them. When I made things for you, you barely looked at them, and the boys would tear my pictures up and never get into trouble.'

I cast my mind back to those days when the twins were little. True, Lucy did start school when it was probably a difficult time for her, but I tried to give her the attention she needed. Clearly I had failed.

'Lucy, I am so sorry if that's how it seemed to you...'

'No, it's not how it seemed – it's how it was!' She was angry now and I was horrified.

'Yes, Sam and Jake did take up much of my time and

244

energy, and if you felt neglected, then I'm sorry, but it certainly wasn't intentional. You were special and always will be. You're my firstborn child, my only daughter, and I love you more than life itself!' How could I get her to understand? My explanations seemed feeble and weak, excuses even.

'Lucy, it seems I've made some mistakes, and I don't want to make excuses, but you got every bit as much attention as the boys did in your first few years. Perhaps even more as you were the sole focus of our lives then. Maybe you don't remember the years before the twins came along, but they were good times. We had fun; we spent summer days in the park with picnics, just you and me, and Dad took us out at the weekend. Dad and I doted on you, and we both still love you more than you'll ever know!'

'But Dad left us. He didn't want me in the first place – neither of you did!'

'It's true, and you weren't planned. We were so young at the time, but as you grew in my womb, I fell in love with you, and so did your dad. Yes, it was a shock, and our parents weren't pleased with us either, but even before you were born, we all longed for you and loved you! A first child is special; I adored you then and still do now.' I struggled to find the words to make Lucy understand. I've never thought of myself as the perfect mother, but I couldn't love my children any more than I do, and I wanted her to know it.

'I always thought it was my fault when Dad left. You stopped laughing after that, except at Sam and Jake. They could make you smile, but I couldn't.'

'No Lucy, listen. Dad leaving had nothing to do with you. He didn't leave you; he left me! It was me he wanted to get away from. He's always loved you and still does. We both do.'

So much for my degree in psychology! Why did I not pick up on the signs of Lucy's despair before? I thought back to those early years after she was born. We didn't have much money, but we were happy and our baby daughter brought such pleasure into our lives. I wished she could remember those early days before the boys were born. She was only four when they came along and had been the focal point of our lives until then. The timing of the twins' birth wasn't great in that shortly afterwards, Lucy started school. To her, it must have felt as if we were pushing her out in favour of the twins. Why had I never seen it? I tried to give her the attention she needed, but obviously, I'd failed. There was rarely time to spend with only Lucy; if one of the boys was asleep, the other was usually crying or getting into mischief. Even out of the house, being the mother of twins draws people, and we would often be stopped while the twins were admired. Poor Lucy must have felt like a spare part. Why on earth hadn't I seen it? But she appeared to cope well with all the changes her baby brothers brought, or so we thought at the time. Children are so amazingly resilient, but in saying so am I looking for excuses – a peg to hang my failures on?

The timeline forming in my mind didn't bring me any comfort or inspiration as to why Lucy felt as she did. As a four-year-old child, Lucy didn't understand or have the vocabulary to express her feelings or let me know of my failings. I can only assume the results of these past mistakes, by Paul and me, had been suppressed until recently. The incident with Brad, the tattoo, and the attitude are perhaps symptoms of past unresolved traumas. Even rolling the timeline through my mind, over and over again, I couldn't pinpoint any specific instances which would help me to understand. The difficulties Lucy had experienced lately were most probably a culmination of past anxieties which were not picked up on at the time. I'd failed my daughter. But was it too late to make it up to her now?

I tried to verbalise some of these thoughts and apologised for making her feel the way she did.

'Can we begin again?' I asked. 'I promise to try harder, but I need your help. Please tell me anything that worries you, no matter what it is. No more bottling things up?' I pleaded.

Lucy nodded and allowed me to hug her again. She went back to her schoolwork and I watched, troubled. There was still a melancholy air around my daughter which I longed to have the power to expel, to set her free and reassure her of just how much she was loved.

To continue talking about Steve seemed inappropriate after this conversation, so I shelved it, hoping for another opportunity to come along later. Perhaps I was selfish in wanting to have a relationship when Lucy so obviously needed my time and attention. Could I give Steve up? Should I give him up? I needed time to consider what to do – seeing Steve would only complicate things. The way it was looking at the moment, taking our relationship any further was simply not going to happen.

Chapter Forty-Three

Our emotional conversation was not brought up again by either of us, although we would need to discuss the issues again. However, Lucy was still recuperating and determined to work hard and catch up on her studies, a dedication I applauded. But she needed reminding to rest. On the Thursday of her week at home, I suggested we visit her dad, Zoe and Imogen. Lucy hadn't met her little sister, so a visit was long overdue. I rang Paul, who was still on paternity leave, and he said the afternoon would be perfect for them. Zoe still didn't feel well enough to go out much, so visitors would be welcome. When I told Lucy, she looked somewhat puzzled.

'Are you going to stay with me, or are you just dropping me off?' she asked.

'Oh, I'll be staying too. I can't miss the chance of a cuddle with a new baby.' I smiled at Lucy's surprise and felt an explanation was due.

'When Zoe went into labour, your dad was away at a conference in Norfolk. Your grandparents were away too, and Zoe called me for help.'

'You're joking! What did you tell her?'

'I went round to take her to the hospital, of course.' My daughter looked stunned.

'Close your mouth, Lucy!' I laughed. 'She hadn't been able to get hold of your dad and when he did get the message, she was already in labour. Zoe was scared. She'd missed many of the antenatal classes and didn't know what to expect. I ended up being her birthing partner, it was an amazing experience, and I'm rather glad I was there.'

'I don't believe it! Surely you should have told her where to go! She stole your husband!' Lucy gawped at me.

'Which was my first thought too, but it did give me a chance to get to know her a little better, and Imogen is so sweet. You'll love her. Maybe I've been judging Zoe too harshly and it's time to drop all the ill-feeling. I was partly to blame, you know, it wasn't only your dad and Zoe who were at fault. With hindsight I can see and accept that now.'

During the drive to Paul and Zoe's, I was aware of Lucy occasionally shaking her head in disbelief and it made me smile. Maybe my attitude to Zoe had coloured Lucy's own opinions. I should have been more circumspect. But was it too late to change things now?

When we arrived, Paul opened the door and hugged Lucy. He knew about some of the conversations I'd had with her of late, and Paul also felt we had much to make up for our daughter. Zoe was sitting on the sofa with Imogen asleep in her arms.

'Aw, she's beautiful!' Lucy said, instantly taken with her little sister.

'She's a lot like you were as a baby,' Paul declared. Lucy looked to me for confirmation.

'Yes, she is!' I nodded.

'Can I hold her?' Lucy surprised us all.

'Of course... just watch her head and put this cloth over

your knee. She has a habit of being sick after her bottle, which she's just had.' Zoe passed the baby gently to Lucy, who held her with such awe etched on her face.

'Don't look too enamoured with her, Lucy – they'll be looking for babysitters soon.' I said it as a joke, but Lucy was thrilled.

'Could I, Dad? I'd be very careful with her,' she asked.

'Of course, it sounds like a great idea to me! If you get to know her and become familiar to her, you can babysit anytime!' Paul grinned. Lucy seemed to take to her baby sister immediately, but who wouldn't? She was a little bundle of loveliness. After a few minutes, I asked for my turn at a cuddle, but perhaps I shouldn't have. All those dormant, maternal feelings came rushing at me like a tidal wave. Maybe I would compete with Lucy to babysit!

On the way home I asked what Lucy thought of her sister.

'She's gorgeous! Do you think Dad was serious about letting me babysit?'

'I'm sure he was, but it'll probably be quite a while before Zoe feels like going out. As well as recovering herself, she'll be very possessive of Imogen. The first few weeks after a baby's born is a very emotional time.'

Back at home, Lucy wasn't quite so animated and returned to her studies. I still didn't feel confident of everything being right with her, but maybe my expectations were too high. She was certainly much better than the sullen, downright rude teenager of a few weeks ago. I followed my daughter's lead and began to work on an article which had been buzzing around in my head for a while. Although we were not on the breadline, I was conscious I needed to earn a living.

Our house began to resemble a library until Sam and Jake arrived home each day. I could tell Lucy was making an effort with the boys, asking them about school or football and listening as if she was interested. But did I want it to be an effort for her? There were still times when she appeared pensive as if in another place, mentally at least, but then I reminded myself it was still early days, and Lucy had a lot to process. I shouldn't expect to be her confidante after recent events.

I did consider her quiet moods could simply be embarrassment about the 'Brad' incident or the tattoo, but she'd talked quite openly on the subject, and I'd done my best to let her know it was, as far as Paul and I were concerned, history. We had no intention of bringing the subject up again.

The week passed, and it was time for Lucy to return to school. Her leg was sufficiently healed to leave the dressing off, and she wore thick black tights with her uniform. We'd talked about what she would tell her friends, and I suggested she said as little as possible without lying. Lucy seemed to think it would be better to wing it and decide what to say and to whom, as it arose. My daughter had matured over the last few weeks. It was a good plan.

I hadn't seen Steve for over a week. We'd spoken on the phone when I admitted to having second thoughts about our relationship. I could tell he was unhappy about it, which in a distorted way was a compliment. I asked for time, trying to explain how my family needed to be my priority. Graciously, he agreed to stay away for as long as I felt it necessary, but I missed him so much! When alone in the house, my thoughts would turn to Steve, and I longed to see him again, to be held and comforted by him – but I knew it couldn't be. Therefore, it came as a surprise when I found him standing on my doorstep on Monday morning after the children had left for school. I was torn between running inside and hiding, and flinging my arms around him and begging him to hold me. As a compromise, I stepped aside, an invitation to come in, which he accepted. I automatically went into the kitchen and put the kettle on; it was times like this when I craved a chocolate biscuit.

'I know what you said, Laura, but it's been such a miserable week, and all I can think about is you.' His face was pale and missing its usual smile, making me feel terrible for having done this to such a wonderful man.

'Couldn't we see each other occasionally, every second week or something?' His eyes lacked their usual sparkle too. I automatically made two cups of coffee and passed one to Steve while I held mine in front of me like a shield.

'Please, Laura?'

'I'd love to say yes, I'm missing you more than I ever thought possible... but it's not fair to ask you to wait, and I have to put my children first.'

'It's okay. I understand, as long as we get some time to ourselves.' The telephone rang, interrupting him, and I moved away to take the call. It was the school secretary; Sam had been sick and was running a temperature. I told her I was on my way. Was this a portent to remind me to stick to my resolve?

'You see?' I looked at Steve, who'd got the gist of the conversation. 'I'm a mother, which means putting my children above my own needs and desires. I'm sorry, Steve, but I have to go.'

Chapter Forty-Four

S am had one of those twenty-four-hour bugs and was off school the following day and furious because he'd missed football practice. After I'd tried to persuade him it wasn't the end of the world, he stomped off to his room, a typical Sam gesture. As expected, he came down cheerful enough when he was feeling better and hungry.

Lucy survived her first week back at school. I didn't ask too many questions, she would talk to me if she wanted to, but I made sure she knew how concerned I was. There would be no more misunderstandings if it were up to me. When she did engage in any kind of conversation, I was pleased to hear her mention Molly again. When Molly's mother told me the girls had fallen out, I was saddened. They'd always been so close and, at times, seemed joined at the hip. Lucy would need her friends so the reconciliation could only be for the better.

Lucy's leg was healing rapidly, but there was still an air of sadness around her, a melancholy which I noticed when she was unaware of my scrutiny. It was difficult to know quite what to do with such a fine line between showing concern and being downright nosey. Then the idea of seeing the school counsellor came to mind. I'd made enquiries before when Lucy decided to leave school, and Mr Bennett said they did use a counsellor, and if Lucy was willing, they would make an appointment. It came to nothing but it might be a solution now, so I decided to mention it to Lucy. After the boys went to bed, I grasped the opportunity of talking to my daughter.

'You've been through such a lot, Lucy, and it must still be on your mind. Would talking to a counsellor help?'

'What kind of counsellor?'

'A therapeutic counsellor, it's someone who's professionally trained to listen and help with all kinds of problems.' My experience of counsellors was limited, but I'd known of people who had very positive results from the experience. I'd also suggested it occasionally when answering a letter as '*Ask Laura*' if I thought it appropriate.

'Is it like a psychiatrist?' Lucy asked.

'No, not really, it's simply someone to talk to who might be able to help you get over any issues which are troubling you.'

'I don't think anyone can help.' A look of sadness crept over her face.

'Lucy, you made a mistake, but you're trying so hard to put it right and I'm proud of you for the effort you're making. Whatever you've done in the past is history. We don't ever have to refer to it again unless you want to talk about it. She shook her head, and tears suddenly filled her eyes.

'No, Mum, I've done something worse than Brad and the tattoo.' I moved to comfort my little girl, who was still so troubled. She let me hold her close.

'Shh, don't cry, Lucy. Whatever it is we can get over it, sort it out. Nothing's going to come between us again, I promise.' My mind was racing. Could she be pregnant? The thought was awful, but it wouldn't be the end of the world. After all, Lucy had been an unplanned baby, and she knew it.

We remained silent for a few moments as I held her, stroking her hair.

'It was me.' She only said those three words, and at first, I didn't understand.

'What was you, Lucy?'

'It was me who sent those awful letters...' Her voice trailed off, and she looked at me, tears staining her cheeks, as she waited for a reaction.

I couldn't speak, couldn't process what she'd just told me! Those foul words, the veiled threats – it couldn't have been my daughter – my little girl? I was frozen in my thoughts and Lucy, obviously frightened, ran upstairs to her room.

Time must have passed, but I wasn't aware of it and didn't know how long I remained sitting in the same spot. Was Lucy lying? Perhaps it was Brad who'd sent them, and she was covering for him, but why would she? Now she'd seen Brad for the person he really was, why would she cover for him? He'd deserted her when she was so ill. Did it perhaps begin as a joke?

Nothing seemed plausible and I was left thinking Lucy must have hated me so much to have done such a thing. But she'd confessed, and I'd been telling her for days that what was past was past, and we could have a new start. Would I have to report it to the police? What had Steve said, they never actually close a case if it's unsolved? I couldn't face telling the police my own daughter had sent those spiteful letters! Terrible thoughts crowded into my mind until I just wanted to close my eyes and forget it all.

But what must Lucy be feeling? To have admitted this was quite gutsy. I tried to think of the worst thing I had ever done in my life and how I would feel if people knew about it. No, I must protect my daughter. If anything, her revelation made me love her even more. She must have been so miserable to do such a thing, my poor, sweet girl!

Having decided to protect Lucy, I was aware of how strong motherly instinct could be. I would still do anything for her and always love her. It also seemed something of a relief that it was Lucy behind the letters and I no longer had to fear an unknown enemy – a twisted sort of logic, I know. My glass was half full.

The clock chimed, and I realised it was 10pm and I'd been sitting rooted to the same spot for over an hour. I jumped up and ran upstairs to Lucy's room. She was lying fully dressed on her bed, still sobbing with her face red and swollen. I ran to her and gathered her up into my arms.

'My poor girl. How awful you must be feeling!' We cried together, for how long, I don't know, but eventually, I lifted her face to look at me.

'Lucy, I love you! All this makes absolutely no difference to how I feel, do you understand?' There was a look of confusion on her face.

'Don't you hate me?' Her voice was thick from sobbing.

'No, I could never hate you; you're my flesh and blood!'

'But it was such a hateful thing to do! I wrote such terrible things, but I didn't mean them. I'm so ashamed, Mum, but at the time, I just wanted to hurt you! I'm so sorry.'

'I know you are, and I'm so glad you have told me; it's such a courageous thing to do. But now I want you to forget it. You need to get some sleep, or you won't be fit for school tomorrow and when I've had a chance to think about it properly, we'll talk some more.'

'Will you have to tell the police, and Dad and Zoe?'

'I don't know yet. That's one of the things we need to consider. For now, though, it's getting late, so into bed with you, don't worry anymore and sleep well.' I kissed her damp cheek then left her to get ready for bed.

In my own room, exhaustion caught up with me, understandable really after such a shocking revelation, and my hands were still trembling. I undressed and crawled beneath the comfort of my duvet, willing my mind to stop churning and let me sleep. Decisions would have to wait until I'd had time to consider the best way to handle Lucy's confession.

Sleep evaded me, my body was tense and my mind wouldn't close down. Perhaps this was the ultimate betrayal; it was indeed painful and challenging to get my mind around all the implications. Did Lucy do this because she hated me? After the week we'd just spent together, I couldn't believe she did. Maybe she only thought she hated me and acted impulsively. If Brad knew about the letters, I was pretty sure he would encourage Lucy. But all of this was supposition. Perhaps I would never know why Lucy did this, and I don't think she fully understood herself. At some point, I must have drifted off to sleep and woke when I heard the familiar morning sounds of Sam and Jake in the kitchen.

I showered and dressed quickly before going downstairs to supervise breakfast, or rather the clearing up; the boys would have helped themselves by then. There was no sign of Lucy, and I hoped she was still asleep; she could have another half an hour before getting ready for school, and I would happily give her a lift if she were running late. But she didn't sleep much longer and appeared in the kitchen doorway looking pale and exhausted. When her eyes met mine, I smiled, wanting her to know things were good between us, but she looked away, embarrassed. When her brothers ran upstairs to collect their school things, I asked Lucy if she'd managed to sleep.

'No, not really.'

'Perhaps you should stay at home today; you're still recovering from the infection, I don't want you to be ill again.' The school would understand, and it would allow us to talk.

'No, I've missed enough school. I want to go.' Again, Lucy couldn't meet my eyes. I sat down beside her and gently turned her face to look at me.

'Lucy, I know how bad you must be feeling about this, but I want you to know I forgive you, and I understand a little of why you did it. I actually think I'm partly responsible, I've failed you and can see it now. What would really make me happy is for you to forgive yourself. Until you do, it will always be there, between us, something which neither of us wants. By all means, go to school if you feel up to it but don't go just to get away from me. If we avoid the issue and don't work at moving on from it, then neither of us will be happy.' Perhaps discussing it over a table littered with the detritus of the twins' breakfast was not the best place or time to work this out. I did, however, worry Lucy might be so upset she would do something silly. Self-loathing is a potent emotion.

Her tears again began to fall, and she put her head on my shoulder, so clearly troubled and exhausted. I decided she wasn't up to going to school, so I told her we would have a quiet day at home together. She nodded her acquiescence and the matter was settled. After the boys left, I rang the school office and told them Lucy wasn't well enough to go in. The secretary was very sympathetic and said that she'd probably gone back to school too early, which was quite true. I then told Lucy to go for a long soak in the bath, after which we would put our heads together and decide what to do.

Using the time she was in the bath to organise my thoughts, I came to a conclusion. We really must tell the police. As it would be embarrassing going to Steve (and he would think I only ever wanted to see him to sort out my troubles), I thought I should ring DC Amy Peters. Naturally, I would talk to Lucy first. What worried me the most about this was what they would have to do to close the case. Would Lucy be charged and prosecuted? I couldn't bear it if she was, or would she get away with a caution and no one else would need to know? Going to the police was clearly the right thing to do, I was convinced. By not going, I feared we would be guilty of withholding evidence, or obstruction of justice, something like it anyway, and we could be in more trouble in the long run. Hopefully, if I said I didn't want to press charges, they might drop the case, but the reality was it was the Crown Prosecution Service who made the ultimate decision.

We drank fresh coffee and sat in the lounge, which was brightened by the early spring sunshine. Lucy looked better for having bathed and dressed; her hair hung wet on her shoulders. Small talk was inappropriate, so I told Lucy I thought we should go to the police. She looked horrified.

'Hear me out first. Initially, I thought we could just do nothing, but on reflection, it could probably land us in more trouble. Although the police are no longer actively looking at the case, they won't close it until it's solved, and periodically it could be reviewed. We would, in effect, be withholding evidence, which in itself is a crime. I want to ring and see if I can speak to DC Amy Peters. She's very understanding and will be able to tell us what happens now.'

'What about Steve Radcliffe, aren't you seeing him?' Lucy asked.

'I was, but not anymore, so I'd rather go to Amy. The police can be sensitive, and hopefully, they'll settle the case with a warning, but this is only me talking, and I honestly don't know what will happen.' It was hard for Lucy to take this in, but she'd been so brave up to now. She nodded thoughtfully.

'If they decide to charge me, it will be no more than I deserve.' Lucy frowned, biting her bottom lip as if preparing herself to take the punishment.

'I'm hoping it won't come to that, but I'm convinced this is the right decision.'

Chapter Forty-Five

My call was transferred straight to DC Amy Peters, who picked up the phone and said her name.

'Hello, it's Laura Green here.' I paused to let her remember me.

'Oh yes, Mrs Green. How are things with you?'

'Getting better, I'm pleased to say.' Lucy was watching me, and I smiled at her when I said that. It was true.

'Good, so you're not ringing to report any more malicious letters?'

'No, quite the opposite... I've found out who has been sending them.'

'Really?' Amy sounded surprised; I suppose they don't usually have the public solving their cases for them. After telling her my daughter had been the culprit, I continued as tactfully as possible, explaining how Lucy had been ill and under a lot of pressure. Amy listened to my little speech, and I finished by saying I hoped there would be no charges and could she let me know what would happen next. The DC was very understanding and sympathetic but explained that the decision wasn't hers to make. She told me she'd look into it, take advice, and then get back to me. Even if DC Peters acted immediately, it could be a long wait, and waiting was not my strong point.

Needing a distraction and not wanting to go out in case Amy rang back, I asked Lucy if she'd like to help me with some baking. It was years since we had done such a thing together, and I had a vision of my daughter at four years old stirring cake mixture in a bowl which was nearly as big as she was. I often turned to baking when I was restless. The only problem is I'm tempted to eat whatever I make afterwards.

'What do you fancy?' I asked.

'A chocolate cake?'

'Good, you take the table and I'll work over there on a batch of scones, cherry or sultana?'

'Both!'

And we began our calorie-laden therapy, chatting about nothing in particular yet all the while listening out for the telephone.

It was, however, the doorbell which rang first. DC Amy Peters stood on my doorstep, shivering in the chill wind. Inside, we went into the lounge, Lucy watching from the kitchen. I offered coffee which she accepted gratefully. In the kitchen, Lucy already had the kettle on and offered to make the coffee for me.

'Okay, thanks, then bring it through, will you?' I smiled. Lucy looked terrified, but at least she wasn't running away!

'It's good news, Laura,' Amy said. 'I've spoken to DS Radcliffe, and he sees no reason to recommend prosecution to the CPS. We now have a confession, so we've decided to close the case with only a warning for your daughter.'

'I'm really grateful!' The relief was enormous. It was a massive weight off my mind.

'I do want Lucy to know how serious this is, though. Steve

summed it up by saying it is not in the public interest to bring charges, so we're going to let it drop, close the case.'

Lucy came through with the coffee, put the tray down and turned to leave.

'Lucy, could I have a word, please?' Amy asked. I was unsure how much Lucy had heard, but she came over and sat next to me on the sofa. Amy began by taking out her notebook and flicking it open.

'We've been working on this case for several weeks now. It's involved me, DS Radcliffe and the support of the CSI department. We've interviewed suspects unnecessarily, taking up their time as well as ours and causing more than a little embarrassment. My DS, however, has decided to close the case with no further action, partly because of your mother's request and partly because of your age and previously clean record. I would, however, like to be certain you understand the seriousness of what you have done. It has cost your mother her job and a great deal of heartbreak, as well as wasting taxpayers' money on a lengthy investigation. Do you understand, Lucy?'

'Yes. I'm so sorry, I know it was hurtful, and I really regret it now.' Knowing how Lucy felt and how nervous she was, I thought it was quite an eloquent speech. Despite what she'd done, I was proud of my daughter. Lucy left us then, and as Amy finished her coffee, I thanked her and apologised for all the trouble we had caused them.

'We've had worse!' She grinned.

When Amy left, Lucy came and put her arms around me.

'I'm so sorry, Mum. Do you think they'll give you your job back now?'

'No, it's not going to happen, love. But I don't want you feeling guilty about me losing my job – the magazine was going to finish the page anyway. The letters just gave them a reason to do it sooner rather than later.'

I was to be proved wrong, however. Later in the afternoon, Madeline rang me.

'Hi, Laura, how are you?' She sounded her usual upbeat self.

'I'm fine, thanks, and how are things with you?'

'Good, Laura, thank you. Our legal department received a call from Detective Radcliffe today to let us know the good news. I'm delighted for you; it must be such a relief to know they've found the letter writer.'

I froze for a moment, unsure of what Steve would have told them, but I should have known better. Madeline continued.

'Naturally, he couldn't give the name of the culprit, but I'm sorry to hear it's someone from your past; it must be so upsetting for you. Now, I'm not going to ask you anything about it, Detective Radcliffe said he'd rather the case wasn't discussed, and he asked us to respect your privacy and feelings too. It's been a painful experience, I'm sure, but you know I'm always here if you need someone to talk to?' Madeline chatted away and I was happy to let her. Steve had thought of everything and acted swiftly before I had to face any embarrassing questions. I was grateful for his sensitivity yet unsure I deserved it.

'Anyway, I've got some more good news for you, Laura.' Madeline sounded quite excited. 'We've had so many complaints about your page being discontinued that the board have decided to reinstate it! Please say you'll come back? I do regret this happened at such a difficult time for you, and I've been authorised to offer you a pay rise if you'll consider writing for us again?'

I couldn't believe it and would have jumped at the chance of writing 'Ask Laura' again, without the pay rise. But I wasn't going to refuse it! I accepted straight away, and when Madeline rang off, I couldn't wait to tell Lucy the good news – and the better news – no one knew she was the letter writer. And we would keep it like that, too.

'I know I don't deserve to get away with this, but I'm so relieved. Your friend DS Radcliffe has been good to us, hasn't he?'

'Yes, Lucy, he has.'

'So why did you stop seeing him?'

'It doesn't matter; it's over now.'

'It wasn't because of me, was it?' Lucy looked at me sternly.

'Not really, it just all happened at the wrong time.'

'Oh, Mum, if you like him, you should tell him! You're still young, and we won't be with you forever.'

'What, are you thinking of leaving me again?' I teased.

'In a couple of years, for uni, yes! Go for it, Mum. He is pretty cool.' This was praise indeed from Lucy, but sadly it was too late. I could hardly go back to Steve now after all he'd done. He would only think I felt obligated to him. We'd come through the other side of a long, dark tunnel. My energies now must be concentrated on my children. Steve would be like my novel, a one-day dream.

The letter was pushed through the letterbox later that night.

Dear Laura,

I know men don't often write to you, but this is so important to me, and I know you can help. I've met a wonderful woman who is beautiful and intelligent, witty and very caring. She's the only woman I've ever loved (and yes, I do know it is love), and I can't stop thinking about her. The trouble is, she's the mother of three children, a seventeen-year-old daughter and twin boys who are eleven. I like the children and would love the chance to get to know them better. But their mother seems to think she can't have a relationship and be a good mother to them at the same time! I totally disagree. I know she feels the same attraction to me as I do to her, so how can I get through to her? Admittedly I'm no expert in childcare, but I believe if she is happy, she'll be a better mother, not a worse one! I also think she could ask the children their opinion. They're old enough to understand the situation and would probably want their mother to be happy, as I do.

I will wait for the children to grow up if that's what it takes, but we could be so happy together now if only she'll give me a chance to prove it. From reading your page regularly in the past, I know you are wise and will provide me with a carefully considered answer.

Please, Laura, I miss you so much!

Steve

Dear Steve,

For once, I am lost for an answer. I was wrong, you're right, and I miss you like crazy. If you'd like a fuller response to your letter, please call round, anytime, I'll be waiting for you.

P.S. I love you too!

Laura

THE END

Also by Gillian Jackson

The Pharmacist

The Victim

The Deception

Abduction

Snatched

The Accident

The Shape of Truth

The Charcoal House

The Dead Husband

Remembering Ellie

Author's notes

Thank you for reading Ask Laura. I enjoyed creating Laura Green, a sympathetic character who many mothers will identify with. Laura finds it easier to help others solve their problems, and when her own life spirals out of control, she flounders. If any protagonist warrants a happy ending it's Laura, and I could do no other than devise a knight in shining armour to give her the love she deserves.

To read more of my work, please visit my Amazon author page, or find me on Facebook @gillianjacksonauthor Follow me on Twitter @GillianJackson7 or visit my website, www.gillianjackson.co.uk

Acknowledgements

My thanks as always go to my husband and family for their love and support during the hours I spend writing. And to the amazing team at Bloodhound Books for their help in getting this book out into the world. Each book is a collaboration. I get to do the good bits; inventing characters and weaving plots, while they work on the polishing and presenting. I truly appreciate their dedication, professionalism and guidance throughout the process.

A note from the publisher

Thank you for reading this book. If you enjoyed it please do consider leaving a review on Amazon to help others find it too.

We hate typos. All of our books have been rigorously edited and proofread, but sometimes mistakes do slip through. If you have spotted a typo, please do let us know and we can get it amended within hours.

info@bloodhoundbooks.com

Milton Keynes UK
Ingram Content Group UK Ltd.
UKHW051658140424
R3544500001B/R35445PG440577UKX00001B/1